The Great
Planet Robbery

Also by Craig DiLouie
Paranoia

The Great Planet Robbery

Craig DiLouie

SALVO PRESS
Portland, Oregon

This is a work of fiction. All characters and events portrayed in this novel are fictitious and not intended to represent real people or places.

Although the locale where this story takes place is a real one, various liberties have been taken, and this book does not purport to offer an exact depiction of any particular place or location.

498530/

THE GREAT PLANET ROBBERY
Copyright © 2008 by Craig DiLouie

Salvo Press
P.O. Box 7396
Beaverton, OR 97007
www.salvopress.com

Cover istockphoto Image by Michael Knight

Library of Congress Control Number: 2007940920

ISBN: 9781930486799
1-930486-79-0

Printed in U.S.A.
First Edition

This novel is dedicated to Christine,
my beautiful and hilarious wife.

Table of Contents

Foreword to Our Tale

Of all the countless megabytes written about Federation history, most stories concerning the early years focus on the hardy pioneers, explorers and terraformers who tamed the wild planets and began the era of manifest destiny—the race to the galactic core.

Most historians, unfortunately, too often forget that the muscle of *Pax Humanus* was its soldiery, and that its eyes, ears and legs were the spacers—the pilots, navigators, truckers and other shipmen who abandoned normal definitions of time and space to work in the cosmos.

The soldiers fought and died in the Federation's single war with the only sentient species it had encountered that could trade punches with the Navy. The Navy got the glory, while the soldiers went on for hundreds more years protecting colonists from hostile natives on dozens of new worlds. But the soldiers saw many planets and met alien species face to face. Few men could stand with them and say, "I was there."

The spacers hauled the ore, trucked supplies and dragged the big trains of space trash, fused in vacuum, into the asteroid belts. But they also saw the red clouds of the luminous nebulae close up, hitched rides on comets, played with time at the edges of black holes, slingshotted out of the gravity wells of gas giants, and spent countless hours in empty black space either in cryogenic hibernation pods or sitting awake in a hypnotic trance. The constellations as we know them on Earth meant nothing to this breed.

Soldiers and spacers could live to hundreds of Earth Standard years relative to people living on Earth and other planets because of the phenomenon of physics known as time dilation, and after a while they began to develop a culture unlike any in the colonies or in Capital Province.

Because of their isolation, they were self-centered, full of attitude, addicted to adrenaline and plagued with quirks, but they were also highly skilled and trustworthy.

Part of the Life was to pull a good scam when one could to feed his own personal retirement fund. The Federation knew the value of such men, but paid them little so as to keep them tied to the Service. The Federation was also a giant bureaucracy whose cumbersome administration spanned more than twelve thousand cubic light-years, with some provinces barely tamed, creating enormous opportunities for men who knew how to beat the system.

At least once in a spacer's life, an extraordinary opportunity—usually dangerous if not outright impossible—would come along that offered incredible riches and instant retirement. Spacers usually called this The Holy Grail. The very mention of those words made eyes glass over with visions unique to the individual.

It was during this time, the Golden Age of the Federation, in which our story begins.

It was a time when two soldiers, Lawrence Dobbs and Timothy Muldoon, gathered a group of spacers and made an extraordinary journey to a hidden planet in the Beyond that held the greatest of all Holy Grails.

That part of the tale starts with a map and ends with a moon.

For now, we see them at a somewhat earlier time, in a cigar-shaped steel spaceship with a rest mass of sixty thousand tons, landing on a distant planet on a mission of war. . . .

BOOK I

THE TREASURE MAP

Chapter 1
The Planet of The Cannibals

Welcome to the Stone Age, fellas. The planet of the cannibals."
Hearing his own words made the pilot of the *Merlin* crack up. Next
to him, the navigator, wearing a pair of earphones around his neck,
chewed gum anxiously and smoked a cigarette at the same time, although
it had been a soft landing. The men had just parked the spaceship on a
grassy plain next to a four-kilometer-high heap of rock.

"You know your orders, Marines," he added, addressing the two men
before him who were pulling on their atmosphere suits. "But I will repeat
them so there is no question as to your duty on this operation." He cleared
his throat. "Your orders are to take—to take over the entire planet!" The
pilot had tried to say this seriously, but succeeded too well and began to
crack up again anyway, arms wrapped around his ribs.

Sergeant Major Lawrence Dobbs, pulling on a boot, glanced sideways
at Sergeant Major Timothy Muldoon, who stared somberly at the pilot.
Dobbs was short, slim and blond-haired, almost elven in appearance
especially when he smiled and his blue eyes twinkled (which wasn't happening now), while Muldoon was tall, beefy and wore a massive black
handlebar mustache flecked with gray. Together, they reminded people of
a fox and a bear from picture books about Earth. It had been an odd six
months for them. Gunnery sergeants in the Colonial Marines, they had
landed their first cushy assignment in eight hard years, only to be pulled
out of their beds and sent to pacify this dump of a border planet for annex-
ation into the Federation. While such a job normally would have taken a
fleet of ten ships each dropping three hundred men, only Dobbs and
Muldoon were sent in this lone ship.

The pilot's laughter echoed around the room, down the empty halls, the empty mess hall, the empty armory and the other cramped chambers of the ghost ship.

"What's that laughing?" the Doctor's voice hollered nervously from the rec room on an upper deck, a distant muffled tone. "Who's laughing?"

The pilot of the *Merlin* began to cool off, rubbing tears out of his eyes. "Listen, seriously, just go on out there, make it look good for the cameras, then high-tail it back so we can get the hell out off this rock. This is obviously some sort of joke, and a hell of an expensive one at that—this mission is costing a million a day. You don't stand a chance for five minutes out there in the bush. According to Recon's probes, Doreen's natives are four meters tall on average, big hairy monkey-looking bastards. Each is strong enough to bring down one of those big woolly herbivores on the planet with a single blow to the head with a bone." He made a karate chop motion with his hand. "And if they haven't found a mastodon and they find you instead, they'll cook you for supper, I swear." He started to chuckle again. "I don't know who you pissed off, but—well, see if you can make it back in one piece."

He watched the men check their weapons and give the thumbs-up to open the door to the airlock. "Hey, did you hear what I said?"

Dobbs and Muldoon looked at each other from inside their bubbles, their heads inset in the elastic padding of the suits. Turning back to face the pilot, Dobbs raised his hand and tapped his helmet, shaking his head and smiling. His eyes twinkled.

The pilot sighed and opened the hatch. "That's what I get for being nice. Bastards."

"Sound check," said Dobbs.

"Get off my ship!"

"Reading you loud and clear," said Muldoon. "Prepare to disembark."

The Marines entered the airlock, closed the door and waited. The chamber filled with a hissing noise. When the gauge said go, they turned the wheel on the outer hatch door and pushed it open. Weapons at the ready, they walked down the ramp onto the charred circle burned into the savanna by the ship's rockets when they retrofired for the landing.

"Bloody," Dobbs thought aloud. Any number of people would have finished the sentence nicely.

"That doctor's a good man, though," his large comrade answered him over the com link. "Giving us a cyanide gas cylinder in case we get ourselves captured."

Dobbs snorted. "All we'd have to do is take our helmets off and breathe deep if we really wanted to go that bad," he said. "But I'd prefer a simple zap between the eyes. The Marine way."

"I'll do the honors at the appropriate time," Muldoon assured him.

"Thank you, Sergeant Major." Dobbs looked up at the soupy sky colored with a greenish tint due to the local sun that was a Class K star, about four thousand kelvins in temperature and therefore of an orangish hue. It was now rising in the east, a large disc. "What a god-awful ugly planet. I'm sure the Governor's people picked it carefully."

Muldoon, the fatalist, shrugged. "Let's conquer the place, then we can figure out what we're going to do to him." He looked left, then right, then looked left again and settled there. "I say we go that way."

Dobbs looked up at his comrade miserably. "You do know what time dilation is, eh, chap? It took us more than two years in cryogenic sleep at near light speed to get here. It'll take us the same to get back. By the time we do, the Governor will be dead for about seventy-five years. In fact, at least a hundred years will be gone in all the places we call civilization."

Muldoon's eyes smoldered as this hit him. "Ah, who gives a damn!" he exploded.

Dobbs looked around. "Did you hear that? It was like a rumble."

"Probably my stomach," Muldoon said blackly. "The way that pilot lands a ship, it's—"

The men froze.

The shadow of a large object had stabbed into their leftward peripheral vision. Being experienced spacers, they knew to move their entire torsos to get a good look through the bubbles of their helmets.

The shadow belonged to a giant monster, remotely gorillalike with grotesquely large arms covered with thick matted hair sprouting from where the shoulder blades should have been if it were in fact a gorilla. One of the planet's hairy natives, one of the cannibals. It walked—rather, it shambled on four legs—through the spiked plants just outside of the charred circle that still smoked in spots, looking with childlike awe over its massive shoulder up the entire length of the cigar-shaped metal spaceship that rose twenty-five stories over the plain.

The monster slowly dragged a hand off the ground that held a clublike bone and wiped its nose with the back of its wrist, then sniffed the air. Suddenly, its squat bullet head faced the Marines. The head tilted sideways, tusks chomping.

Muldoon spared a quick glance at his rifle's gauges, then aimed it at the creature, squinting down the barrel. "Should I put him down with a round, Sergeant Major?"

The monster flinched, staring at the humans.

"No, he seems like a reasonable bloke," said Dobbs. "Maybe he doesn't want to scrap. We'll try diplomacy. Give him a friendly wave, Sergeant Major."

Muldoon lowered the rifle and raised his hand in greeting, grinning in his most friendly way.

The creature roared and fled fifty meters in an amazing burst of speed, loping using its four legs and two arms, until it suddenly stopped, grabbed its chest and collapsed.

Dobbs and Muldoon exchanged a glance.

"So much for contact," Muldoon said. "If I had known that was going to happen, I would have shot him instead. The poor bastard."

"Like those Earth beasts we read about in school," Dobbs told him. In the colonial schools, learning about Earth was as vital for children as reading, writing and computers. "Rhinoceros. Mean as a Kiki, but you get them scared and running, and they drop like a meteor."

"Damn, I've got an itch in my suit!" Muldoon exploded.

Dobbs brought his hand up to rub his chin, ended up touching the bubble. "I'd like to get back to the topic of the Governor, if you don't mind. I was thinking, if we look at this the right way, we could be in a right spot of luck if we manage to get ourselves out of here alive."

Muldoon frowned. "How do you figure? Are you looking on the bright side, as in the spacer saying, 'The air tank isn't half empty, it's hall full'?"

"No, I'm being literal, chap," Dobbs told him. "Think about it—the Governor will be dead for scores of years by the time we see our native stars again."

"Yeah, a good hundred years will be gone, so you say. If we keep up with this damned space travel, too much time'll go by on us and we won't recognize the place when we get back. We'll be helpless. It's happened to us once before. Damn, I wish I had a good cigar!"

"I'd go to the Magellan Clouds and back if I thought it'd make sure the old bugger was dead before we set foot in Federation space again. You may want to get revenge, but I just want to get rid of him. This is as good as making a clean get-away. Time will do the job nicely."

Muldoon considered this, then nodded sagely in his bubble. "A wise assessment. It's a fair trade." The logic appealed to him, who was the type of man who broke responses to bad situations into fight or run.

Dobbs said, "Although there is one possibility we haven't considered."

"Oh?" Muldoon was irritated now. "What's that? I thought we had it settled."

"The Governor may have made arrangements in case we got back alive somehow."

"Brilliant," Muldoon said blackly. "His dying wish will be our execution. Or maybe we'll end up prison guards on Cantor V. Nobody can be that cruel! What do we do, then?"

Dobbs grinned at him. "We conquer this godforsaken planet."

"Rich we were supposed to be!" Muldoon inhaled deeply, smelling the rubber helmet lining, and sighed. "We'll take the rover, then?"

"Aye."

They drove the rover south in silence across the grassy plain until they found a ridge. Looking for some nice scenery to go with lunch, they rode to the top and admired the view of a valley cut by a forked river and forested with strange-looking trees that were as wide as they were tall. An exotic insect as big as a rat landed on the windshield and studied the men through the glass with wide, intelligent eyes. Its mouth opened and its mandibles clicked excitedly, as if it were urgently trying to communicate with them. Dobbs flicked it off with the wipers. After lunch, Muldoon got out and put fresh oxygen tanks into the cells.

"You didn't have to be cruel to the poor thing," he told Dobbs.

They moved on until they found another cannibal skinning a herbivore near the river. The monster roared, pounded its chest in defense of its supper, then fled thirty meters into the water, grabbed its chest and collapsed. This went on for two weeks. Each time Dobbs and Muldoon returned to the ship to re-supply after giving more natives cardiac arrest, the pilot had only shaken his head and hadn't said a word, his silence an apparent punishment to the Marines for having ignored him when he was being nice. Terror spread among the natives about the invading witch doctors who slaughtered hundreds with a glance, and they fled the choice regions into the colder mountains. Probes were launched to study the atmosphere for terraforming, the mountains for elements to mine, the land for cultivation and colonization.

Within twelve weeks, Dobbs and Muldoon had conquered the planet.

Chapter 2
Their New Home

Sergeant Major Dobbs saw red. Red dirt, red rocks, a sky filled with swirling red dust. A red world. And it was about to get even redder. A dust storm was coming, the kind that covered half the planet Siren for months at a time. Visibility was already down to only a dozen kilometers through the big window. The dust closed in silently like a veil over the vast empty spaces. It was so fine, it penetrated the cracks in the dome. He could taste its iron grit between his teeth. Bitter.

Sergeant Major Muldoon knew a big dust storm was coming. Although there was no dampness, for some reason he felt it in his leg, which had been skewered by the barbed tentacle of a lobster-headed Kiki a long time ago on another planet. Muldoon sighed, sat and listened. There was already wind—eighty kilometer an hour wind—but he couldn't hear it. Instead, he heard the domed building groan and creak.

"There's a storm coming," said Muldoon. "A big one."

"Aye," said Dobbs, who didn't feel like small talk. He was busy with his brooding.

"That's the second damned one this year. You know that."

"Aye."

Muldoon clenched his fists on his knees. "I hate this godforsaken place. You don't understand. I like the company of living things!"

"Don't worry," said Dobbs. His eyes narrowed. "We'll see who gets the last laugh."

‰

When Dobbs and Muldoon had returned from Doreen, the Prefect of Waldo himself pinned the medals onto their chests in a small ceremony and saluted them as heroes. In about eight years, the news would reach Earth and cause a minor sensation throughout Capital Province. But Dobbs and Muldoon had only wanted to know if the Governor had any further revenge planned in the memory banks of the government computers.

"What are our orders, sir?" Dobbs had asked sunnily, wringing his hands.

"You boys sure like the tough assignments, don't you?" the Prefect had answered.

Muldoon had turned purple.

Siren orbited a dying sun called Gamma Hades. In a sense, a star is a giant furnace, burning up fuel and leaving behind ash. Gamma Hades had burned up enough of its hydrogen that it had begun to die. In time, it would cool enough to glow a rich red, and expand enough to envelop Siren and its sister satellites. Even later, Gamma Hades would collapse into a tiny black hole. But that was still billions of years away.

Siren, the third planet, had once been a healthy world completely covered with water that over billions of years had built up an atmosphere and had been home to millions of species of aquatic life and plants. But when the sun began to die, the temperature changed, then the atmosphere thinned thanks to the impact of a few large meteoroids. The oceans evaporated, leaving behind valuable deuterium, and the fish died, leaving behind organic material in the rocks. In short, the planet became a barren ball of dirt, and the only water left was now frozen in rocks or below ground in aquifer pockets.

When the Federation explorers landed, they chose Vesuvius Mons, the planet's biggest volcano, as the ideal spot to mine for minerals and organic materials left behind by the long-dead fish that were used at the time as an ingredient in cryonic embalming fluid for long-range space flights. Vesuvius Mons measured two kilometers high and three hundred fifty kilometers across. It was surrounded by cliffs about two kilometers tall that had been formed millions of years ago by lava flows. The six mining camps were built there among the grotesque hump-backed sand dunes shaped by winds averaging twenty kilometers per hour and cruising up to more than three hundred at the height of a sand storm. The base and landing strips were set up ten kilometers away on a plain pockmarked with small craters.

The planet was a dump. In fact, the entire solar system—the Province of Good Hope—was considered by the rest of the Federation as little more than a low-tech industrial park.

It was also their new home.

ஒ

Dobbs stared out the window and brooded, while Muldoon leafed through the premiere issue of *Davy Jones*, a comical astronautical magazine. Suddenly, he flung it down in disgust.

"What time do you have?" said Dobbs.

"It's almost three."

"Well, we may as well go and see the bugger now, then. He said three."

Muldoon stood up stiffly. "All right. Let's see what the man wants. Then let's go and see if Cook rustled up those synth-pork chops. I can't take one more spoonful of bean curd!"

They approached a nearby door that read COMMANDER and knocked.

A voice called them in.

Boots clocking crisply on the floor in time, Dobbs and Muldoon entered the Captain's office, removed their caps, and saluted in perfect sync. They were infantry, and they knew the drill. The Captain, wearing field fatigues, leaned back in his chair and inspected them. Dobbs noticed the man's olive-green shirt was open to reveal a brown T-shirt and his bar-coded dog-tags, and that his steel-rimmed round glasses were slightly askew on his handsome young face. His name-tag read WILLIAMSON for George Williamson. From the smell of bourbon in the room, Dobbs concluded that Williamson had been tipping the bottle again. Something about the shame of being assigned to a miserable outpost on a boring dump of a planet, protecting ungrateful dirty miners from giant sand monsters, and all that.

"Reporting as requested, sah!" Dobbs shouted.

The Captain gave them a bored wave. "At ease, Sergeant Major Dobbs, Sergeant Major Muldoon." Originally a Navy man, he spoke like a Terran-American as Muldoon did, while Dobbs had acquired the traditional Marine manner of speech. "I'm glad you could come. I wanted you here to ask you a question, because I'm hard on facts."

"We're at your service, sir," Muldoon assured him.

Williamson folded his hands on his stomach and smiled. "Good. Tell me about time dilation. How does time dilation work?"

Muldoon's grin evaporated and he glanced at Dobbs, chewing on his mustache.

"Well, sir, it's like this," Dobbs said. "Time and space are of the same fabric, like a blanket, as it were. You put an ion grenade on the blanket, and it makes a depression. That's gravity. The grenade has mass. Say it's a planet or a star. Now you put a bowling ball on the blanket, and it makes a deeper depression. Say that's a black hole. When you're in space flight, you approach infinite mass as you near the speed of light, so your ship, normally a ping pong ball relatively speaking, turns into a bowling ball itself. The deeper the depression in the blanket, the slower time goes by relative to the objects making a smaller impression. That gives us the Twin Paradox, where a spacer can get off the grenade and onto the traveling bowling ball, come back after a flight of about a year and find his twin and everybody else on the grenade fifty years older while he's only a year older. Why, me and Sergeant Major Muldoon are almost eight hundred Earth Standard years old ourselves, what with zipping around in space for so long and all."

Williamson sat wearing an amused expression, waiting patiently. Suddenly, he grew as red as Siren's dust. "I'm a Navy Captain, you morons. I know how time dilation works!"

He began typing furiously into a laptop on his desk. "I just got a broadcast from the Commission on Space Trade and Supply. It says you chartered a ship on New France to load fifty tons of brand-new scotch and fly it around at near light speed for a few months, then had it brought back and pass a loophole in the trade regs as twenty-year-old scotch. Because of the time dilation. As we both know, it's not really twenty-year-old scotch." This forced him to laugh. "Jupiter, you increased its value a hundred times!"

The Captain then scratched his head, studying the screen which cast his face in a bluish glow. "That flight must have cost a pretty penny. Did you really make a good buck off this?"

Dobbs smiled sheepishly. "We made a modest profit. It was there and we took it. Can you blame us? I mean, technically, it was twenty-year-old scotch, at least as far as New France was concerned. Who cares how old it really was? A rule's a rule." Next to him, Muldoon stared stonily ahead at the geographical and geological charts on the wall behind the Captain's desk, there for show.

Williamson shook his head, starting to stew again. "Well, you've got to know that the Commission's pissed as all hell, and it's reflecting poorly on me. I'll never get off this rock now. I've got my own share of enemies." He sighed. "So then I figured I'd do some checking on your records. I should have done it when you got here, but I don't ask a lot of questions about the people they send here, for obvious reasons. I mean, I'd really rather not know." He went back to the screen. "It's a weird soup. Numerous decorations for courage in battle. Part of the unit that saved those settlers on Kilroy from the Kikis. Muldoon here fought against the Xerxesians in War VI. Some good soldiering, what I'd expect from Marines. And so on and so forth. Oh, I like this one—single-handedly conquered Doreen." He chuckled. "Yeah, right. Oh, but this is where it gets tasty. In the Yokohama Province, you tapped into the Data Flow out of Capital Province just ahead of the local stock market and used the information to buy and sell technology stocks. Couldn't prove it, but it's here. Says here you ran contraband goods to the black market at a religious commune on the Boxer Dyson Sphere. And what's this about Halifax?"

"Halifax as you know is a small world in the Wolfshead Province," Dobbs explained. "We had some information for the Prefect that might have been something of an embarrassment to him. That man had no heart, what he did to his ol' Mum, and we had him dead to rights that he was a lousy bastard. We got away with some hush money and tried to make off, but he had a change of heart and sent the Gimps after us. Natives."

Muldoon couldn't maintain his composure anymore, and started to laugh out loud.

"Now those Gimps are fast and deadly, but not too bright," Dobbs continued.

"They lived only on the side of the planet that faced the sun, you see, always migrating," Muldoon explained, blinking tears.

"They followed their orders to the letter, they did. They chased us to the dark side and dropped dead right at the border!"

Muldoon began to howl. Williamson smiled patiently, drumming his fingers on his desk.

"Sorry, sir," Dobbs said. "As you can see, we did nothing wrong."

"He had it coming," agreed Muldoon. "What he did to his poor sweet mother."

"All it says here is you killed members of an endangered alien species," the Captain told them. "I didn't need to know the rest. But whatever you did, you ticked off Governor Mandela enough so that even seventy-three years after his death, he still made sure you ended up somewhere unpleasant when you got back from your last mission. And now you've got yourselves in hot water all over again." He leaned over the desk. "Listen, you're good soldiers. You're not the criminal type because to be honest you suck at it. So why make trouble? If Mandela hadn't had a poetic sense of justice, you'd have been court-martialed or worse, made prison guards on Cantor V."

"None of those charges have ever been proven true or accurate in a court of law," Dobbs reminded him.

"They shouldn't even be in the record," Muldoon agreed indignantly, back to staring at the wall, but inwardly he shuddered at the idea of Cantor V.

"They've got proof on this scotch scam you pulled."

"But that wasn't exactly illegal, since there was the loophole," Dobbs countered. Then he rubbed his chin, realizing that Williamson was not his enemy. In fact, he could easily understand them. "Sir, I'd like to ask you something. Why did you sign up for the Life?"

"For the adventure, of course. I wanted to do something for my home world. I was a younger man then."

"Aye, and so it was for us. And still is. But we need to think of our future as well, when we're older men."

"We fought and bled to build this Federation," said Muldoon. "Us, and men like us."

"Aye, and shame on us if we end up poor beggars when there's no more fighting to be done," Dobbs agreed. "That's why we set up the Retirement Fund."

"Think of the time they don't need real men anymore," Muldoon said loudly, his face darkening. "Where will we be then, eh? Jupiter! We've fought hostile natives who looked and made at us like red devils. We've survived poisonous air, cosmic rays, bacteria, parasites as big as cats, landslides, asteroids bouncing off our hull in the deepest blackest space you ever saw." His large hands clenched into fists and he turned to Williamson. "You know the Life, Captain. Where were those cowards then? That's what I want to know!" His shoulders drooped. "Ah, what's the use! The whole Federation's going soft!"

"Sorry, sir," Dobbs told Williamson. "He has large feelings when it comes to right and wrong. For me, I'd just like to see us get what's coming to us."

Williamson stared back at him dryly. "And isn't it funny, that's just what the Commissioners said." He sighed. "Listen. I've given this a lot of thought, and I've heard you out, so please shut up. Technically, I should put you in the brig. But you know what I'm going to do? I'm going to do absolutely nothing." With that, he leaned back again, refolded his hands on his stomach and smiled.

"Nothing, sir?"

"Nothing. I don't care."

Although he was a man who accepted simple things simply, Muldoon was confused. He cocked an eye at Dobbs, who shrugged back.

Williamson appeared to relish their confusion. In fact, the whole scene suddenly appeared to amuse him immensely.

"The Commission people won't make it here for another five months," he told them. "They're sending Troubleshooters all the way from New France to make an example of you personally. Until they get here, you'll continue with your duties. In case you didn't notice, it's almost feeding time. Camp Four's gonna get crabs, and I need men at their posts. You're the only human combat infantry I have here at the command base, and besides, nobody's as good at working with the Cricket levies as you are. That gives you exactly two days for your R-and-R, which I'll let you take as well. I want you good and ready to fight. But you will be back and you will fight if you have to."

"We'll do right by you, sir," Dobbs said. "You can have no doubts on that score."

"Good. When you get back, have the Crickets saddle up and take the Crimea Road to Camp Four, where we had so much trouble last month. The Odessa is blocked by a landslide." The Captain leaned on his desk, sliding his computer to the side. "And I'll tell you something else, man to uh, men. Off the record. If you find a way off this rock after the next crab feeding cycle, you can take your chances. I never said that, of course. But I'll turn the other way for a while. Fair enough?"

Dobbs frowned, doing mental calculations. Muldoon filled in. "May I ask why you're giving us a hand up? It doesn't make sense to me."

Williamson's eyes flashed with sudden clarity. "Yeah, you can ask. The answer is I don't know. Maybe it's because I agree with you, just a little. Or maybe I just hate to see good soldiers put to waste." Then his gaze softened, and he took off his glasses to wipe a new film of red dust off with a tissue. "And you're out of my hair either way, right?"

"Thank you, sir. Is that all then, sir?"

"That'll do it. You're dismissed." The Captain looked tired.

"You're a good egg, Captain," Dobbs said.

"It's hard to imagine that this planet was once an ocean world," Williamson replied. "You know, in Terran mythology, the Sirens called to sailors, and the sailors came and crashed on the rocks." Dobbs and Muldoon watched him swivel his chair to look out the window at the red sky. The sky was darkening. The storm was building.

Chapter 3
The Rescue

Macintosh, part of the Flow of raw materials to the Terran solar system and data and hi-tech goods and technology back out to the colonies, was the largest space station orbiting Siren. It was a truck stop for ships to refuel and ship crews to rest. It also contained a factory that manufactured low-tech goods, pharmaceuticals and crystals for use in solar power cells. Experimental high-yield soybeans were grown at a research farm, and satellites were towed in to be scooped up and fixed in a repair bay. *Macintosh* floated in space at a Lagrange point so that its orbit consistently ran between Siren and Danby, Siren's nearest moon, where a few automated factories churned out boots, cookware and other cheap appliances for the Province. But to Dobbs and Muldoon, *Macintosh* was simply where bars, sextech centers and trading posts could be found—one of the few civilized places in the solar system where a man could enjoy business and companionship.

Thousands of kilometers below, in a scrambler jet, the Marines flew over their sprawling outpost with its barracks, warehouses, reactor, landing strips, giant freighter for carrying raw ore, and the rail gun that fired the smaller, more precious payloads of deuterium into the atmosphere to be picked up by *Macintosh*.

Muldoon burned the rockets and they climbed, the outpost dwindling to a dot and the pockmarked vastness of the red planet filling the screen. Within moments, they left the thin atmosphere and made course for the space station, a distant rotating dumbbell weakly lighted by reflection from the planet and framed by the blackness of space and its cloudy millions of bright stars (for now, it was still just a reddish dot on the screen).

Soon, the stars would be blotted out by the bottom of Danby, Siren's moon.

"With Troubleshooters coming, I know you're planning something," said Muldoon, working the controls. "What gives? It doesn't have to be a secret." Dobbs was the smartest man Muldoon knew, the type who always had a good plan. It made life simple.

"We've got five months," Dobbs answered from across the cockpit, leafing through the second issue of *Davy Jones*. "That gives us four, and it'll take them six. We'll have a nice head start."

Muldoon smiled and winked at him. "They'll find no trace of us here, I'll bet."

"Like we never existed."

Muldoon's smile quickly dissolved into a frown. "But it bothers me, you know. Leaving the Service. I think I'm going to miss the Life."

Dobbs smiled up at his comrade. "We've had some high times in the Service. But I'm sure we'll find something else to occupy a man of your experience and aptitude."

Muldoon grunted. "It'll feel good to get back into Standard *g* once we reach Mac. I weigh only a hundred and twenty pounds down there. I can't believe the men actually tried to play ping pong in the rec room before you brought down the weighted balls."

"And I got the scrambler for us today, let's not forget," Dobbs said absently, reading.

"So you did, Sergeant Major, and I'm thankful. I don't think my stomach could have handled another ride on that commuter rocket."

"You treat your stomach like it was your own mother. Well, we're still ahead of the game. This R-and-R comes at a good time. We'll put out our feelers for a way off this rock."

"I'll get to see Dariana again," said Muldoon. Dariana was a sextech at The Solar Flare, and all professional relationships aside, Muldoon considered her his girlfriend. He noticed with irritation that Dobbs was smiling impishly. "Well, something should be up. But you've made only a few contacts since we've come back from the Beyond. It sure won't be easy."

"There's always a way. Isn't that our motto?"

Muldoon grinned and cracked his knuckles. "Absolutely. I was just thinking about Halifax again. Those dumb Gimps!"

Dobbs chuckled. "That Captain's a good chap after all, aye? Nice sense of humor."

"He's a good man," agreed Muldoon, his large jaw now set. "Another man who deserves a fair share. Too bad he's a boozer. I'll turn up the heat a little if you're cold."

"He'll receive his share straight from you and me, I swear it."

They flew in silence for a few minutes, listening to the ventilation system exchange carbon dioxide for recycled air that blew through the supply grille as dry heat.

The heat dried Dobbs' throat. "I think the humidifier's gone and crapped out again."

Muldoon checked the indicators, looked out the window into darkness, then glanced back to the indicators. "Something's up. We've got an object."

"It's probably space junk," Dobbs said. "Or a satellite. The computer'll fix course."

"No, it looks like it's a trading ship." Their broad solar sails gleaming, small trading ships commonly passed between *Macintosh* and space stations orbiting the other planets, such as Polyphemus, the gas giant where they mined and processed Helium-3.

"Can't be, though. There's a solar flare due any day now, according to the reports. Every trader's in dock, if he knows what's good for him."

"That's what I was thinking. But the parallax measurements show it's a ship. Look now. You can see there on the viewer, that dot. No, there. He's flashing his lights. See?"

Dobbs went back to his magazine. "It's a routine courtesy. Flash him back."

"That's an S-O-S, Sergeant Major. Old Morse code. He's in trouble."

"Radio in for help, then. They'll send out a rescue-tow. Please."

Muldoon grunted. "I suppose we'll have a go at it. You wanted adventure, right?"

Dobbs was usually left to do the thinking while Muldoon did the heavy lifting. But when Muldoon fixed his mind on a diversion, usually some wasteful venture to help somebody who got himself—usually herself— into a jam, Dobbs knew better than to argue with him. Muldoon could be pure stubborn bulldog. He sighed. "Suit yourself, it's your R-and-R."

Muldoon began working the controls, braking, then firing streams of gas out of the jets in a slow, painstaking roll. The guidance system supplemented manual with small corrections in thrust.

"It doesn't look promising, I can tell you," Dobbs said, his nerves shot already. "They don't make scramblers for this, Sergeant Major. Let's consider our options carefully."

Muldoon nodded and fired the rockets until they hit 1.5g, terminated acceleration to continue at the same velocity for a few minutes, then began braking. As they closed on the damaged boat, an ancient-looking tow-barge, they saw a jet of gas spraying into ice crystals from one side, pushing it sideways toward Siren. Every few moments, a strong burst of gas fired from the other side's roll jets, keeping the boat roughly straight.

"He's a good spacer, that one," said Dobbs. "That's not his guidance system doing all that lifting."

"Yeah, I don't know how long he can keep it up with that hunk of junk, though."

The pilot came through on the radio, his voice fading in and out with static.

". . . in sector four-two-eight Siren repeat require assistance rupture in . . . repeat, mayday, mayday, this is REP-4 in sector . . . Siren. . . ."

"Ask him if he can stabilize long enough for a rescue," Muldoon said.

Dobbs picked up the radio. "REP-4, this is—blast it, what's our call sign?"

"We're Romeo-2."

"REP-4, this is Romeo-2, proceeding along elliptic on convergent course to your coordinates, will correct to parallel at seven-zero-twelve in eight minutes. Maintain your present course. Over." He turned to Muldoon. "Mars, I can't remember all this spacer garbage."

The pilot of the tow-barge laughed over the radio, accompanied by a harsh burst of static. "Who are you boys? You don't sound like Rescue Patrol. But who cares? Whoever you are, I'm sure glad to know you. I'm running low on spit and tape here. Some jackass, probably on Danby, threw a champagne bottle into orbit and it hit my boat at more than a hundred kilometers a second."

Muldoon sat impatiently. "If he doesn't stop jawing our ears off, he'll run out of fuel and then to hell with him."

"Can you keep her stable long enough for us to reach you?" Dobbs said into the radio. "Over."

"My gauges are still in the yellow, but yes. You can pull up alongside me. Wait. Yes. I'll string a line across, climb into your airlock and cut the connection. Over."

"Roger that. Hang on, man. We're on our way." He turned to Muldoon and tossed the magazine into the back, where it floated serenely through the air in zero gravity until it came to rest on ceiling. "This was a bad idea from the word go, if you ask me."

Muldoon nodded and feathered the thrust until they were in a path and velocity parallel to the boat, which continued to slant and appear to be trying to right itself.

"I've got you in visual," the pilot said. "Don't go anywhere. I'm coming over."

Dobbs turned in his seat and looked back at the floating magazine with longing, suddenly realizing this was going to take forever. Next, the pilot would want to repair his boat, which could take the rest of the day. He sighed. So much for R-and-R.

Muldoon checked the instruments and swore. "Tell him he's getting too close!"

"He's got another rupture," Dobbs said, pointing to the screen that showed the view from the left side of the ship. "I'm only guessing, but he's firing like mad to balance."

"Yeah, you're right about that. Jupiter, that's his air!"

"I've got problems," they heard over the radio. "Hold on."

"Well, it's screwing him up nicely," Dobbs said, breaking into a clammy sweat. "He'll have to add more thrust or he'll head right into us and we've all had it."

"Aw, what the hell now," the pilot said.

"Let's hope his jets can handle the lifting, then," Muldoon told Dobbs, staring at the screen. "We're practically kissing his ship. Why did I get us into this? Me and my big mouth!"

"Holy cow," the pilot said.

"Just be good and ready to open the outer hatch when the time comes," Dobbs said to Muldoon, then said into the radio, "You've got another rupture, REP-4. Correct your thrust!"

"What do you think I'm doing?" came the reply. "My roll jets are at full thrust now, and I'm even working my pitch jets with my feet in my spare time. This ain't no Ship of the Line, kids! Listen, when I come across, we're scuttling the boat. Prepare for evasive maneuvers in case the roll jets get swamped and the boat kicks into your flight path. I'm starting now. Wait for me. Out."

Dobbs holstered the mike. "You heard him. He's going to scuttle his can. Should be quite a sight. Keep your bloody eyes peeled."

"He can suit himself," Muldoon said, unlocking the hatch. "He must be good to steer a piece of junk like that. There oughta be a law against flying those boats."

"Now you know why I wanted to call for help, old boy." Dobbs mopped sweat from his forehead. "You've never done an evasive maneuver in your life. We're not pilots."

Muldoon frowned. "You know, I never told you this one story. I was assigned to a new landing field on Poltava, which we had just taken from the Xerxesians in the last war. One day, a supply ship was taking off. Even seeing them from a distance, you had to admire the power of those rockets. It went into full burn, and the thrust began to shoot that big steel cigar into the atmosphere. Then they had a failure, and the ship wobbled, then started to list."

"God almighty," said Dobbs, grateful to take his mind off of a collision. Muldoon was always the cool one in situations like this, fearless, a pillar on the battlefield. "What was the failure? Xerxesian sabotage?"

Muldoon looked sheepish. "I never did find that out, although I'm sure it'd make for a better story. But I'd say it must have been, because who ever heard of such a thing. The rockets cut out as the ship went down over a distant plain and threw dirt in the air high enough so we could see it from kilometers away. We certainly felt it, it shook our bones. Imagine forty thousand tons of steel hitting the ground that hard! Some of the crew—" He pulled a lever, and they heard a series of muffled booms. "Okay, I think he's in the airlock. This is too close! The boat's going to tumble."

"Look, his roll jets cut out!" Dobbs was clinging to the instrumentation panel. "It's coming right at us!"

"Wait a second. Is he in?"

"Retrofire! Retrofire!" Dobbs screamed. "Hit the bloody brakes!"

Muldoon hit the rockets hard to brake and Dobbs crushed against his harness at 4g until he saw stars. The magazine came back from the ceiling and smacked him in the back of the head with the force of a baseball.

"Hail Mary!" Muldoon shouted over the roar of the rockets.

Dobbs came to in time to see the pilot's boat cross their path on the forward screen, large enough to read REP-4 on its side, spraying twin streams of crystals that, besides its momentum, were now its only source of propulsion. It began to tumble as it picked up speed. A sensor broke off along with little pieces of debris and joined Siren's orbit. Within moments, the wreck of the tow-barge receded into a fuzzy dot framed by the broad red curve of Siren.

Dobbs caught his breath. "That was too close. I'm going to be sick."

Muldoon grinned. "Look at her go. Right into the mother." He reached up and rapped on the wall behind him. He heard a series of taps in reply.

"Now what's he doing?" Dobbs said.

Muldoon laughed. "It's old Morse code. He says good spacing."

"So our boy survived the retrofiring, and no hard feelings to boot for smacking him against the wall. Now let's see if we can get ourselves out of here with my fillings still in my teeth." He rubbed the back of his head and swore. "Bloody magazine!"

Muldoon watched the pilot's ship disappear. "Do you think she'll burn up? She's going to make the run pretty steep."

"No, she'll go all the way," Dobbs told him, still irritated. "The atmosphere's too thin for a good burn, you know that, that's why you see those ugly craters." He filled his lungs with recycled air and exhaled in a loud sigh. "So what happened next in your story? Thanks to your little adventure, we've got plenty of time."

"Oh, that. Well, some of the crew were still alive, caught up in the safety nets, but there was a radiation leak from a crack in the reactor, and they didn't have much time. We were ordered not to attempt a rescue until the medevacs showed up."

"What could you have done anyway with a reactor leak?"

"Not much," Muldoon admitted. "But something could have been done, I'm sure. You see, by the time the medevacs got there—I mean, they were on another continent, I don't care how fast they can go skimming the stratosphere—those Navy boys were stone dead. We sat huddled in the control tower around the radio, and we heard their calls for help until the end. It froze the blood to ice in our veins to hear it. Imagine twenty men, standing, totally quiet, not even breathing. Then I remember the radio operator—Franklin, his name was—threw down his headphones in disgust and marched out of the room. He didn't want to cry in front of the rest of us. And I always thought I could have done something."

"God almighty," Dobbs said. He was nodding sagely, knowing well how soldiers lived for second chances. "Well, you did your good deed today, chap."

"Yeah. This guy's going to bring us luck. You'll see. I've got a good feeling about him."

Chapter 4
The Map

"Faces like lobsters, they had, remember?" The old pilot of the tow-barge leaned against the table, smiling a smile so wide it almost reached the large flaps of his ears. The Astronaut's eyes were set on his drinking partners, bright blue against a permanent sun-tan common among spacers. As it turned out, this was the second time they'd saved the man—the first time being ten years ago on Kilroy, when they'd been part of a small unit that had put down the Kiki Rebellion.

"And if they spit on you, by God you'd—no, worse, if they got their hairy tentacles on you and took you alive, you'd wish you had a friend in the Marines nearby."

Muldoon nodded soberly. If a soldier got wounded in action on a foreign planet, and the medevacs couldn't haul him out, the best thing that could happen to him would be for a comrade to put him out of his coming misery with a zap between the eyes. During the Rebellion, with Dobbs lying wounded on the ground and enough weapons charge in his pistol for one last shot, Muldoon had swung the barrel away from his comrade and blasted a Kiki with it and then, through sheer luck and stubborn refusal to sit down and die, had gotten them both out alive, although his leg had gotten skewered in the bargain.

"When the Governor paid Fort Christine an inspection visit, he never should have done that—thing—to the locals," said the Astronaut. "He should have known it was their mating season. No cultural training, boy. Earth-born, I'll bet. Another fresh young face to say, hi, I'm here, what can I do to make things better? He made a hell of a mess. But you boys saved my skin, didn't you? We only had twenty hours of air left in that chamber, and the Kikis were throwing their bodies down the shaft to jam up the pump. Mars!"

The servobot appeared with a tray. Dobbs accepted the drinks and tapped the machine on the head, a sign of appreciation that servant robots were designed to understand. The servobot whirred with pleasure, turned ninety degrees on a dime, and jerked back into the bar crowd, squawking, "Pardon me, excuse me, thank you."

"And now today you pulled my ass out of that tin can," the Astronaut continued. "My atoms would be blowing all over Siren if you boys had not shown up. It's like you're my guardian angels. I mean, I don't see you for Lord knows how many years, and suddenly you show up to save my life again. It's a bonafide miracle."

Dobbs picked up his shot glass and drank. "We were glad to help." He glanced at Muldoon. "Really. But you were about to tell us more about Neverland."

The Astronaut reached a large hand up his bullet head and ran it over the bristles of his crewcut. "Yeah, right. Neverland. I can't hear my own voice in this place, much less keep track of what I'm saying. This new music, it's just noise!"

Muldoon smiled and raised his eyebrows. "Rivers of gold. . . ."

"Yeah, right." The Astronaut blinked hard. "That was a beautiful rock, that was. The whole planet's like a buried treasure. Breathable atmosphere. And the gold!"

♀

Dobbs and Muldoon had pulled the pilot out of the airlock on their way to *Macintosh*. The man had passed out and was moaning gibberish about a planet called Neverland, then bolted upright and said now he'd never get the gold. It took a booster shot to revive him, but the man's luck continued to hold—thanks to the thick padding of his old-fashioned spacesuit, he'd escaped the hard brake with only a light concussion and a sprained ankle. Within minutes, he was awake and recognized the Marines from the seventy-three bloody days of the Kiki Rebellion. The Kikis had taken some cultural insult and started slaughtering the colonists. The ones they took alive, they dissected to see how humans liked it. The Astronaut had been saved, and had struck up a brief friendship with the two Marines. It had now become a very special friendship.

Within a few hours, Muldoon had docked the scrambler with *Macintosh* and paid the fare with his debit card. Shaped like a grotesque dumbbell, *Macintosh* rotated slowly to provide Earth-Standard gravity for its occupants. Dobbs, Muldoon and the Astronaut had strapped themselves into the elevator seats for the ride down into the tube. During the fall, the artificial gravity was gradually introduced so that grounders and space rookies wouldn't throw up in their laps. The men agreed to spend the evening in one of the bars.

At the end of the ride, a thought had been nagging at Dobbs, and suddenly he remembered. His eyes twinkled as he smiled at the Astronaut and said: "Commander, I hear Neverland's a promising young planet. Ever been there?"

ട്ട

The Astronaut leaned back against the booth rest and swallowed his shot in one gulp. Dobbs noticed some spill near his name tag on his left breast, ROBINSON. Yes, that was his name. Buck Robinson.

"So you want to know about Neverland. Graham brought his team to the planet because the penguins at Mission Control in the Yokohama Province thought they'd picked up some low-grade radio signals from that direction, then some egghead swore it was communication from an intelligent species." Robinson sighed. "Somebody else we could bomb into submission. But I'm sure it was just the reflection of a supernova or something. The bastards on that rock were in the Stone Age."

"Penguins, Commander?" Dobbs asked him.

Robinson's forehead wrinkled into creased folds. The man was an ancient mariner, as they say, but Dobbs noticed that nothing else on his face wrinkled except his forehead—he had that limber, fatless, ageless look of the hardcore space jock. "Yeah, the bastards think they got their wings, but can't fly. You know, Mission Control types."

Muldoon swirled the brandy in his glass and pulled his cigar out of his mouth, releasing a burst of smoke. "We call them officers, Commander."

"You call me Buck. You saved my life twice, for crying out loud!"

Dobbs pressed the button for the servobot. "It's amazing you've been there. I'd heard of Neverland, but I thought it was just a story you tell children."

"Yeah, well don't go planning a vacation there anytime soon anyway,"

Robinson said, then roared with laughter, haw haw haw. Dobbs smiled politely, rubbing the bump on the back of his head, and Muldoon twirled the ends of his handlebar mustache with amusement, already happy from being able to enjoy a good meal, a drink and a cigar.

"My job was to pilot the ship to Neverland so Graham and his people could check it out. We started a little blind because the Neverland system is in the Lighthouse. I mean, we didn't even know the planet was there until we went there and found it."

Muldoon, who had never been to the Yokohama Province which neighbored their Province of Good Hope, shook his head and shrugged at the term "Lighthouse."

Robinson leaned forward as if to hear better. "What's that? Oh, the Lighthouse. It's a glowing cloud of hydrogen gas about two hundred light-years long, just outside Yokohama in the Beyond. All the starnauts in that province navigate by it, so we call it the Lighthouse."

"Caulfield's Nebula," Muldoon said, nodding in understanding. "Marines call it the Bloodstain. You can see it pretty well from here in Good Hope."

"You should see it close up sometime. With all the stars in it, it glows like a beautiful G2 sunset. Gorgeous. But it's never been explored. It's just too massive and the big telescopes can't see into all that glowing gas. And why bother? Nebulae almost always hide only new stars, so why look for a planet to colonize when chances are there ain't one?"

"But Neverland was there," Dobbs said. "So its sun must have been older. The Neverland system must have gotten married to Caulfield's Nebula somehow."

Robinson winked. "You got it. So anyway, we penetrated the Lighthouse, and then we could see pretty good on optical. We followed the signals for a while, and I was just thinking what a big waste of time, when all of sudden we bumped into the Neverland system."

Muldoon grinned. It was a good story—a new star system!

"But everything went wrong," Robinson went on. "Neverland's near an asteroid belt, see, which we skirted and came into a geosynchronous orbit. We had a short-circuit that blinked out the frontal out-boards for a moment. When the panel came back on-line, we saw we had thirty seconds to avoid this big mother rock coming straight for us! Not even enough time to say Amen. We floored it, but the rock punched a hole in the ramscoop and we hit the atmosphere ass-first in a shallow descent, bang, and skipped like a stone. Yeah, I said ramscoop, this was a long time ago. That's the funny thing about moving at near-light speed, every time I'd come back from a mission, technology'd moved ahead and they had some newfangled engine or ship I had to buy. A racket, that's what it is. They made ships real complicated in the old days—one thing went wrong, and a chain reaction happened. Sure, we had redundancy. Backup systems for the backup systems. But all the conduit for these systems were in the same cable trays, and a four-foot length of it got smashed at starboard. So almost everything failed. It's a godsend we didn't go into a tumble. But we did crash on the planet. That's when we actually had a patch of luck, because where we landed was good ground."

"Pardon me, excuse me," the servobot was working its way through the crowd. "You called for service. May I take your order?"

Dobbs ordered another round. Then he sat back, undoing the gold button at the collar of his dress uniform. Like Muldoon—and most spacers— he loved a good tale, and the idea of rivers of gold still piqued his interest. "Chuffin 'ell! So what happened next?"

A man across the room roared with anger, followed by a scuffle. A plastic stool clattered onto the floor and a woman screamed. They turned to see two men fighting near the bar, teamsters from the look of their flight jackets. One of the teamsters was getting clobbered.

"Look at that, will you?" Muldoon said in a fury. "That man's twice his size!"

"Let it go, Sergeant Major."

Muldoon rose, pulling up his sleeves. "Why, I never saw such a—"

"Mars, will you sit down! Not tonight. You've done your good deed for the day."

Muldoon slowly sat back down, his eyes still on the fight. Robinson looked at Dobbs.

"You crashed," Dobbs prompted him.

"Okay, so we handed out the aspirin and tried to get the systems back up, with some success. That's when Graham checked the on-boards and said life forms were approaching. Couple hours later, the dots left the screen. Graham suited up and went out with the others. They didn't come back. Two days later, I took the other rover and went out. I thought I'd find Graham being worshipped as a god, you'd know what I mean if you knew this guy. One of the great Federation explorers. The best of his class."

Muldoon nodded, drawn back into the tale since the fight ended as quickly as it started. He and Dobbs had heard of Graham. But it was the stuff of myths, a long time ago.

"I found Graham and the others. I knew it was them because their rover was nearby, empty. They'd been burned alive. Charred bones. Spears, simple stone jobs, lying around. I drove like hell back to the ship and made some repairs using the backup generator. But I didn't get bothered. I was able to take off. I never did see any locals, and when I got back, the government and its partnering consortium wrote off the expedition—I mean that almost literally, there's practically no record of it left in any of the big Data Banks. The insurance company lost millions. I have no idea how much money that would be today, but it'd be a hell of a lot. I never talked about the gold, even during my trial when the government tried to charge me with negligence, so the planet stopped being of interest to the authorities, and it got named Neverland. Others call it Valhalla, the final resting place of all mariners." Robinson paused, made a little teary by the image. "That planet is a rare gem."

Muldoon handed the man his liquor. "So there really is gold there? A lot of it?"

Robinson's face broken into an awful grin, showing twin rows of strong white teeth. "Aw, hell, you're not going to believe an old mariner's tale, are you?" And he laughed again, haw haw haw. "I got lots of good stories. I saw a supernova once, close enough that I could see the bones in my hand even with my eyes closed. How many people can say that? Another time, I remember, my ion drive went to half power. I rode into a comet and hitched a ride straight to Galileo on a piece of its tail!"

Muldoon frowned in disappointment, starting to think that he'd been goofed. Dobbs' entire being appeared to sag like a deflating tire.

Robinson leaned forward, his face suddenly fierce and gloating. "Don't you worry. Yeah, there were rivers of gold, gents. Rivers of it! I mean in the literal sense. Pure stuff, untainted, high-grade gold grain. You could make a hundred thousand light converters out of it. Or a million miles of spec-grade plating and wiring, take your pick. I was too damn scared to go out and scoop it all up myself and get rich. I wished I had, because I'm broke right now. I could use a hand up. I'm an Unknown Sailor, you know, and it's a bitch."

Dobbs eyes twinkled like blue fire as he pictured it. A million miles of specification-grade wiring with almost no overhead. Enough to make a man a multimillionaire at least.

Muldoon asked Robinson, "What do you mean by that, 'Unknown Sailor'?"

"I've been in this racket for forty years. That's forty years at close to the speed of light, kids, and I'm not counting all the years I spent in cryonic hibernation. They had a supercomputer on Earth in a vault to keep track of us who'd been in space a long time, make sure they kept up with the pensions. But a long long time went by on Earth while I was on my forty years of missions, I'm talking eighteen hundred Standard years or more due to the time dilation, and a terrorist incident or something over the years wound up making a fire that damaged the computer, vault or no vault. All record of me and about four hundred other poor souls was lost, the early guys, the oldest space jocks. I still exist in computers in most of the provinces, so I can get around, but I can't get my pension from Capital Province, see. To them, I don't exist anymore."

He scooped up his glass, gulped down the liquor and slammed it empty back onto the table. "Local stuff, but not bad. Yeah, I'm broke. You'd think that after all I'd done for the Federation, launching probes, scouting sites for space stations, laying satellites and all the rest, I would get taken care of in my old age. I mean, I'm almost two thousand Earth-Standard years old, follow me? I'm practically immortal! Now I scrape by as a satellite repairman, flying a thousand tons that were barely space-worthy. What is that? It's humiliation, that's what it is. Bullshit work. But my memories could come in handy, see. They have value, and I'm not talking about writing my memoirs. I still got something to sell."

Dobbs and Muldoon seemed to consider this. Robinson faltered, adding, "Well, to the right enterprising types, that is."

Dobbs opened a breast pocket of his tunic and produced a cigar, which Muldoon lit it for him with a steel lighter. He tasted the tobacco and enjoyed it for a moment. His heart was pounding, and he was sure his cheeks were flushed, but otherwise he kept his cool. Still looking at the cigar, he finally said, "Well, Commander, if there were, as you say, rivers of gold on that planet—if, I mean to say, your information were reliable, I should think Sergeant Major Muldoon and I might know a party interested in a purchase."

"Good! How would you like the introduction to go? In my day, we—"

"No need for the usual customs, confidentiality and commission," said Muldoon. He jerked his thumb at Dobbs. "Because what he's saying is we're the interested party."

Robinson's mouth dropped open. "You want to buy it directly? Hell, that's even better!" He pressed the service button this time. "We're talking business now. I don't know about you, but business gives me an awful thirst. And we're celebrating, right? You saved my life!"

"Of course," Dobbs continued, "since we're dealing with flight into a nebula, you'd have to be able to produce reliable astral charts, radiometrics. . . ."

Robinson put his elbows on the table. "Hell, I got it all. Now you and ol' Tim Mud-doon here seem like enterprising gents to me. You know your way around artillery, I know that firsthand. Men like us, we've got to think of our future!"

"That's the truth," Muldoon said. "Nobody else is rushing to do the job."

"I always kept the information close to the chest because I thought I'd get back there one of these days and get the gold myself," said Robinson. "I used to have dreams about it even. But look at me, there's no way I'd be able to pull it off now at my ripe age. Today was an omen I can't hold onto this anymore—I mean, I really thought I'd bought the farm. But information has value in these parts. There's a whole thriving black market, just for information. We mariners know everything. I want to cash in my chips."

Dobbs looked sideways at Muldoon. "What do you think, Sergeant Major?"

Muldoon shrugged, making it Dobbs's call as usual. "We've got nothing else planned, Sergeant Major. And he's right, you know, we have to look out for the future."

Dobbs nodded. Rivers of gold! His heart was racing. He turned back to Robinson.

"Yes, you seem to know a great deal," he said, smiling.

"I know a good opportunity when I see one," said the Astronaut, winking. "For men who like a good challenge, I mean. Not for wimps!"

"The Federation is a realm brimming with opportunity, even in a backwater province," Dobbs told him.

"And let's not forget adventure," said Muldoon, his teeth clenched on his cigar.

Dobbs raised his shot glass. "Now let's drink to that, shall we?"

ৡ

That night, Dobbs and Muldoon stood over a document, enjoying the taste and heady effect of cigars and brandy sipped from large snifters. The material of the document was a rare parchment, heavy-weight fibered Mantillia. The script itself was a rarely used flowing ancient Earth callig-raphy called cursive that the men had learned at the colonial schools. The warm, dry air was filled with tobacco smoke that moved in a slow current toward the return air grille. The bottle was nearly empty. The men's faces were hot and red. Their eyes smoldered blue. After some quiet talk between them, they leaned over the desk and signed the paper.

They toasted in silence. To the Retirement Fund.

They had located the Holy Grail sitting in the middle of a nebula, and they were going to get it.

BOOK II

THE VOYAGE PREPARATIONS

Chapter 5
Muldoon and Dariana

Muldoon loved Dariana, a Class I sextech who had needed only minimal cosmetic engineering to perfect her curves and full figure. She lay on the bed next to him the next morning, exposing the full length of her body, fast asleep and reminding him of an angel.

Muldoon had known many women over the years, and he remembered them all. Memories of the sex—although he had partaken in many strange and pleasurable experiences with sextechs and other women—were not readily available. But his brain was a treasure chest of coy glances, birthmarks, tinkling laughter, warm snuggles and good female advice. He was not particular in whom he loved, but he loved his women fiercely. A professional soldier, he thought he could never have just one woman, accepting the transience of romance as he accepted all other facts of spacer life, but he was monogamous. He loved only one woman at a time, then gave her unconditional love.

Dariana awoke and stretched. "Mmmm. You had quite a night, huh?"

Muldoon smiled with boyish embarrassment. "That's for damn sure."

"You were only about four hours late."

"Well, Darry, time dilation and these infernal distances create a special code among spacers. Me and Lawrence, being half-spacer ourselves, have learned to respect it."

This piqued her interest. "What sort of code?"

"You see, it's hard to make friends since after your next trip you probably won't see them again. The custom is if you make a friend, you have a drink, and if you see him again, you spend the night in hard drinking, given the odds of meeting up again. Lawrence and I picked up a man we met in the Kiki Rebellion."

"I love that story!"

"We left him sleeping under the table. The servobots probably vacuumed him up."

Dariana laughed, sat up and began brushing her long black hair. "You must be pretty hung over."

"I don't feel a thing, that's the whole truth. God, you're beautiful in the morning."

"I'll make some tea."

Dariana stood and threw on a robe, then went to the kitchenette. Muldoon heard her put a kettle in the microwave. Yes, he thought, that's what he liked about her, and would remember. She was a sextech, but there was nothing impersonal or contrived about the way she made love, the way she made a home for Muldoon after a long night of lovemaking. This was his retreat from hard colonial life, and a refuge from thought itself.

Something stirred in him again, and he remembered crying out in his sleep, Dariana gentle as a mother, soothing him. Not like him at all. Spacers had to watch out for such things, especially crying jags. But he knew there was a deeper reason.

"Darry," he said.

"What is it, dear?"

His mouth hung open. "Nothing, my love."

She let it pass. "So you didn't get yourself into any brawls last night, did you?"

"There were two fights," Muldoon said. "Teamsters. But I behaved myself." He listened to her rattle cups and plasticware.

"Tim?" she called.

"Yes, my love."

"Did you really make love to Crickets on Tattoo?"

Muldoon chuckled quietly. "Yes, I have made love to their women."

"But those god-awful heads! And they live in honeycomb!" She came in holding a tea service. She handed him a cup. "Nice and strong, the way you like it."

"I'm a good Marine, I am," said Muldoon, accepting the hot cup gratefully.

The Crickets were bluish humanoids from one of the first worlds to trade with, be conquered by, and subsequently be absorbed into the

Federation, thereby benefiting from Federation "administration, technology and culture." Fair in intellect and about one-and-a-half times stronger and faster than humans, Crickets had a feature disturbing to most humans—a praying-mantislike head. The Crickets had loved humans so much that they had rapidly evolved humanlike bodies from insectoid ones and embraced Terran culture, but couldn't lose the head. Since native-levied colonial armies began mutinying many years ago, the Crickets were found to be a loyal and capable stock colonial soldier and policeman, and were distributed throughout the Federation. Muldoon trusted them in a scrap as much as he trusted any good Marine. He and Dobbs commanded about thirty of them at the base.

"Listen, Darry, about the Cricket women. Tattoo had no human women within a parsec, but there were plenty of Crickets at the settlement. All of the men at the fort, uh, took pleasure in them."

"But the head!"

"They have the most beautiful bodies, perfectly proportioned and very human—they can't hold a candle to you, of course, but they are quite beautiful. I feel a great kinship to the Crickets. They are a good hard-working people. I am not a specist."

"What ever was it like, Tim?" Dariana was not jealous, but instead showed a professional curiosity.

"Well, their skin is as smooth as marble, and hairless, going back to the days when their flesh was a form of chitin, insect skin," said Muldoon. "The idea is that you have to move a lot to get real friction. During love-making, the pincers reach up and clasp on both sides of a man's head."

Dariana sipped her tea. "And why do they do that? Does it hurt?"

"The pincers ensure the propagation of the species. They are actually additional erogenous zones, ensuring the female clasps your head with them. At the same time, they prevent her from reaching up and eating your head in the throes of climax."

"My goodness!" she laughed. "That's amazing!"

"Yeah it is," Muldoon said seriously, finishing his hot tea. "It's pretty amazing."

"What if you had children with them?"

"You can't. We're separate species, even though they've copied most of our genes."

"But what if you could?"

"I can't imagine, Darry. Who knows?"

Dariana nestled close to Muldoon, who put an arm around her shoulders. "If you think that's amazing," she said, tickling his chin, "I've just been trained in a new astral projection massage technique that will make your mind leave your body for hours, and take away all those aches and pains from fighting crabs all day."

"That sounds smashing," Muldoon said, imitating Dobbs.

"Tim?"

"Yes, my love."

"Why were you crying last night? You did, a little while you were sleeping. Then you called my name."

Muldoon looked for an escape. "Crying? The devil you say!"

"That means you were feeling upset and helpless. I've seen you upset, but never helpless. So I could only think of one thing that would make you feel that way. You're leaving me, aren't you? I mean, you're leaving the Province." Her voice was soft, without anger.

"Well, I must be taking a brief trip soon, that's right."

Dariana looked up at him. Her genetically engineered green eyes flashed with intelligence, or perhaps it was intuition. Whatever it was, it was a distinctly female ability to cut through the layers of a man such as Muldoon. "A brief trip. At close to light speed?"

"Yes," Muldoon said sheepishly. "Listen, I have to meet Lawrence for lunch."

Her voice had full volume now. "I could be old when you return! Or dead!"

"We will always be with each other, Darry," he soothed.

"Yeah," she said dryly. "We always had *Macintosh*. Pardon me while I write my memoirs. Tell me about your trip. Where are you going?"

Muldoon set his jaw. "I'm not allowed to talk about our plans."

"Why? I could be killed? Interplanetary intrigue?"

He normally enjoyed her mocking him, it was a sort of foreplay. But he felt trapped and pressured now. "No, it's just that it's. . . ."

"It's what?" She elbowed him. It smarted. "What?"

"It's a man's game, Darry. You know."

"Bull," she said bluntly. She pulled away from him, leaned to the end-table and produced a cigarette, waiting. Muldoon reached into his trousers on the side of the bed, retrieved his lighter and lit it for her. She demurely took a drag, then said, "Women have been Prime Minister, and thousands of them are astronauts, pilots, even Marines. It's because I'm a sextech, isn't it? That's why our trade is the oldest, fifteen thousand years old! Not for pleasure of the flesh, but for the power a man feels being around a submissive woman."

"Damn it, Darry." Muldoon had heard that speech a dozen times. "You must be in the consortium we're forming. You have to be bound by the contract. That's how it works. I don't make the rules!"

"I've got an idea! I'll join your consortium."

"But you have no special skills that we require," said Muldoon, then flinched when he realized too late what he had said. "Gaw!"

"You're a pig, Timothy Muldoon. An absolute pig! Screw your contract. I don't want a percentage. I'll work for my passage."

Muldoon thought of Dariana with men he knew, and flinched. "You—not in my life!"

"I'll talk a few of the other girls into coming to work for the other men," she said. "I will be all yours. It will make the trip much more fun, and much less serious."

"That's what I'm afraid of," said Muldoon, sagging.

"It will be horrible here without you, Tim. You're the only nice man who calls on me. The rest are disgusting truckers and pilots. No manners. I've simply got to go too."

Muldoon sighed in surrender. He knew he should have saved himself the trouble and told her right away. "All right. I'll tell you, and then I have to go because I promised I'd meet Lawrence for lunch at Maxwell's, and I'm starving. He's found us a pilot. Okay, here's the score. Lawrence and I bought a map leading to a planet in Caulfield's Nebula that's loaded with gold. There are hostile natives, and we have to get past the Border Patrol."

"Border Patrol!" she said, putting the cigarette out. "They have Patrol at the border, too? To protect against what? There hasn't been anything in the Beyond advanced enough to attack the Federation since Xerxes, and that was long ago."

"You are a silly girl," Muldoon told her. "The Border Patrol are the flyers who keep smugglers and gunrunners from leaving the Federation at one point, spacing around undetected, and reentering somewhere else without interception."

"Oh," Dariana said, nestling against him again. "And gold, too. This is so exciting!"

Muldoon put his arm back around her. "We will go to the planet—it's been named Neverland—and loot the place from the floorboards to the rafters. First, we're going to have to put together a very professional crew, a ship and clearance for space flight. That's Dobbs' department, so my job is simple. It's supposed to be a gem of a planet. G2 sun. Breathable atmosphere. Reasonable sunrise-to-sunset cycle. Nice and warm."

"It sounds like a fun adventure you've cooked up, Tim."

Muldoon grinned. "The best one yet. Something a man can sink his teeth into. Some call this type of opportunity the Holy Grail, others I've heard call it the Fountain of Youth."

"People could make a home on that planet. Outside the Federation. All on their own. Pioneers!" She squealed. "Now that would be a real adventure."

"It might just be, Darry. But I can't think of that. We're going to be rich. In any case we have to leave the Province because. . . ." His face grew hot.

"What is it?"

"Lawrence and I are in a little trouble with the government." He looked for a moment as if he were in agony, and Dariana scratched his head, encouraging him. "We've only got five months before this Commission of Something or Other comes for us, and they'll bring Patrol with them, I'm sure. So we have to leave the Service either way, it looks like."

"Why didn't you tell me about this, Tim?"

"Well, Lawrence and I are good Marines, but we've gotten ourselves into little side ventures every so often when we have time. We call it the Retirement Fund. These ventures aren't always exactly legal." He looked to her for a reaction, then crossed his arms. "I never wanted to tell you before because I didn't want you to know, that's all."

She smiled. "You're trying to protect me," she said. "That's sweet, but I'm not that frail no matter what you think of me. I forgive you for all crimes past and future, but not for withholding information. Because then I have to go through the trouble of figuring it out for myself or prying it out of you. Not that prying isn't fun in itself, but—"

"Aw, Darry, I do want to protect you." He held her close. "It's going to be dangerous as hell on Neverland. Something could happen to you, and I'd kill myself!"

"My knight in shining armor!" Dariana said. "But there you go being a pig again. My whole life I've spent in these space stations. It's the most boring existence you can imagine. I've lived hundreds of adventures by hearing good stories. I'm tired of that, it doesn't satisfy me anymore. I want to have an adventure of my own."

Muldoon grinned in admiration. "My woman has guts."

Dariana suddenly smiled and frowned at the same time. "Actually, this adds a whole new dimension to you. You're very clever, Tim."

"Lawrence is the clever one. I'm just going along to keep him from getting himself killed. He's always thinking of something."

"You took a Kiki dart in your leg for him, didn't you? I know that story."

"I couldn't leave him behind, and I couldn't put a zap between his eyes. I had to take him with me."

"What good friends you are. Well, if you think I'd be in the way, maybe I shouldn't go. But I'd miss you, and I want to tell you I love you for at least telling me." She kissed him lightly and looked into his eyes, probing.

Muldoon knew he was in a Catch-22. When he and Dobbs got rich, there'd be no more adventures and they'd settle down. Muldoon loved Dariana and wanted to marry her because he admitted to himself that he'd never met anybody else like her, and probably never would again. But to go and get the gold, Muldoon would have to leave Dariana, and she'd be dead for at least four hundred years by the time he got back.

If he tried to take her with him, Dobbs would have a royal fit. Mars!

Muldoon sighed. "I suppose I could talk to Lawrence about it. Which again reminds me, I've got to go and meet him."

Bells chimed, signaling somebody at the door.

"Oh, I think I've got a problem," Dariana whispered. "I know who that is. It's this man who keeps bothering me. A customer."

"What's that?" he demanded.

"He wants me to do strange things, you know. He's very nice, but strange."

Muldoon was already stepping into his trousers. "What did you say?"

"I'll let him in. Maybe you could reason with him."

He stumbled after her, pulling on his pants. "Where are you going?"

"But I forbid you to hurt him. He's really very nice. His name's Caspar."

Dariana went to the door and welcomed in a tall, young, grinning man wearing the rumpled leather uniform of a Patrol flyer. "Hi, sorry I'm late, kid," the man said, sweeping back a lock of blond hair from his forehead.

"Oh, who's this?"

Muldoon socked him in the jaw. "Learn how to treat a lady!"

"What the hell?" the man screamed, then ran away, holding his cheek.

Muldoon slammed the door after him and wheeled on Dariana. "Is that how they treat you? How dare he!"

"It's part of the trade, Tim. I told you not to hurt him. What am I supposed to do?"

He pointed a finger at her and opened his mouth. Then a thought hit him like a zap between the eyes. He knew he'd been goofed. If he weren't so angry still, he would have roared with appreciation at the play. But the point was made.

"You're—" His voice dropped in volume, deflated. "You're coming with me and that's final."

Dariana threw her arms around him. "My knight in shining armor!"

"Jupiter!" Muldoon said, his shoulders sagging "I fell for that cheap stunt, at my age!"

Dariana studied him. "You don't have to swear. Okay, I made a vid-call to a regular customer last night when I guessed what the score would be. Can you blame me? I like you. And I want to chase my own Holy Grails too."

Muldoon grinned. "It was a good play," he admitted. "Although now I feel bad about clobbering that kid. You made your point loud and clear. And I love you."

"So can I really come with you?"

He nodded. "I suppose there's no stopping you, and it looks like I'm going to miss lunch too," he said, and kissed the woman he loved.

৯

Sergeant Major Timothy Muldoon was born on the planet Grommet in the province named after the great explorer Kilroy. Grommet's population grew rapidly in the first five hundred years of the Federation. The local sun, a warm Class F star, provided ample sunlight. The sunrise-to-sunset cycle and the soil, rich with dead plants and a thousand species of mammals, were conducive to growing kilometers of magnificent crops. While the atmosphere was not quite breathable to humans, terraforming would make the world fully livable when funds and resources became available. And as a reward for good behavior. Grommet was a prison world, where repeat offenders on Earth went if they accepted the offer to go off-world with their families to start a new life and grow crops for the Federation. In all of five hundred years, the Federation Ministry of Public Order and Corrections had faced only one criminal who refused, a young woman. She was jettisoned into space with the next garbage payload off Ganymede—fused in vacuum with thousands of other tons of trash and sent into the Asteroid Belt—and although she became the stuff of legend on Grommet, only the supercomputers now remembered her on Earth.

Muldoon's ancestors received their freedom after six generations of rough living on Grommet, and decided to stay as freedom did not come with a ticket for space travel. After another three hundred years, the Prime Minister signed a bill from the Parliament of Capital Province that abolished the prison-world system, and later resulted in the terraforming of Grommet. From poor stock, Muldoon's people stayed poor through the centuries, farming and trading in the rough streets of the cities until the men began a long-standing tradition of enlisting in the Colonial Marines. Timothy Muldoon was the twelfth generation of Muldoons to do so, and was proud of his rank of Sergeant Major as well as his wide travels at close to light speed around the Federation. He never forgot his family, however, although his immediate loved ones had long since returned to the soil of the planet. Whenever possible, he deposited money into an account that helped pay for his sisters' distant direct female descendants to attend the University at Paradiso. Muldoon hoped that with their natural beauty and an education, they would marry rich men or at least launch proper careers that would get the Muldoon clan back into a lush quality of life in Capital Province.

To Muldoon, life contained few maybes. He hated his enemies and loved his friends. He was loyal to family and clan, and considered Dobbs, the Prime Minister and all Marines to be part of his family. He admired people who were good at their trade or had special skills or talent, and respected people who worked hard to improve themselves, which was why he enjoyed the company of Crickets while most humans looked down their noses at them. He exemplified the martial spirit, but his soul was the natural poet. He defended the weak avidly, which usually resulted in brawls. He showed hot courage and cool leadership in battle, commanding a natural soldier's respect from rankers to officers, and could be stubborn and quick-tempered. He had nerves of steel, he was resolute in all decisions he made, and he excelled at games of chance. Like Dobbs, he had excellent taste in liquor, women, cigars, hovercars and other aspects of gentlemanly lifestyle. It was true that he wore his style on his sleeves, betraying his lower-class ancestry, but he had a decent, solid style. People appreciated his frankness and interest in their welfare, admired the way he could admit he was wrong. He quietly held an unshakable faith in God, and knew that God had a plan just for him.

Chapter 6
The Cat in The Box

All and all, I want to live my life, then end my life, with meaning," the Pilot explained. He wore a brown leather Space Cav jacket and baseball cap, and smoked a cigarette. He kept a working antique .45 on his hip. A veteran spacer, he was as comfortable in a weightless environment as he was in gravity. Despite the perils of space travel—solar flares, cosmic rays, meteoroids, dust swarms, space junk—he was cool, even nonchalant in the pilot's seat. The type who knew he would live through any crisis, but didn't care if he died. Dobbs sat across from him and his navigator at Maxwell's, wondering what kind of trouble Muldoon had gotten himself into. But he knew he could easily guess if he tried: Dariana. The Navigator was a world apart from the Pilot, a quiet little bearded man whose eyes shifted nervously.

"With meaning," the Pilot said again, and buried his face in his mug of beer. "Here's how I want to go. I hijack a small tourist cruiser, it's got lots of windows. I take her into the nearest black hole, a nice big one. While I'm moving toward the center, who knows how long you've got before you're turned into spaghetti? I only want five seconds, because dig it. The mass of a black hole is infinite. Just the concept blows my mind. Infinite. I've been close at ninety-nine percent of speed of light, but I've never achieved infinite mass. Not even God can do better than infinite! I could do that in a black hole, it happens whether you want it to or not. While I'm flying down the toilet, I can look out and see it happen. I mean, I'm at infinite mass, at least theoretically, right? Time practically stops for me relative to the rest of the universe because of the time dilation. Generations of people all over this arm of the galaxy will watch me, and ask, did he move yet? Huh? Nope. More generations will pass, then more. I will appear to stretch across the black hole's event horizon. I'm going in feet first, cowabunga! Millions more generations pass, then the local sun dies. Other stars die. They all die. I'm watching it happen in comical fast-motion. The universe expanding rapidly into the dark unknowns, the distant lights twinkling and going out in the blink of an eye. Total darkness. Space dust."

Dobbs took a sip of beer and set the empty mug down quietly, respectfully. He was still experiencing a Neptune-sized hangover from the night before, but business demanded lavish entertainment of the vendor.

"That's how to end your life with some meaning," the Pilot said.

"But I wanted to talk to you about something else," said Dobbs. "Something better."

"What's that?"

"How to make a lot of money. I've got a big job for you and your partner if you're up to it. A heavy freighter. Two-way passage."

Kilroy frowned at Dobbs' clumsy segueway. "I was getting to that. I figured maybe we'd try and get to know each other first, see if our core philosophies were compatible and all that, I mean, there's nothing worse on a flight than bad vibes."

"I don't have the same need, frankly," Dobbs told him.

"Don't you even want to know if I'm related to the great explorer Kilroy? Everybody asks me that."

"I did my background check. Although you're in fact not related to the great explorer, you came highly recommended by people of excellent character, and I understand you're looking for work."

"Aw, shucks, who said that."

Dobbs smiled. "People of excellent character." As he considered all spacers. He knew and couldn't help that he was a complete snob to almost everybody else but this breed. Spacers, due to their ongoing war against time and space, held a distinct culture, lifestyle and universe-view which Dobbs had been raised in and preferred.

Grounders, on the other hand, thought spacers were nuts—adrenaline-addicts who were self-absorbed, were socially dysfunctional in general, and wore enormous attitude on their sleeves. Dobbs had to give a nod to that point of view. But who cared? Good spacers were reliable, trustworthy, extremely talented and understood the doctrine of mutual gain.

Kilroy tapped out a few bars of a song with his hands on the tabletop, then laughed. "Whatever. All right, yes, you got me. We're looking for a mission. Trade's not good this year. Technology takes too long to reach this province. Makes the businessmen scared of risk and that means less spacing. What kind of job do you have in mind?"

Dobbs thought for a moment. "Since you're interested in eternity, have you ever heard of the Fountain of Youth?"

Kilroy frowned, his mouth open, a mug of beer in his hand. The Navigator's eyes, previously darting around the room, suddenly flickered and focused.

"Okay, I'm hooked," Kilroy said carefully. "Tell me more."

Dobbs smiled and produced several sheets of paper made of heavy-fibered Mantillia parchment. He handed them to the Pilot. "Sign and accept the oath of confidentiality."

Kilroy whistled and accepted the document as if it were a beer filled to the rim. "Real paper. Nice production. Excuse while I do a little reading." He read the contract, pausing to ask questions which Dobbs answered. Then he turned to the Navigator.

"Tommy. Tommy."

The Navigator glanced at him.

"This guy's serious. Give me a pen."

The Navigator's hand darted out, holding a pen. Kilroy drew his mark with a flourish. He in turn handed it to the Navigator, who looked at it as if he'd been handed a snake. He scratched out his name without even looking at it and gave the papers back to Dobbs.

"Now you can tell me where we're going," Kilroy told him. "This had better be good, because I'm sick of jokers."

Dobbs smiled, his eyes twinkling. "We're going into the Beyond to a planet called Neverland. It's in Caulfield's Nebula, and we have a map."

"Neverland!" Kilroy roared, and slapped the table. "Mars, that's a good one. The final resting place of the mariners, right? So we really are going to the Beyond. This isn't gun-running. That's what I thought at first—I see a lot of Marines do it."

"Don't say that around Sergeant Major Muldoon. He's a patriot."

"So what are you going to do, take the place over? I know a Marine colonel who did that once. Went into the Beyond and started his own kingdom."

Dobbs smiled and explained the entire story, starting with meeting Buck Robinson.

"You've got the Holy Grail," Kilroy said when he finished, nodding soberly. "The holy of holies. Or we're both real big suckers going into a friggin' nebula with a bogus map."

"We've got nothing else planned," Dobbs said casually.

"And you're going to hijack that beast of a freighter at your base for the mission."

"Nothing else is available for free, I'm afraid. It'll have to do. We need a freighter of this size."

"I know, our trading ship is too small for this. No problem. Those big freighters are basically good ships, just clumsy is all. A question of mass. I will modify your ship as needed and fly it. We'll have to bring some of our own stuff. Integration might still be a problem. Do you have a good engineer?"

"The best," said Dobbs. "Mr. Travis, from the base. He hasn't been approached yet, but I know the man well. He's in."

"Good, but well, here's another one of your engineer's problems," said Kilroy. "This model of freighter you described to me usually travels unmanned, so it falls like a rock most of the way after it enters atmosphere, braking hard every so many kilometers. This means the crew will have to endure the misery of free fall for quite a while unless your engineer can rig up heavier retrofiring on the bottom for a nice soft ride. Free fall doesn't bother me personally, though. Actually, I think it's liberating. You got the charts?"

Dobbs took three rubberband-bound stacks of thermal paper from a briefcase and laid them on the table, then put a battered hard drive on top that held the heavy data. Buck Robinson had delivered it all that morning as promised.

"Where'd you get this dinosaur?" Kilroy said, inspecting the hard drive. "We should be able to read it with our nano, though. What else you got there?"

"Astral charts, some hand-drawn, I'm afraid," said Dobbs. "But of finest workmanship, as if from a navigational computer. Printouts on old thermal paper, but clearly legible. We'll need a course that will bring us into geostationary orbit at the point where Graham's ship crashed." He pushed the stack of documents toward the Pilot.

Kilroy laughed, jerking his thumb at the Navigator, his elbows on the table. "Give that crap to him. Do I look like the Navigator?"

The Navigator sneered as he accepted the documents, then began dissecting them, poring over key charts with his face inches away from the paper.

"So what else?" Kilroy said.

"We need a freelance weapons expert," Dobbs told him. "The planet is full of hostile natives. I was wondering if you could recommend a good man for the job."

The Pilot rolled his eyes, then closed them, thinking. "Ah." His eyes flashed open. "Brandon Fritz. He's in the Province. A ball turret gunner. Hey, now I know what you're thinking. They don't come nuttier than ball turret gunners. But this guy is into heavy metal. Hardcore. He could rig up a dental laser to blow up a small moon."

Dobbs shrugged. "If he's good, he's good."

Kilroy appeared a little sheepish. Dobbs could tell this was a rare occasion, and shrugged again to prompt him. "You should know up front that he's a little wigged out, even for a turret gunner," said the Pilot. He and Dobbs leaned forward together. "A long time ago, he was in War VI. In one action, he sawed up a Xerxesian transport and it must have been too close, because when the reactor went up he got blinded by the explosion. Every action he was in, he would get blinded for a time. After a while, it took some cards out of his deck, if you know what I mean. Then he served on the Berry for three years. You know the Berry. Big fat slow-moving sloth of a planet. A one-hundred-and-forty-two-day sunrise-to-sunset cycle. That's a long time to spend in the dark for a man who had learned to hate and fear it. He ended up taking light treatments, then went AWOL and jumped in a scram and flew nice and slow around the planet just ahead of the darkness, chasing the sunrise until his fuel ran out. That was dumb. Space Cav gave him a Section Eight."

The servobot dropped off their drinks, and the Pilot drank thirstily.

"He wakes up every night, screams for a while, you know," he said, belching.

Dobbs produced a cigar, which reminded Kilroy to smoke a cigarette.

"Perihelion," the Navigator mumbled to himself.

"As long as he can perform his duties, I could not refuse him," Dobbs said.

"No prejudices," said Kilroy through a cloud of smoke, shaking his head and smiling. "Tons of self-interest, with a slight moral streak. I think I like you." He jerked his thumb at the Navigator. "Tommy likes you, too." The Navigator did not look up. "Excuse Tommy, he's absorbed. And sometimes, Tommy don't hear so good. His last partner was a bastard and a fool. Went against Tommy's nav program on a mission and decided to hot-dog it. Planetstorming. Stupid. They dipped into the atmosphere too steep, and almost burned up. The noise was too loud—you know, the turbines overloading and all—and now he can't hear too good, especially when he's absorbed."

"Well, I'm told you're both the very best in your trade," said Dobbs, moving onward.

"I also hear your pal's not so bad with a scrambler. Word gets around these parts."

Dobbs laughed. "You should try landing with him. You'll lose your lunch. Anyway, we're only looking for men of quality for this job. Guiding a ship through a nebula's no small task. So I am pleased to have you aboard."

"Oh, I'm glad to be aboard," said the Pilot. "I'm glad either way, as a matter of fact. I mean, I'm glad to be aboard and not be aboard."

Dobbs stared at the man.

Kilroy laughed as if to say, gotcha. "I subscribe to Quantum Zen. You should really consider it yourself. Have you heard of it?"

Dobbs shook his head. He knew that minor physical or mental problems such as tics, compulsive habits, crying jags and phobias were nothing odd with veteran spacers—in some provinces, it was actually a sort of badge of distinction. So he was not disturbed by the information regarding the ball turret gunner and the Navigator, for example, and he was live-and-let-live about odd philosophies such as Quantum Zen. So long as they could perform their trade with appropriate skill, all was well. The only ones to watch for, Dobbs had learned, were the burn-outs, the suicidal ones being the Untouchables.

"It's not too far out," Kilroy was saying. "I mean, nobody stands in space stations and hands out implants about it. It's actually quite practical. Actually, I sleep nights because of it. Well, you know about quantum mechanics, Schroedinger's Cat and all that. There's a cat in a box with a radioactive atom and a bottle of poison. The atom might decay within the hour, it might not. It's fifty-fifty, clean right down the middle. There's a Geiger counter in the box, too. If the atom decays, the Geiger counter will tick and that tick will break the bottle and release the poison, killing the cat. Now, we can't hear the tick ourselves or the bottle breaking from where we are outside the box. That means at any given moment during the hour, the cat could be alive, it could be dead. Nobody but God knows. Like I said, it's fifty-fifty. So what is the mathematical probability the cat is alive? Fifty-fifty. In terms of physics, the cat is alive and dead at the same time. Don't look at me like that. This is the stuff that helped Tracey prove the existence of wormholes."

"So anybody who's not here in this room with us, because we can't see them, is both alive and dead, according to the odds of them being dead," said Dobbs incredulously, although he was wondering how much a good bookie could make if a syndicate were set up. "That is, I mean, if they're not being observed by another sentient being?"

Kilroy pressed the service button this time. "Don't worry about the tab—since you're hearing me out, I'm buying this round. You're looking at this wrong, pal. What the paradox tells us is that alternate universes are possible, dig it. Like old Newton said, for every action there is an equal and opposite reaction. So what if every action we take has an opposite action that breaks off into an alternate universe? You know what that means? I'll tell you what that means. Either way, I'm okay. In an alternate universe, I'm refusing you right now. So say I'm making a big mistake going on this mission with you—say we've been had and there's no gold there, or say we make a little flight error and forget to check the fuel gauge or something and end up millions of kilometers off course, out of fuel and food, which is as horrifying as being buried alive—in my alternate universe, everything is A-okay because I turned you down. That's why I'll sign on and take my chances, and I'll sleep tonight. Dig it?"

"Heavy," said the Navigator. The man grinned fiendishly. "That's heavy, I said." Then he went back to the charts. "Bad light in here. If you really think you're so brilliant and existential, oo, wow, you can handle the simple question I asked you earlier."

"But it's stupid!" cried Kilroy. He turned to Dobbs. "He asked me Einstein's old joke, suppose you're in a spaceship and look out the port-hole, and see another spaceship. That spaceship is moving. Or is your spaceship moving? Then he looked at me as if he'd found the Theory of Everything. It's like asking if God can make a galaxy that he couldn't rotate. Yuck. Boring. The real answer is it doesn't matter, there is no answer!"

The Navigator sneered at him. "That's my point. It's a philosophy. I signed on because it really doesn't make a big difference what job we score next."

This made Dobbs smile. These men were typical spacers.

Kilroy waved him off. "Nihilism. Like I said, boring. But back to Quantum Zen. You know, if I were brilliant, which I'm not, I'd find a way to bridge the universes. I'd simply jump into the alternate universe where I made the right choice whenever I could throughout my whole life. That would be like having as much power as God."

"Yes, I'm sure," said Dobbs, accepting his drink and tapping the ser-vobot on the head. "But I simplify such a philosophical outlook by say-ing, no worries. Sergeant Major Muldoon and I can do anything that suits us if we hold to that time-tested motto of our partnership—that, and 'There's always a way.' My comrade often serves a nobler purpose, but I'd have no qualms about finding a way to control your bridge between the universes and charge a toll. Now that'd be a nice fat annuity I could live with."

Kilroy laughed, charmed.

"And all thanks to no worries," Dobbs added grandly. "Because the same great God that watches over the Prime Minister and the Federation watches over us, and our protection and good fortune are assured by the inner workings of the Divine Plan."

"Predeterminists!" said Kilroy, who seemed genuinely pleased with his new employer, and led a toast. "Well, more power to you, Marine. Here's to the biggest gamble of all. We'll make all alternate universes tremble with envy!"

This made Dobbs laugh, and he got over his hangover and warmed to the fun again, aided by switching from the strong local beer micro-brewed from seaweed to good synth brandy, a gentleman's drink.

They passed several hours in philosophical musings and discussion of the mission until the Navigator looked up as if in a trance, which almost made Dobbs spill his drink.

"This is complicated," said the Navigator. He had filled half the table with the charts and some ancient-looking books from his knapsack, open to coffee-stained pages crammed with astronautical tables and formulas. "The target is close to its sun, and there's another planet, a gas giant, rip-ping the place apart. Tidal forces suck asteroids from the local belt into high-speed orbit past the planet. It's all volatile, we'll probably find your little pet civilization extinct from an impact. These radiometrics are crap, ancient. We'll have to go optical to navigate when we get there. We'll have to upgrade the guidance system to get some fancier footwork out of the ship. We'll aerobrake to save fuel if we can and achieve geostationary orbit right where you want to park. The best scenario for a one-way trip will be seven-point-six years at ninety percent of the speed of light including acceleration and braking time. Christ, I wish we had an anti-matter drive!"

"My partner's a mystic, as you can see," Kilroy said with humor, good and warmed by his beer. "We've never gone into a nebula before, Tommy. It should be fun, don't you think?"

The Navigator either didn't notice him or pretended not to. "If we live through all that, we'll use the gravitational pull of the planet to swing us by the local gas giant, which in turn will slingshot us back to the borders of the Federation."

"So we're in business?" said Dobbs.

"We're in business," sneered the Navigator.

"Bravo," said Dobbs. "He knows his trade. I like that in a man."

"And now another toast," said Kilroy.

"What shall we drink to this time?"

The Pilot laughed. "To the great planet robbery!"

Lawrence Dobbs IV was born in the present-day province of Wolfshead on Olivia, the fourth planet from a Class F star. His ancestors had arrived there twelve hundred years before in the early pioneering days of the Federation, before cryogenics, back when the space arks were complete worlds in themselves where generations passed before reaching a final nesting spot. Upon landing, they farmed and mined the land, and many more generations passed. Bellwether's discovery of a wormhole just out-side (in astronomical terms) the solar system made Olivia one of the hottest places to own property in the Federation. The Dobbs clan moved from farming into pharmaceuticals and the manufacturing of new alloys and perfect metal spheres at a string of space stations around the planet. This wealth was passed down from generation to generation through arranged marriages along with high culture and eugenics to keep leukemia out of the gene pool before the Great Cure was discovered and rippled its way out to the provinces. Passed down, that is, until Lawrence Dobbs II gambled away the family fortune, all of the untold millions, at the great casino space stations orbiting Saturn in full glorious view of the remaining rings that hadn't been mined for water and were now protected by environmental laws. Lawrence Dobbs IV, from penniless aristocracy, joined the colonial Marines to help carve and defend wild planets that became zones for free enterprise for men who could grasp opportunity. He had been decorated, promoted up to lieutenant with the promise of making captain, and was finally busted—for gambling—down to sergeant major and master warrant officer, a rank more compatible with his outside interests.

In many ways, Dobbs remained a product both of the aristocracy bred into his genes and life migrating through space and time, which made most relationships transient and turned men and women into rabid opportunists. Muldoon made the perfect partner for Dobbs's schemes. A wily cat to Muldoon's bulldog, Dobbs ran the diplomacy and business of the liquor table, while Muldoon supervised the hard work and the platoon on the battlefield. Muldoon went along for the ride because it always guaranteed adventure.

Dobbs had a simple way of answering life's greatest questions: He knew who he was, why he was here and where he was going with perfect confidence and satisfaction. Unlike Kilroy's grand plummet into a black hole, Dobbs's goal was simply to make a lot of money, have a good time with the profits and see if one really could take it all with him. Self-interest may have fit him like a glove, but creating situations of mutual self-interest suited him best. He was neither shallow nor actually greedy, and his schemes rarely hurt anybody. He never minded sharing, he respected skills and intelligence, he secretly hated violence and he helped people in order to gain a later favor that he knew he probably wouldn't need.

He had a simple way of looking at problems as well, as fixed or variable.

Fixed problems included Federation laws, broken pumps, overheated plasma rifles and the like. He liked fixed problems the best, since people of skills, talent and ability working together almost always solved them or at least found the way around. Fixed problems were solved via a simple Western Terran outlook on causality. And the larger the consortium and the greater its montage of talent, the easier solving the problems became.

Variable problems, on the other hand, made his hair stand on end.

Dobbs had rightly guessed immediately after he left Muldoon last night that the fool would ask Dariana to come along on the voyage. Or rather that she would make him ask her. Dobbs felt sorry for Muldoon; time dilation was the enemy of love. After even a short spurt in space, a man could come home and find out that the academy sweetheart he'd sworn eternal love for was married and had five children, or more likely was already dead and fertilizing a vegetable garden. In Dobbs' experience, space life bred hard men and women who lived on their wits and operated alone or in business partnerships with other hard men and women. Together, they sometimes formed consortiums to tackle large jobs. Spacers were a breed apart from the normal trash that tended to collect in the backwater provinces, and Dobbs liked them because they shared his understanding of the truth of mutual self-interest. Spacers could like other people, they could admire and respect somebody, but they never loved anybody.

Muldoon, on the other hand, had a heart the size of Neptune, the poor bastard.

The man had apparently reached that crazy age when he was ready to settle down. This caused a problem, since Dobbs and Muldoon had always been loyal first to their partnership, watching each other's backs in battle, and when they had the chance, the Service and the Retirement Fund. The code of their partnership, which had endured twenty years, demanded absolute loyalty to these things, as divided loyalties between them and women, strong drink, gambling or some other pleasure often led to disaster. Dobbs knew that Muldoon felt he was in a Catch-22—he wanted to settle down with a woman, and he had flipped over Dariana, but he wanted to get rich first so he could marry well. To get rich, he couldn't leave Dariana behind, because she'd be long dead when he returned.

To serve two masters, a man had to have both strong character and the ability to rationalize like Lucifer so as to integrate sometimes conflicting demands. Dobbs wondered if Muldoon had the stuff, and then he remembered when they had first met.

It had been fifteen years ago, when his unit from the Third Guards had been assigned to protect a gas mining settlement on Jordan, a gaseous planet. The settlement and fort floated on the hydrogen slush, magnetically repelled and anchored at the same time to the planet's magnetic metal core thousands of kilometers below their feet. As a low-gravity planet with a thick atmosphere, most animal life had evolved to fill the sky niche, where competition was brutal in a pecking order from giant brainless sky whales and flimsy pterodactyls down to bugs and translu-cent floating creatures that ate the plankton flourishing in nutrient-rich air currents. It was a Marshole. Like most Federation settlements, theirs was built before the planet had been properly studied, and was set almost on a spot where three major airflows converged to make an eternal storm five hundred kilometers to the east. These airflows provided some wind energy for the colony, but, carrying food, were also migration routes. Within a year, an endless cloud of shrieking winged monsters converged on the settlement, inserting themselves in all shapes and sizes into every available air lock, crack and exhaust vent. Dobbs figured out that a giant cargo tank could be lowered off the bottom of the barge into the slushy surface where the winged monsters wouldn't imagine going even if they had the power of imagination. Muldoon helped him rig it up. Dobbs went down as quickly as possible—word had somehow spread among Jordan's natives that an unprecedented food reservoir had been located. Muldoon stayed above and killed monsters by the thousand until his rifle overheat-ed, then tried to convince the miners and their families to join his flight. The homesteaders refused valiantly, believing they were winning, and that the first wave was the last. Muldoon abandoned them and went below, and later he and Dobbs received a Parliamentary Citation for hero-ic action, the sole survivors.

More important than this typical life example of deception-meets-reward was that Dobbs had immediately admired something in this man. It was related to the fact that Muldoon could be principled enough to fight the monsters with all his powers, but intelligent enough to abandon those silly people when he had to.

Dobbs thought about it. Their first experience in mutual self-interest together, added to their complementary natures that had bonded them in friendship and partnership, had indicated that Muldoon both had charac-ter and could rationalize like the devil if need be. So maybe the man could share allegiances both to Dariana and to their partnership, especially when it came to this mission, the Holy Grail itself. But at the same time, Dobbs doubted. While he seemed more capable of being the Pilot's cat, two things at once, Muldoon was more Pavlov's dog, all programmed responses that oriented him toward life as sure as his sense of balance was guided by his inner ear.

೪

Dobbs and Muldoon flew through space toward their base in silence, watching the vastness of the red planet fill the screen. Muldoon kept his eyes fixed on the sea of red dirt that steadily revealed the details of canyons, plains, mesas, mountains and volcanoes. They were over the equator now, just above a few sparse clouds of carbon dioxide. Soon they passed into the northern hemisphere, over the growing sandstorm that rippled over half the face of Siren.

"How long do you think the storm will hold up?" Muldoon said.

Dobbs was brooding, pretending to read *Davy Jones*. "Long enough, I should say. It'll probably starting letting up just before we lift off. The perfect smokescreen."

"We couldn't have planned it better, Sergeant Major."

"Aye, a right bit of luck, that," agreed Dobbs.

They rode in a silence that was thick with unspoken questions, as murky as the dust storm under their feet. Muldoon seemed thoughtful. He put the scrambler into autopilot and stared at the view-screens.

"A long time will go by in the rest of the Federation while we're gone," he said. "How much will the gold be worth then, do you think?"

"We'll rig up a modeling program. We project the value of gold as an industrial material into the future when we return from our journey. We factor in, I should say, one-point-six rebellions, zero-point-four provincial wars, seventy or so discoveries of new gold deposits on existing Federation worlds. Plus another thousand or so other factors."

"Try three thousand, for starters. Look at that storm. It's like a bowl of tomato soup!"

"Aye," said Dobbs, back to brooding.

"The traders weren't up and about today, did you notice?" he said.

"They're still waiting for the solar flare," Dobbs explained.

"So what's next? We've got a pilot, navigator, map, and soon we'll have ourselves a ship we'll have to get ready. I'll take care of getting the Crickets on-board. I guess that leaves the Base Engineer and the Mining Engineer as the main guys on our list. And after that, we've got to fight the crabs again at least once and clear them out of the area for good so we don't let the Captain down."

He paused and glanced at Dobbs, who sat with his arms folded.

"And it could be dangerous fighting those crabs. I could be killed. Then you'd lose your best friend." Hearing no response, he continued to bait. "I am your best friend, ain't I?"

"Damn you for a fool, Timothy Muldoon!" Dobbs suddenly cried, pounding the instrumentation panel. The panel whirred in response. "A bloody fool!"

Muldoon grinned. Since Dobbs had brought it up, Muldoon roughly knew the score.

Dobbs continued, "God almighty! All right, then! She'll go!"

Muldoon began to rumble his deep baritone laugh.

Dobbs had turned purple. "Just keep her out of my bloody way."

"You have my thanks, brother," said Muldoon. "She's spoken with two friends who will come along too and be good to the rest of the crew. Me, I hope they'll find husbands. I think you know Drew and Rachel. They're good eggs."

Dobbs groaned. The addition of more women compounded the variable problem, although Muldoon meant well. Dobbs began to make nonsensical calculations in his head. One could not plan for the likelihood or timing of Pandora's Box being opened, even if one had bloody Pandora sitting right there next to bloody thing. Inside the box, there is a cat—now it's open and not open—Jupiter, thought Dobbs, I'm going balmy.

Variable problems made his hair stand on end. Grounder women!

"You'll like my Darry, she's a wonderful cook," said Muldoon cheerily. "She'll fix us up a great supper when we come out of hibernation and get real blood back in our veins."

Dobbs didn't have the heart to remind Muldoon that mechanically prepared food was mechanically prepared food, period. But he guessed correctly that Muldoon was focused on the hands that fed him, being the damned silly fool he was. He found himself happy again that he had never been a fool for love or any other reason.

"I'd like to discuss the outfitting of the ship, if you don't mind," said Dobbs. "I suppose by now you know we're going to take the freighter and refit it."

"I figured that was going to be our ride," said Muldoon.

The scrambler was in the storm now, finding its way on its programmed course, correcting vector and orientation after each buffet of the winds.

Muldoon chewed his mustache. "Aw hell, Lawrence. I need to talk to you about what's on my mind."

"Where in hell are we?" said Dobbs, starting to panic. "I can't see a thing. It's all red dust."

"The scram's on autopilot," said Muldoon patiently. "She knows where to go. Listen, there's no escaping this. You have to hear me out."

Dobbs slumped in his seat, surrendering. "I said she could go, but you can't let me be. You're going to marry her, aren't you, you crazy bastard? I knew it!"

"I've thought about it for a long while now," said Muldoon, looking forward resolutely. "I've never met anybody like her, and I've known a few women. When I'm with Darry, I wouldn't trade places with the Prime Minister himself. There are hundreds of millions of women in the colonies of our Federation, and I feel like I've found the one woman among them all who could make the rest of my life a happy time. I couldn't just let her go." He grinned. "I may even have children. Now you understand that, can't you?"

Dobbs groaned again, seeing that Muldoon was serious.

"You've said that kind of thing before, you big oaf," he said. "Why don't you follow the example of every sane spacer in history and keep control of your emotions!"

Muldoon frowned. "Because they're a part of me. I couldn't cut myself off from them any more than I could cut off my right arm. You should try it. It would do you some good to feel something!" He pounded the instrumentation panel and a row of lights blinked out.

Dobbs turned purple again. "I feel plenty!"

"Ha! You're a full-blooded spacer! You think the universe revolves around you."

"Emotions are fine and dandy, old man. But you get mixed up with a woman, and in the end you end up going arse over kettle and feeling bad. And you do it over and over!"

Muldoon's face relaxed, and he eventually grinned. "And every time it's worth it. Every time is brand-new, and I enter with no idea of what'll happen next except I know I'm hoping for the best. And while it lasts—how I can describe it to you, if you've never been there? You're a full-blooded spacer!"

"Get off my back about that, I'm warning you."

"And besides, how can I know how it'll end? Did we know we'd get off of Doreen alive, or that we'd be assigned here afterwards? I like not knowing the future. And look at this woman—I've found the one, I told you. I feel good. She's important to me."

Dobbs crossed his arms. "She knows how to handle you, that's for sure. But you know our loyalties. Our necks first, the Service second, the

Retirement Fund third."

"The Prime Minister and Federation come first," Muldoon told him seriously.

"Whatever. But we've gotten through many a scrap by sticking to business."

"Yeah, and I've given up so much real happiness because of it. This time, I'm taking a stand for what I really want. And besides, I figure that if we're rich after this, we'll have our Retirement Fund and there'll be nothing left to do but retire and live life. Ever thought of that? I'll bet you haven't!"

This seemed to dawn on Dobbs dramatically. "Once we get rich, there'll be no more enterprise."

"And no more adventures," said Muldoon. "What then? I know what then. I've been thinking about this ever since we decided to leave the Service. I'll need to be married to a proper woman. And you might do just the same for yourself. That's right."

Dobbs was quiet.

Muldoon clapped him on the shoulder. "Sorry about all this, Sergeant Major."

"No apologies needed, old man," said Dobbs, shaking his head. "I hadn't thought it all through. But your logic is right and proper. Damn! And damn me for a fool for crying on."

Muldoon grinned at him. "But we've had some high times in the Service, haven't we? The Kiki Rebellion. The civil war in the Commonwealth. That crazy Sultan. And those Gimps!"

"High times, old man," said Dobbs. "And the best is yet to come. Well, at least you're coming instead of staying. I'd hate to do this party without you."

"This will be our biggest adventure yet. The Holy Grail. I wouldn't miss it for my own planet. But you have to promise to get along with Darry. It's important to me."

"Oh, aye," said Dobbs. But he suddenly appeared lost.

"Get ready for the shock," said Muldoon. "Here she comes."

The wheeled landing gears of the scrambler, splayed like an eagle's talons beneath them, pounded the runway, making Dobbs say, "Oof!"

"I wasn't ready for that," Dobbs said.

Muldoon wondered exactly which shock in particular he was referring to.

Chapter 7
War Against The Crabs

Jwant in," the Engineer shouted as the heavy winds swept clouds of red dust over them. "If you don't let me in, I'll kill you!"

"You're on the com link, Mr. Travis," Dobbs said inside the bubble of his helmet. He took a step back, then forward, going with the wind.

"Yeah," said Muldoon, "you don't have to shout."

The Engineer was an expert in mechanical, electrical and electronics engineering in both the design and applied sciences. An answer man for any technical problem at the base, he was at home among wires, turbines, motors, transformers, grease and electrowrenches. He was the most highly paid man on the planet. And he wanted in.

"I designed a Dyson Sphere, and nobody cared. I was a terraforming engineer in a previous life, one of the great Planet Builders. I helped terraform New Maxis. And nobody cared!" He inserted a box into an outlet at the rear of the long rectangular troop rover. "Fuck 'em!" Unsatisfied with the reading, he grunted and pulled a thick black-insulated cable and inserted it into the outlet. "This I'm gonna do for me. I want in."

Dobbs turned so he could see Muldoon. "Are the Crickets on board?"

"Yeah, they're in the back of the rover all set to go."

"Well, we should be on our way, then. Let's take Mr. Travis with us. We'll circle the freighter and have a look at the mother." He turned to Travis. "Mr. Travis, the crabs just ate a miner at Camp Four. We haven't got all day."

Travis, somehow graceful in his atmosphere suit heavy with the cylindrical air tanks on his back and the weights in his boots, pulled the plug and shut the lid. He was still shouting. "Perpetual motion machine? I probably could have done that too, if they had bothered to ask. Okay, you've got enough juice for the trip now. It's fully charged, and then some." He stood for a moment, holding the cable. "Hey, why don't I come with you guys? We can talk. You need my expertise, you know. Don't leave me out of this! I signed that paper, right?"

"Mr. Travis, come on, we're waiting for you."

Dobbs and Muldoon had already entered the rover's cab. Muldoon reached down and gave the Engineer a hand up. He grunted. Travis was a stocky, compact man—he'd been raised on a planet with almost 2g's of gravity—making Muldoon wonder why he seemed so powerless sometimes.

Safe inside the cab, Travis pulled off his helmet and exhaled. "Ah." Dobbs and Muldoon did the same. They instantly smelled their own sweat mixed with dry forced air and a whiff of gasohol, whose combustion started the engine that would then be powered by a battery. After Muldoon turned the engine over, the rover lurched forward.

"You'll need the Mining Engineer, too," said Travis. "He's at Camp Four, so we're in luck. He's the only man who has the know-how to move that much gold—look out!"

Out of the clouds of red dust a massive robot-truck lumbered by, carrying raw ore rich with iron and the titanium from which spaceships were built. The truck was headed for the outpost, where it would be processed and sit in the warehouse until enough minerals, plus mined helium, hydrogen and silicon, were stored up to fill the freighter. Small payloads of rarer elements were shot into orbit by the nearby rail gun, whose action created plasma that destroyed the rails until robots created new rails for the next launch.

We'll take those robots with us, Dobbs thought, rubbing his chin, and leave the mess for the Commission chaps to clean up. And it'll serve them right. Coming all the way from New France! How much money would that cost, he wondered. Well, they intended to set an example. It made Dobbs want to laugh. If he had a penny for every credit the government spent on setting examples, he'd be the richest man in the Federation, and buy his own planet.

Muldoon threw the transmission into a lower gear and stepped on the brake. The transmission howled. Then he turned, the box of the rover lurching on its wheels and treads, and turned again to follow the robot-truck toward the freighter.

"You should land a scrambler with him," said Dobbs. "You'll lose your bloody lunch."

Muldoon grunted, reminded of food. "We had bean curd for breakfast again."

"Where are we headed?" Travis peered out a side port. "The crabs are going wild in this storm. We ought to be getting to Camp Four."

"We're going to have a quick peek at the ship first," Dobbs told him. "You wanted in, aye?"

Travis suddenly didn't seem to care about being in so much as he cared about not being left out. He kept quiet and pulled at his beard.

The giant ship, resting on its legs, looked like a cross between a giant sleek submarine and an insect. The legs were retractable landing gear, distributing the ship's thirty thousand tons of rest mass. Even so, the concrete under the leg pads was cracked and sunken from the last landing. The sides were ridged with fins and small wings. Heat shields and radiation guards protected the cargo from the radiation of solar flares and the cosmic rays of space. The ship's belly housed four vast cargo holds and was girdled with a great iron ring. On the front of the ship bristled an ugly collection of infrared and UV sensors, magnetometers, charged-particle sensors, cameras, cosmic-ray sensors, spectrometers, plasma sensors and communications gear, unsightly as acne. The ship's call sign, 77X19, was etched onto the side of the ship in chipped fluorescent paint along with its name, BIG BERTHA.

"As you can see, it still has a ramscoop coiled up in the front," said Travis, pointing to a box attached to the nose of the ship. "I guess they figured they'd keep it on there for backup energy after the upgrade. Don't want to lose this cargo, ha ha. We ditch that piece of crap. Lose a little mass, less fuel to burn." As was the Engineer's habit, when he talked technical he lapsed into thought fragments. "Yeah. Needs a little work. See there? Corrosion. Oh, and that crack. Looks like some piece of junk hit the ship at a sweet velocity. Quarter-inch impression on the front plate I got to patch. See it there? Ah, you missed it, stupid dust."

The rover jostled over rocks and came up along the flank of the ship.

"Okay, here you've got your cargo holds, processing plant, airlocks. Big momma in the plant. Lose that if we can. We'll have a fish pond, hydroponics farm, chicken hatchery, you name it! Solar! There it is. Ah, now here's my favorite part." After a few minutes of driving along the enormous length of the ship, Travis angled his head to look up and out the window. Dobbs and Muldoon caught a glimpse of the giant exhaust funnels through the waves of red dust clouds, the great cylindrical fusion engines. "That's your engine room there. Generator room there. Requires almost no maintenance once she's up and running. I'll rig up some of the forward areas like the bridge to have their own artificial gravity."

"Earth Standard," Muldoon said with relish.

"We'll need better radiation shielding," Travis mumbled to himself. "Great hydraulics—she'll land wherever you put her. Cruising speed of about a hundred thousand kilometers per second. But I can bring her up to ninety-one, maybe ninety-two percent of light speed."

"That's good," said Dobbs, rubbing his chin. "That's quite good."

"She don't look like much on the outside, but they don't make them any better."

Dobbs turned to Muldoon. "Sergeant Major, let's bring her around and make for Camp Four. Use the autodrive and make haste. Can't let the Captain down, now can we?"

"No," said Muldoon firmly. "We won't."

Travis leaned forward from the back seat, between them. "Hey, what are you going to do to the old cry-baby?"

"The Captain?" Dobbs turned in his seat as best he could to put a twinkling eye on the Engineer. "Oh, I shouldn't worry about him."

"You bastards!" Travis said with admiration, smiling. "Take her easy on ol' puff-n-stuff, he's just a kid. I'm glad you fellas asked me to join in. I've been waiting for this my whole life, only I didn't know it until you asked. Fuck 'em!"

"Now we'll take off, I assume, using those chemical rockets at the base of the craft," noted Dobbs, taking a bite into an apple with a crack that made Muldoon hungry.

"Hey, where'd you get that?" Muldoon demanded.

Dobbs ignored him. "The atmosphere's thin, we get off this rock with little fuss. But the ride is long and hard. How do we get good acceleration toward light speed without burning a bloody lot of fuel?"

Travis appeared delighted to hear somebody speaking his native tongue. "You don't know? That's an easy one! The ship's packing four main fusion reactors. They run on deuterium, tritium and helium. They can carry a load big enough—they're tough, let's just leave it at that. I can retrofit them to run on deuterium and Helium-3, and we economize on mass."

"But where will we get the Helium-3?" Muldoon said. "I'm just asking."

"Why, haven't you fellas noticed that there's a gas giant in this solar system? Ol' Polyphemus. They mine Helium-3 there, all you want and more. Of course, it's, it's not. . . ." He stumbled. It was not his department.

Dobbs smiled back at him, his cheek bulging with apple as he chewed. "No worries, Mr. Travis. We'll procure the Helium-3 and you'll have—how did you put it? All you want and more. I have the perfect plan. All legal. We'll simply requisition it."

Travis laughed, a little embarrassed. "Yeah, well, I was saying. Now, the fusion reactor'll get us there. But the real problem is not fuel capacity, but raw engine power. How quick we can get to maximum velocity, I mean. We'll need some hardcore acceleration. It could mean a big difference in the length of the trip. "

"The sooner we return safely, the sooner we're all rich and we might be able to recognize something familiar with all the years that'll fly by back here."

"We'll launch from the Coil Gun. If you want the quickest trip, that would do it."

"What's this about a gun?" Muldoon said.

Dobbs whispered to him: "Sergeant Major, be a good fellow and put more air in the tires. It's too rocky. The Crickets will be barfing back there, and I don't want to see what they've digested or eaten."

Muldoon grumbled, "There's nothing wrong with what they eat," then pulled a lever until he was satisfied with the air gauge. The ride grew less bumpy.

"The Coil Gun is a giant fly-tube made up of coils in orbit near Macintosh," Travis was saying. "A dedicated solar power unit sends current through the coils. That metal girdle you saw around the belly of 77X19 is an armature. The coils create electromagnetic fields that pull the ship and shoot it off into space.

"The mass driver," said Muldoon, nodding.

"Brilliant solution, Mr. Travis," Dobbs said. "You are a master of your trade."

"You think that's good," Travis said, beaming and pulling at his beard. "You should see what I could do if we had a decent antimatter drive!"

The radio crackled and Dobbs picked up the receiver, exchanged salutations and listened. He hung up the receiver and turned to Muldoon.

"The crabs are getting spunky," he said.

"What's the situation?"

"They've got Kepler and his two foamnecks bottled up in a maintenance shed at Camp Four, with one man wounded, while the miners are
shut up in the base. They're under siege and no way out. Step on it, man,
the Captain's worried as hell."

Muldoon yanked on the lever to brake the rover, pitching Dobbs and
Travis forward in their seats.

"What the devil?" cried Dobbs.

"We've got company up ahead."

After the oceans died on Siren, virtually all life became extinct except
for several species of giant sand crabs and the parasites that lived in them.
The hologram movies of the crabs sent back by the Federation explorers
caused a minor sensation in the Capital Province of Sol, since the monsters somewhat resembled Earth crabs. But given the spectacle of life on
other newly explored worlds, some intelligent or at least sentient, Siren's
crabs were all but forgotten on Earth in the past few hundred years. This
satisfied Heller's Theorem, which stated that the larger the Federation
got, the less its citizens knew about it.

On Siren, however, the crabs remained a nasty problem. Since the
oceans died, they had gradually evolved to become smaller and smaller to
adapt to the new environment, but they were still monsters as far as
humans were concerned.

Most of the time, the crabs burrowed deep into the sand, where they
slept and hatched their eggs in the warmth radiating from the planet's
core. But when Danby was at its closest to Siren every two hundred days
(local), the crabs were awakened by the moon's tidal forces and had a
feeding and mating frenzy, expending on the surface all of the heat they
had stored up underground. The crabs chewed on rocks, feeding on minerals, organic materials and frozen water, similar to the way Earth ele-
phants chewed on rocks for salt with their giant molars.

The crabs did not like competitors.

There was one particularly big animal standing just ten meters in front
of Dobbs, Muldoon and Travis, barely visible between the gusts of red
dust soaring over the dunes. An adult female from the size of the creature,

grinding her molars which made the enormous chin bob up and down. The large pincers appeared to be waving a greeting, while the two smaller, four-taloned pincers under the giant mouth snapped open and shut.

Muldoon put the engine into idle, took the com link and said into the mike, "Marines, stand ready. Helmets on, guns warmed up. We've got a crab about ten meters directly forward. Sergeant Major Dobbs is going to hit her with the cannon. If we run into trouble, I'll give the order to get out and dispatch the animal. Understood?"

A screeching noise exploded over the speakers.

Muldoon snapped off the com link and turned to Dobbs, who was wriggling a pinkie in his ear. "Sergeant Major, fire when ready. Then we're on our way again."

Dobbs brought down the scope and firing wheel and sized up the crab in the cross-hairs. He took a final bite of his apple and tossed it into the back with Travis.

"You stay right there, brother."

He pressed both thumbs on the firing wheel in his hands. The rover rocked as fifty-millimeter shells shot at the sand crab. Smoke and a chance gust of red dust enveloped the creature.

"Did I hit it? Blast that sand! Where is the bastard?"

"It's a she," Muldoon corrected him.

An object hit the rover on its left side, and the vehicle rocked sideways.

"What the hell?" said Muldoon. "Is that the same one? They don't move that fast."

An object hit the right side now, rocking the rover. Then the left again.

"Who said these crabbies aren't intelligent?" said Dobbs. "It's a bleeding trap!"

"Actually, they're not really very intelligent," Travis said, his voice shaky. The man was pale. "They're simply evolving defensive and hunting strategies against new—"

"Somebody make him be quiet!" bellowed Muldoon, silencing Travis. Then he turned and added, "Sorry, Bill."

Travis stared back with wide eyes, nodding. "It's okay. Go back to doing your thing."

The rover rocked again under an impact, harder this time.

"Yes, we're all under a lot of stress," he added.

Muldoon was scratching his head. "This is the farthest I've ever seen them from their nests. They shouldn't be here. Let's give 'em another dose of the cannon, Sergeant Major. Fifty mike-mike again. I'm going to turn on the infrared and see what the hell's out there."

Dobbs hunched over the fire wheel and pressed with both thumbs. But only one blast sounded. A loud whine emitted from the right side. A misfire.

"It's the bloody sand," he said with disgust. "We've got a jam."

Muldoon watched the infrared monitor as it warmed up and showed eight green dots circling and converging on the big red dot—the rover.

"A misfire?" said Travis, chuckling. Then he stopped and pulled at his beard. "Doesn't that mean we have a live round over our heads?"

"Yes," agreed Muldoon, thinking. "It happens."

"These rovers can go in reverse," Travis added helpfully.

"We're surrounded, in case you hadn't noticed."

The rover rocked to the right hard, groaning. It swayed, almost off balance, then the sheer weight of the vehicle brought it back, making the shock absorbers squeal.

"I do hope you've got an idea, Sergeant Major," Dobbs said, breaking into a clammy sweat.

"Looks like the Crickets are going to barf after all," said Muldoon. He pulled down the com link mike, told them the situation and ordered them to disembark, Tactical Orders Nine and Twenty-Five. He threw in Sixteen for good measure. "Fire at will. And watch your butts!"

Muldoon turned to his comrades now. "Let's get our helmets on. Bill, you stay here and put your cork on too, just in case. We'll be back in a minute."

Travis was nodding vigorously. "Thanks. I'd like to stay here."

The Marines pulled on their helmets, locked them, then loaded their field rifles. They positioned themselves in their seats facing opposite sides of the cabin. Shouting the sharp "Ha!" of the colonial Marines, the men pressed on the hatch releases with their boots, opening the doors simultaneously, and stepped out. They immediately heard the report of the rifles of the Crickets, a muffled and distant bass.

The Crickets had formed a defensive perimeter around the rover, and were firing when visibility afforded a target.

"Shoot straight, men!" he told them.

He looked into his large rifle scope at the little red dot, firing a few test rounds into the wall of flying dust, and waited for the infrared to warm up.

"Choose your targets! You're the best soldiers in the galaxy."

A crab, a bull from its smaller size and surprising speed, came clambering down a dune, causing a minor avalanche of sand. The legs slid for a few yards, then the animal launched itself against the rover, rocking it almost onto Dobbs and his Crickets on the other side. Near Muldoon, an unlucky Cricket who had been in the bull's way slumped to the ground, his helmet broken, dying instantly from the poisonous atmosphere, his antennae wilting and his gloved hands curled in front of his chest.

"Damn!" said Muldoon, dropping to the ground. The crab was staggering a little, stunned from the collision with the rover. Muldoon fired without aim toward the crab's unprotected belly. After putting a few dents into its shell, he scored a hit on flesh. The animal scampered sideways, then backwards, until it dropped to the sand and retracted its limbs into its shell. Muldoon spared a glance at his scope and saw the green dots.

There couldn't be that many crabs.

"Color Sergeant!"

A Cricket appeared at his side, firing his rifle. He paused. "*Scoru-nok-grom sah?*"

"We've stumbled onto a whole nest of them, Pete," Muldoon said.

"*Man-nok-man-rangu-grom,*" the Color Sergeant observed. "*Kem-bahu sah.*"

"That's what I was thinking. All right. Get them up on the roof. I'll cover from here."

Behind Muldoon, the Crickets began to climb the ladder bolted onto the side of the rover. Two bulls appeared and hissed at him, reaching at him with their claws. Muldoon retreated, firing steadily. The crabs hesitated, then advanced after him. What made Muldoon's skin crawl the most was the way the bulls, unlike the larger, lumbering females, could transform their own sluggishness into surprising bursts of speed for the kill.

A scream filled the inside of Muldoon's helmet, the sound of a Cricket in pain. Muldoon glanced left and saw the man holding onto the ladder, one of its legs held in the large pincer of a crab claw. The crab reached up with its other claw and tried to capture the Cricket's other kicking leg.

"Give that man cover fire!" Muldoon cried in frustration.

The crab gave up pulling and settled on putting the captured leg into its chomping mouth, where there were large teeth designed to grind up rocks into nutritious digestible minerals.

"What the hell is happening over there?" Dobbs said over the com link.

"Aren't you on the roof yet?" thundered Muldoon, switching to plasma and firing, *crack crack crack*. The crabs cringed under the impacts, spurting blood, then scrambled away. Plasma was good for fighting crabs, but a serious risk to the soldier when shooting a target at close range.

"Aye, I'm almost at the top. Get your arse up here too. The Color Sergeant says you're the last one down there from your side. Are you trying to win a medal?"

Muldoon turned and bounded on weighted feet through the low gravity as if running in a dream. Near the front of the rover, Travis' panic-stricken face appeared in the window, his eyes wide, his mouth forming an O and his hands pressed against the glass. Muldoon reached the ladder and started up, then turned to look down into a large square lipless mouth hissing up at him over the hill that was its chin, the rim caked with red dust, the crab's large tongue dripping with hot digestive fluids.

He knew he shouldn't fire a rifle set to plasma so close, especially one-handed, and debated it for a microsecond. Then he fired, the rifle bucking out of his hand. A shard of a broken tooth clattered off the bubble of his helmet and a burst of blood splashed up his leg. The crab retreated, coughing.

"Try that again and I'll throw a grenade down there too!"

Grunting, he climbed onto the roof and joined Dobbs and the rest of the platoon of Crickets. Dobbs stared at him with disapproval.

"You look like a mess. Where's your rifle? It'll come out of your pay, you know."

Muldoon shook his head sourly inside his bubble and turned to watch the crabs circle the rover, occasionally bumping into it. The oldest crabs had beautiful multicolored shells marked with ridges, spikes and knobs shaped by the whim of the planet's winds. These designs made the crabs attractive to each other for mating, a fact of life that drew them into the gusting winds of the sandstorms.

"We'll have a rough time getting through those shells," said Dobbs. "They're as good as any battle armor. Plasma might do it, but I wouldn't advise it when we're all packed together like this. Who's bleeding idea was it to come up here?"

"What do you think we should do, then?" Muldoon said with irritation. "We were sitting Gimps down there. But in a minute, they'll start throwing themselves at the rover again. And besides that, it's only a matter of time before that misfire goes off under our feet with all this rocking back and forth. Then we'll lose our Engineer."

As if on cue, a crab launched itself against the vehicle's rear, making it lurch against the brake. The Marines went to their knees to steady themselves.

The Color Sergeant pointed at the ground. "*Ak-grom-mari-mari sah!*"

A Cricket had fallen off the rover and was being alternately picked at and fought over by two bulls as he tried to crawl away. A tank on the rover had also been ruptured, spraying oxygen in a stream that ended in snowflakes.

"Pete, stay where you are," Muldoon told the Color Sergeant. "Give him cover fire, but do not leave the roof!"

Some of the Crickets provided cover fire, while others pulverized the crab that had hit the rover and found itself on its back, its limbs writhing.

Muldoon reached and helped the fallen Cricket back up onto the roof. "*Nak-naka-grom-malitek*," he said sternly, giving the alien's arm a fatherly squeeze. Then he saw the dead crab on its back and turned to Dobbs. "Sergeant Major, I have an idea."

Dobbs reached up absentmindedly to wipe sweat off his forehead and ended up tapping the bubble of his helmet. "I'm all ears."

"We'll have to use grenades, round or no round under our feet." Muldoon handed one to Dobbs and held one himself.

"I agree," Dobbs said quickly.

"Fire in the hole!" they said, pressing buttons on the charges and throwing them down among the crabs.

One of the grenades landed on the back of a crab and went off, startling the animal and sending it scrambling sideways. The other hit the ground, bounced twice and exploded upward, flipping a crab onto its back.

One of the Crickets fired into the exposed flesh of the crab. The legs flittered, then the animal went still, its underside a blue mess that quickly froze.

"Excellent suggestion," said Dobbs.

"I'll give the order," Muldoon answered. "Pete, tell the men to use grenades."

"*Ak-grom Muggoon!*" the Color Sergeant screamed, saluting, then gave the order.

The Crickets sent grenades down among the crabs, bagging two more of them by the same method. The rest of the creatures scattered.

"I doubt we've seen the last of them," Muldoon said. He checked his scope, which showed green dots moving to the north and regrouping there.

"Men, form up! Tactical Twenty-Two!"

The Crickets clambered down the front of the rover and formed a firing line on the ground, men alternately kneeling and standing.

"Switch to plasma, we're in the clear. Now then, fire! Fire at will!"

The Crickets fired the plasma bursts into the sandstorm, the guns cracking, then echoing continuously afterward, a loud bass rumble like distant thunder. Muldoon listened with great satisfaction. He knew the ground. There wasn't much open space out in front in the pass created by two large craters, and there was a good chance to hit one of those animals with a rifle, storm or no storm. Dobbs appeared at his side, peering through IR glasses.

"Look, one's lost a leg, I think," he said.

Muldoon stepped in front of the firing line, off to the side, and raised his right arm. "Come on, Marines, let's have a go at them!"

Muldoon's helmet filled with a harsh scream that sounded close to "Ha!"

"Charge!"

The line moved forward, the Crickets firing as they went. Their weighted boots stepped over torn limbs that were big enough to belong to adult females. The pass quickly became a lake of bluish liquid as a number of the giant crabs, lacking a leg or two and losing blood, heaved and collapsed onto the sand, quivering until death took them.

Muldoon stopped, almost out of breath, and laughed.

He heard Dobbs over the com link. "Have you gone mad?" He had switched to a private channel. Muldoon did the same.

"I'm getting too old for his. I'm losing my mind. Look at me, I just led a charge against giant crabs. Nonsense! We're leaving the Service at the right time, if you ask me."

"Consider it training for Neverland. A hundred million savages!"

"We'll need that ball turret gunner after all," Muldoon said thoughtfully. "Get some real weapons if we're going to do this right, in case it comes to violence. Damn, I've got an itch!"

"I'll have him down here in a few days," Dobbs answered. "He's in the Province at a, uh, clinic. For now, we've got the Crickets, an engineer, a pilot, a navigator, a ship and a map. Now all we need is clearance for space travel and the ball turret gunner, and we're as right as rain. It'll be done in seven days, then all that's left is detail work."

"And the Mining Engineer," Muldoon added. "We'll get him right now."

"And the Mining Engineer."

"How will we get the clearance for travel? Damn, I wish you'd gotten me an apple!"

Dobbs appeared at his side and socked Muldoon's shoulder, making him jump.

"You'll see. Our man will be here in two days time, and we'll get our clearance. It's all arranged. No worries."

Muldoon sat on a boulder, felt its cold surface through the padding. "The sooner the better. I'm really getting too old for his. Let's recall the men."

"You can be proud of your foamnecks today. They earned their pay."

Muldoon looked at Dobbs with surprise. "They're the best soldiers in the galaxy."

🙢

When they returned to the rover, Muldoon cursed himself. He was getting sloppy, leaving no rear guard, and some crabs had somehow gotten around them and finally turned the vehicle onto its side. In the cabin, Travis had fainted and urinated, which is a colossal mess in an atmosphere suit and took him forever to mop up. Meanwhile, the Marines cleaned out the misfired round while the Crickets got their dead comrades on-board.

They reached Camp Four without further incident. Muldoon sat, again thinking perhaps he wouldn't miss the Life after all. Travis didn't say another word the entire time. That's when Muldoon started feeling a strong and sincere endearment for the man, treating him very well and making him feel like he was a part of the conversation nonetheless.

The Mining Engineer greeted them with open hostility. A burly, black-bearded and foul-mouthed man, he unleashed a storm of obscenities at them about showing up late that drowned out the roar of the turbines and the megawatt drills as well as the sand storm that now covered most of the hemisphere and rumbled under their boots, a remarkable feat.

Dobbs and Muldoon took no offense, as McDonough treated all men equally badly. They told him the plan and put the contract and a pen on the table.

McDonough sat across the table in the cramped room and looked at the document as if trying to read his future, rubbing his dirty face and plucking at his beard. He took his grimy cap off, ran his hand through his black hair, and put it back on. Dobbs and Muldoon felt pulsing vibrations under their feet from a nearby transformer and waited.

McDonough grunted and nodded once, deep in thought. Then a smile slowly spread across the man's mouth like a sunrise. Dobbs smiled back, his eyes twinkling. McDonough roared with laughter. He laughed for a good ten minutes, tears washing his cheeks.

He slammed the table with his two open hands and bellowed, "I'm in!"

Then he put some shot glasses down and they shared a shot of synthesized rum in the kind of satisfied silence that bonds men.

Chapter 8
Hacking Into The Flow

"What must be him now," said Muldoon. "So this man's a profession-al, you say."

Dobbs watched the scrambler emerge from the clouds of dust on the landing strip, then turned to Muldoon. "He's highly recommended. He's one of the very best in his field. He'll brag about his bionic eye."

"Can we afford his like, then? A bionic eye's a serious piece of over-head."

"We're no stranger to making hard bargains."

Muldoon shrugged. "Let's hear what he has to say, then."

Dobbs and Muldoon greeted the Hacker at the western airlock.

"Welcome to Siren," Dobbs said cheerily. "You must be Mr. Chip."

The Hacker barked a short coughing laugh. "Chip is my computer name on the InfraNet. Unless you're on the InfraNet, you call me Amazing Phil."

They went to a cramped conference room that stank of old coffee and was dimly lit by two blinking electroluminescent panels in the ceiling.

"I'll have some of that coffee, Larry," said the Hacker. "Tons of milk and sugar."

Dobbs put a mug in the machine and pressed a button marked WHITE-S-X, waited until it had filled, then handed it to Amazing Phil, studying him the whole time. The Hacker was a tall, thin boy with two different-colored eyes, a mop of red hair and a scraggly goatee. He wore a Space Cav field jacket, the current rage with kids in the solar system, which meant that it was probably the rage on Earth a century ago and like all other things, took its time reaching the backwater provinces.

"We would have been happy to meet you in the station," said Dobbs. "Treat you to a pleasant evening of amusements."

"Old-fashioned way of doing business," Amazing Phil told him, grunting with satisfaction over his coffee. "Vendors get drunk and they loosen up on the price. I mean, it's stupid, for old men." One of his eyes turned to focus on Muldoon, while the other kept its icy stare on Dobbs. "I like to do business the way I like to do business, Larry. You boys got any problem with that?"

"We'll do business the way you fancy it," said Dobbs with a forced smile, gritting his teeth. "You may proceed. There's a good fellow."

Amazing Phil slurped his coffee. "Jesus, that's quite a Marine accent you got there. So it sounds like you boys need to register a freighter, normally reserved for wormhole cargo flights between Siren and Earth, for a flight through Governor Takeshi's solar system into the great Beyond."

"Aye, that's the start of it," said Dobbs.

"Yeah, that's what we boys want," Muldoon added with irritation.

The Hacker added, "Then you want new identities for about ten people for your return. Plus these Crickets you mentioned. Why you'd want to give those animals a ride back is beyond me. Plasma fodder."

Muldoon's face darkened, but Dobbs silenced him with a glare.

"Aye, and that's the last of it," he said.

"Not easy, boys, not easy." The Hacker cracked his knuckles and took a laptop out of a leather backpack. "It's a good thing for you I know my craft and I'm available, or else your asses would be hung out to dry somewhere near my underwear right now. And as a bonus for your particular project, you should know that I had a chip inserted so that I can recite all nine hundred megabytes of the space regs by heart."

"You came highly recommended."

"Okay, let's get on with it, then," Amazing Phil said with irritation, staring at Dobbs as if he had been wasting the Hacker's time. "I cooked up a presentation that I give to all my clients so they understand the real dynamics involved with me breaking into the Flow and playing with its neurons. My business is pretty complicated stuff, a dangerous field, no place for amateurs. Only real cowboys and superheroes allowed. If I go too fast, you tell me."

"We're all ears," Muldoon said dryly.

"Do proceed," said Dobbs patiently.

"Okay." Phil hit a key and a timer appeared in the upper righthand side of the screen. "You're paying for my time starting right now. I'll give you no more than thirty minutes, unless you've got chicks in this Marshole, then I'm off like a prom dress." He pointed at the screen. "I can do this in 3-D too but I didn't feel like bringing the hardware. Just wanted you to know that too. Okay, look at the screen. The Federation formed over two-thousand-and-change Earth years. It's shaped like a very rough circle with Earth and the Terran solar system at the center. The entire Terran solar system is heavily populated and rich in wealth, culture and quality of life. But the central government of the Federation is on Earth and is a giant, bloated bureaucracy that not even its kilometers of supercomputers can handle efficiently. Me and my friends could run the place better."

The Hacker touched the screen, and new colorful images filled it.

"Why is the system so inefficient? An imperial style of government, although as we all know people in the Terran solar system—Capital Province, I mean—can vote in elections for the Earth Parliament. Ha ha. Over the course of the development of the Federation, planets were colonized right and left. Planets found populated with intelligent life were traded with, conquered and made to join the Federation as part of the *Pax Humanus* policy—thereby, as they say, benefiting from Federation 'administration, technology and culture,' another joke. The colonies stay enslaved to Capital Province to get high technology and hi-tech products. Raw materials are processed and shipped to Capital Province, and hi-tech products are shipped back. This is called the Flow.

"Two great discoveries made the Flow and far-flung colonization possible. You boys might actually know this. The first was the life-prolonging medical techniques and cryonic drugs that allowed suspended animation for long-range space flight. The second was Tracey's discovery of wormholes throughout the galaxy that permitted unmanned probes, then freighters, to pass through. Humans disappeared without a trace during hyperspeed, and one physicist apparently showed mathematically that they were converted into pure energy, haunting the hyperspeed dimension as ghosts or something, I don't know, I don't care. The long and short is wormholes made the relatively rapid movement of raw materials and goods possible. All in all, though, it's still pretty darn slow. Wormholes weren't always conveniently located. One was conveniently located at the center of Capital Province, ensuring Terran prominence. But other wormholes were far from some provinces, delaying the transport of new technology and products. Separated by time and space from the rest of the

Federation, they turned into dumps, like our very own Marshole here."

The Hacker grinned. After showing off his computer and his take on history, the next event was apparently his knockout punch.

"But the Flow is not limited to raw materials and products, right? It also covers information, right? Information flows through the wormholes both ways. The entry and exit points of the wormholes therefore form bottlenecks. As data transmissions leave the wormhole, local distribution is handled by substations and relays spread throughout each solar system. This is where a rare breed of men like me come in."

"You know a way to break into the Data Flow, then," said Muldoon.

The pupil of Amazing Phil's bionic eye dilated. "Very good. Like I said, if I go too fast, let me know."

Muldoon clenched his fists.

"As I was saying, it's all garbage in, garbage out over vast distances, with lots of concentration points for massive streams of data." The Hacker turned off the laptop, closed the lid and put it back into his bag. "In other words, like I said before, there are information relays and substations that have to take the pure data streams coming from Terra through the local wormhole and distribute them throughout the province."

"And these substations are vulnerable to some sort of enterprise," Dobbs prompted.

The Hacker snickered. "Oh, sure thing, Larry. That's where I can work my magic."

"And what sort of magic are we discussing? As it applies to us, I mean."

"Well, the biggest data user in the Province is the Transplanetary Mining & Distribution Company. We'll tap into their line and chances are it won't be noticed. It also makes sense in that you've got a freighter. I'll fake an order from Earth, right, that authorizes you to move through Takeshi's province and into the Beyond. You'll be incorporated as an independent exploration and mining company that sells materials to the TM&D. You can have it one of two ways. Either I set up a bogus contract that you have to give the standard twenty-five percent to the TM&D, or you sell all of your materials at a price lower than the free market value. With the latter, you're taking your chances."

"We'll take the former," said Dobbs.

"Good, that's classy on your part. I'm impressed. As a finishing touch, I'll put a virus into the system that will drop you into the next census with new identities, even for your animal friends. Voila. I am truly awesome."

"How much does all this cost?"

"It's not very difficult, but there's the amount of labor involved," Amazing Phil explained. "You can't just get into the TM&D Company. I also have to get you into the Interplanetary Space Agency, the Federation Agency for Space Exploration & Trade, the Federation Commission on Space Trade & Supply, the Federation Business Bureau, the Federation Archives and eight other agencies in the big fat bureaucracy we call government. I'd have to send some data both ways. The Border Patrol may have to be penetrated, which is pretty risky. We're talking some heavy lifting. I'll let you go with four hundred thousand."

The Hacker's price was incredible, and besides it exceeded the Retirement Fund.

"Your proposal is very tempting," said Dobbs. "I think we can talk business."

"You bloody savage," Muldoon said.

Amazing Phil choked on his coffee, growing red as his hair. He turned, mouth open.

"Listen to the way he talks about the Motherland and the great work of our Prime Minister," said Muldoon. He turned to Dobbs and jabbed a finger at the Hacker. "He's a radical!"

"Whoa, I—"

"It's sedition, that's what it is. Talks about the gift of administration, technology and culture as if it's some sort of joke! He probably hates missionaries too."

Dobbs winked at the Hacker. "It's all right by me if a man wants to criticize Capital Province's handling of some things. Too many tiresome laws, I say."

"Don't you ignore me, Sergeant Major!" Muldoon said.

Dobbs ignored him. "Right, Mr. Chip? I think we can do business. I know you could use a new client, since the information trade's slow right now."

"How'd you know that?" The bionic eye turned green.

"I knew that the minute you said you were available."

"Do business with him?" Muldoon said. "A separatist? You know how I feel about separatists."

"Aye, I do at that," Dobbs said gravely, rubbing his chin.

"I'm a good Marine, I am. But I don't care to see this one hang, just kiss off. He doesn't like how we do business, says it's old-fashioned and stupid. He charges for an exploratory interview, then gives us a preschooler lesson on how the Federation works, just to fill up the time. He—" Muldoon exploded. "He's a specist. He called Crickets animals!"

"Sergeant Major, this man here has services we require." Dobbs turned to the Hacker. "Let's negotiate a little on that price, though. It's kind of steep."

"Well, I guess I'm mostly charging for my time," the Hacker began, his bionic eye glancing at Muldoon. "It's a volume job. Let's say three hundred thousand, in thirds."

Muldoon pounded the table. "Three hundred—"

Dobbs shook his head. "You've got to help me out here."

Amazing Phil growled and pointed to his eye. "See this? If you haven't noticed, it's bioelectronic. With this, I can see and move data in virtual reality as if I was making a tuna fish sandwich!"

"Sedition!" Muldoon said. "Where's the Captain? We've got laws here."

Phil threw his hands in the air. "Mars! How much you guys got?"

Dobbs rubbed his chin. "I think we could pay two hundred and fifty."

The Hacker scratched his chin, then appeared to deflate. "All right, but not a credit less."

Muldoon glowered at Dobbs. "Two hundred—"

"And tax-free, too," Dobbs said. "Done!" He turned to Muldoon. "Sergeant Major, give him the bank number and credit the account to eighty thousand as a downer."

"You're getting a great deal, believe me," said the Hacker. "Bargain basement prices. I've got a lot of overhead. I didn't even tell you I had another chip inserted that allows me to speak any language in the Federation, in case you needed it." His mouth contorted. "I can even do a good Marine accent."

Muldoon's face began to lighten. He smiled earnestly. "Well, now, that's good to hear. You know, you're not so bad, really. You know your trade. I like that. Now, then, come with us and have supper. Cook's found us some pork chops to go with the bean curd."

"Well, I've got to get back, you know, but thanks," Amazing Phil said, growing red again. "I want to get started right away. Like I said, there's labor involved."

Muldoon stared at him as he hurried out to the airlock. He turned to Dobbs.

"Kids these days," Muldoon said, shaking his head. "Called the custom of the liquor table old-fashioned. Comes in here crying about the Prime Minister, calls us old men one minute, boys the next, then has the gall to tell me the men in my command are animals."

Dobbs nodded. "Times are changing. Must be all the hardware they put in their heads. Affects the mind. It's a new generation."

"They're just dumb kids."

"Those chips make them smarter than we are. But they still don't know a standard good cop-bad cop routine when they see one, and they cave in a minute if they're in the least bit the insecure type. Fool's mate. He failed the simplest test, and we didn't have to really negotiate." Dobbs shook his head in wonder. "It was almost too easy."

"They're just dumb kids," Muldoon asserted. "They should learn the way how."

Dobbs smiled slyly. "Even with you laying it on so thick."

"That kid had it coming—you know I'd never lay it on otherwise. And ho ho, what about your performance? I thought you were the master at this. You practically kissed his ass. I'll take some of that coffee. Black, please."

"Why didn't you just pistol-whip him, that's what I want to know. Poor dumb kid."

"You're a lousy bastard," Muldoon said. "If I hadn't nailed him, and he had it coming, he would have wasted our time and charged us for it all day. The way I played it, he barely fired off a mention of his eye."

"Well, it was my closing skills that did the score with the little bum nugget, in any case."

Muldoon darkened. "You always say that and you're always wrong."

Dobbs laughed. "Come on, man. I'm just goofing you. Don't drink this swill. Let me buy you a proper drink."

"And you'll throw in one of your Olivian cigars in the bargain, unless you're hiding another apple. I have large feelings."

"Now all we need is our weapons expert. He'll be here tomorrow. If the storm clears up a little more, why don't you take him out later on and test the weapons on the crabbies. We can't leave the miners unprotected, and we can't let the Captain down ever, can we?"

"No, we won't," Muldoon agreed, his jaw set, then grimaced. "Kids these days! Dumb as Gimps!"

Chapter 9
The Ball Turret Gunner

he last of the thousands of incoming ballistic rockets had been destroyed long ago, detonated by lasers or exploding on impact and taking a battleship with it. Scarred and bruised with long black streaks along their hulls, enough of the fleet's ships remained to carry on the fight. The planet would not surrender. Ultimatums were passed back and forth through the void at the speed of light. Then the Marco Polo bumped into a space mine. Nearby crews watched its seventy thousand tons of titanium alloy crumple and scatter in a series of soundless explosions. The nearby ships had to correct their course to prevent collisions as the burned-out hulk tumbled away into black space doing incredible somersaults. Fed up, men made decisions based on data and scenario-outcomes provided by super-nanocomputers the size of an ammo box. From the *Achilles*, a small blue orb was jettisoned into space on a trajectory that would cause it to intersect the planet in three days once it reached peak velocity. The fleet fired up its rockets, retreating at a speed that made the buckled-in crews feel dizzy from the increased gravity as the blood rushed from their heads to their toes. The blue orb sailed onward, serenely, at its incredible speed until it approached the planet, where it appeared to slow. The men on the *Achilles* watched all of this on-screen. The Commander was excited—there were no interceptors, and now it was too late and resistance was futile. The orb disappeared into the atmosphere. It contained a charge of antimatter. The charge armed itself just before the orb struck the planet's equator. The planet exploded. The solar system was liberated. The screen went black.

The ball turret gunner woke up screaming in the darkness.

◈

In the red desert of Siren, three five-meter-tall manlike machines strode down the hump of a dune, leaving deep tracks quickly covered by fresh torrents of sand carried by the wind. Two of the machines were Mules, carrying men. The third, leading the troop, was a John Henry Class VII mining machine that looked like a grotesque robot-man on muscle steroids.

The machines had crossed forty kilometers, pausing only once in the morning shadow of Vesuvius Mons. One of the riders had gotten out in an atmosphere suit to lubricate the Mules' joints and change a battery that had prematurely leaked its charge. The John Henry robot had stood motionless, oversized arms at its sides, performing its own internal maintenance. The man then laboriously climbed back up into the cabin of his walking machine. Their motors revving, the Mules continued to move northeast until lunch time, Siren's dying red sun directly over the men's heads, barely visible in a pink sky.

"Halt, John Henry," said Muldoon in one of the Mules.

The John Henry shortened its steps until it came to a halt. The small bullet head pivoted to set tiny red eyes on him. The oversized jaw did not move, but Muldoon heard the loud baritone over the crackle of the com link.

"JOHN HENRY HEARS AND OBEYS."

Muldoon tried to stretch in the cramped compartment of the Mule. "I'm checking the scanner. It's not easy to get a fix here. Too much interference from Vesuvius Mons. My guess is the nest is north of here, so we'll correct our course a little."

The ball turret gunner's voice buzzed from the speakers. "Let's eat first. What did your fiancée pack us for lunch?"

Muldoon looked out the window and tried to catch a glimpse of Brandon Fritz in the other Mule, but he only saw a hazy outline through a sudden burst of swirling red dust.

"Darry packed us some nice big Jovian sandwiches. Do you see yours?"

"Here's the lunchbox." He added, "She made this? But it's synthetic."

"No matter," Muldoon said with a grin. "Darry added her own personal touch. And you won't find an ounce of bean curd."

"You've got a fine gal, there."

"Dariana is my intended. She's the finest woman in the Federation."

"I understand she's coming with us. Isn't that bad luck?"

"Gimpcookies. Her being with us will be a blessing. You'll see."

"I understand she's bringing a few friends." Fritz paused. "Single friends."

"Yeah, they're two charming, educated ladies. You'll like them."

"I mean, they're sextechs, right?"

Muldoon frowned. "We'll not speak of that now, thank you."

They talked a little more, but when they began to eat, Muldoon accepted the silence with gratitude. The ball turret gunner wasn't very good at small talk. He wasn't a boring man, but he seemed to be severely depressed. It was only when he discussed the technical nature of heavy weaponry that he brightened and his personality became colorful. Muldoon guessed that the man was like some of the old spacers who refused to "come back to the future" and reenter grounder life, instead living for their trade to protect themselves from becoming suicidal or a complete burn-out. But in Fritz's case, his trade was mass destruction.

After lunch, Muldoon ordered John Henry to lead the way north.

"JOHN HENRY HEARS AND OBEYS."

Muldoon was agitated. The voice grated on a man's nerves.

"You are about to see the demonstration of your life," said Fritz, perking up a little. "This robot-man is my masterpiece. I have now become the Leonardo da Vinci of destruction."

Muldoon took a drink from the tube of his water bottle, the way hamsters drink in a cage. "Does this mean that you're ready to tell me about its capabilities?"

"Oh, I could bore you with armaments," Fritz told him. "Like an HMG and two LMGs on the fore, eight hundred rounds a piece. Armor-piercing exploding bullets I brought with me that can pierce a crab shell and a concrete wall behind it—I'm surprised they don't issue those to you standard here, the guys in charge must really hate everybody on this planet. An RPG and a flame thrower, although I admit the range and duration of the napalm is limited. I'm working on that. A fifty mike-mike cannon, plenty of ammo. He can handle the weight and still maintain a good speed— I upgraded the motors and the drive. All he's missing is a CD deck to play *Ride of the Valkyries*. He's loaded."

"Dobbs said you're the best at your trade. Any defensive capabilities?"

"I left that pretty much the way it was. I mean, it was built to take boulders bouncing off its squat little head while extracting iron, so how could I improve on that? Heavy armor plating, coated with a layer of ceramic to beat off heavy atmospheric pressures. Kevlar protects its internal organs such as the driver, pistons, cooling unit. Titanium alloys—almost the same stuff they use to build spaceships—to beat corrosion. It'll handle the sticks and stones those spearchuckers on Neverland have, believe me."

"Well, you know, we're not sure what type of weaponry they will have," explained Muldoon. "More than eight centuries have gone by on Neverland since Graham's expedition, if Commander Robinson reported its mass correctly. About two more by the time we land there."

Muldoon heard Fritz snort over the com link. He realized the man was laughing.

"What, then? Flintlocks? Cannons? *Pistoleros*? Who cares, John Henry's loaded. But to give you peace of mind, if our boy really runs into trouble, I equipped him with a self-destruct that would go off like a one-megaton firecracker. That was my first signature."

The robot heard its name and something clicked. "JOHN HENRY'S LOADED."

Muldoon glanced nervously at the broad back of the metal colossus marching just ahead and to the right of his Mule.

"Communication protocols?"

"Oh, don't let the speech freak you out. It's mostly cosmetic. I mean, he barely knows what he's saying, only reacts to his name and certain instructions. He's not really loading anything. He won't accidentally blow up stuff unless you give him a pretty specific order. But you should know he can act independently."

Muldoon was startled. "He can make decisions? What kind of decisions?"

Fritz snorted again, another laugh. "It's not like he has a major AI chip and is going to go self-aware on us. He's not a combat android, just a dumb brute. But I wired in a new molecular computer into his brain. That's where he gets the speech, but get this. The chip has a fuzzy logic processor—he can handle yes, no and maybe. I wired a transistor from the brain to his weapons and limbs. Within programmed limits, he can make decisions in microseconds, such as, 'Which weapon is most appropriate for killing the foe of my masters?' Besides the usual 'This is a boulder. Should I go around or walk into it?' Then he can act by sending a signal that activates the right pathways in the electronic switch in the transistor, then a second amplified signal that contains the order to move, fire, whatever. There's a Kevlar coating on the signal cable for protection, of course. Decision-making was my second signature. Muldoni, meet the ultimate fighting man. The only warrior who could actually kill a man twice over, make him twice as dead. You'll see."

"I'm impressed," Muldoon said, scarcely concealing his disgust. The idea of John Henry doing the fighting—and the idea of utterly destroying an enemy—struck him as unmanly or at least not very aesthetic. But he had to remind himself—he heard Dobbs in his head saying the words—that they were would be up against an entire planet of savages, and items like the scramjet and the John Henry Class VII could be a tie-breaker.

"I can read your mind," said Fritz. He sounded as if he meant it. "John Henry is a shock trooper. He must work with people to effectively pacify an area. He also does the heavy lifting, the kamikaze stuff, only he doesn't get killed."

"JOHN HENRY . . . WORKS WITH PEOPLE. ERROR. JOHN HENRY CANNOT AMALGAMATE INPUT."

"There are still a few glitches in the speech programming," Fritz said sheepishly. "He barely has more speech capability than the right hemisphere of a human brain."

"Silence, John Henry," Muldoon was saying.

"SILENCE IS JOHN HENRY."

Fritz continued. "Listen, we'll need all the help we can get. I've done the best I could do with what I could scrounge up combined with the equipment at the base and the crummy armaments they supply you here. We've got a scramjet, the John Henry and I'll have at least one of these Mules retrofitted with heavy weapons. The scramjet's even got a rack of seismic charges and small nukes left over from the stock used to open up the mines."

"JOHN HENRY RETROFITS HEAVY WEAPONS."

"I'm picking up a reading just one kilometer north of here," said Fritz. "You got it too?"

Muldoon was saying, "John Henry is a dumb piece of lard."

"JOHN HENRY IS DUMB LARD."

This made Muldoon laugh. "I wish Sergeant Major Dobbs was here to see this," he said merrily, warming to the robot now. "Mr. Fritz, let's head north to intercept."

The Mules bucked into motion. The machines walked like ostriches, swaying comically as they took their strides. The cabin rested on enormous shock absorbers to minimize the movement, but Muldoon found himself holding onto the oh-shit bar again.

"I think you'll like the demonstration," Fritz said sullenly, apparently unhappy with Muldoon's joke. Muldoon spared a look at the other Mule and caught a glimpse of the ball turret gunner. Long blond hair, a blond beard, a tall and lanky frame in a ball turret gunner's standard-issue black leather cap and jacket. Sensitive brown eyes, even sad, juxtaposed against an honest and almost boyish face. Fritz caught him looking, cracked a wry smile and waved before Muldoon's view was blocked by a wave of sand carried by the winds.

"Mr. Fritz, you look tired again. Are you sleeping okay?"

"What did Kilroy tell you, or that little snitch of a navigator?"

"I know it's none of my business," said Muldoon. "I'm just asking."

"No harm done, Muldoni. I will tell you one thing, though. Man to man. Since you're a military man like myself."

"If you want. So you were in the Wars, then?"

Another snort. "Gee, how old do you think I am? I was in War VI, for its last five years only. When I enlisted, I wasn't even old enough to drink."

"Yeah, I remember it well, although I didn't see the final destruction of Xerxes. I was fighting on the ground, on Poltava, while you fought in space. A long time ago." Muldoon barely recalled that the planet had been named Xerxes by the Terrans to make it appear more sinister. Before intelligent life had been discovered there, it had been named Marion. The natives called it *Idid-ethyua*, which roughly translated as, "Mother."

"It was a long time ago," Fritz agreed. "But I'll tell you, all the fighting didn't bother me until I noticed something that put the fear of the Lord into my head."

As a professional soldier, this interested Muldoon. "And what was that."

"During the War, it first hit me when we broadsided an enemy transport and I opened fire from a flank turret. The twin blasts of the lasers came down like one of those Army sewing machines they use to stitch a limb back on. I mean, it was surgical. I ran up the length of the ship with it, trying to knock out some of its heavy weapons on the first pass, but then I must have hit the reactor just right because a big explosion evaporated the back of the ship, and it sort of rippled its way up to the front until there was no more ship."

"That sounds like an excellent piece of work," said Muldoon with admiration. He was no warmonger, and did not relish killing for sport or for its own sake. He could not bring himself to kill alien women and children, even if they looked like red devils, and had never killed creatures who did not intend himself or others harm. But Muldoon was a patriot, and on an abstract level he found great satisfaction that the Federation had won all of its conflicts with other intelligent civilizations, particularly the big one with the Xerxesians, the only civilization that had had the technology to match the Federation's best warships.

"There was a blinding flash of light, then the deepest, blackest black I ever saw," Fritz continued. "You're not supposed to look at the big explosions dead-on, you see. You're supposed to turn away quick. But that time I was caught off-guard, and I got blinded. Total darkness. I looked into that darkness, and I saw it."

"What?"

The speakers were quiet. Muldoon glanced out the side window at the other Mule, but Fritz did not look back. Behind him was a giant wall of rock marking an ancient lava flow leading up to a cliff two kilometers high, at the foot of Vesuvius Mons, where the miners had found fossils of a hundred species of exotic alien fish buried in the rock. It looked like an impressionist painting behind the veil of dust thrown by the storm.

"The true face of war," Fritz finally answered. "No satisfying fire, no body dropping in the cross-hairs, no loud booms to make your adrenaline rush, no flags or victory. Just cold space, the void and total quiet. I mean the marvel of the act of creation in reverse. There was something there, you squeezed on the triggers, and now there's nothing there, and you almost doubt those people ever existed. It practically screams at you, but it's completely soundless, of course, the real screaming comes from your gut. And if you scream loud enough, you can keep that darkness out of you. You don't want that darkness inside you, man. If you look into the void and it becomes a mirror of you, reflecting off each other, then, well, then you're fucked." Fritz repeated with conviction, "You're fucked. You see a ship erased like that and it's bad. You see a planet erased like that, and it's, it's. . . ."

Muldoon said nothing.

"Aw, nuts," said Fritz, sounding a little embarrassed. "I guess I spent too much time sitting in my bubble counting stars. I never told—I figured, since you were a veteran, too . . . I don't think I'm making any sense. You probably don't know what I'm talking about. But it felt pretty good to say that. Thanks, Muldoni."

Muldoon slumped in his seat. He began to feel hot in the thick padding of his atmosphere suit. Fritz's speech was the most depressing thing he had ever heard, even worse than the "out brief candle" speech at the end of *Macbeth* he'd read in the colonial schools where they taught kids Earth history and culture before everything else.

"Why do you keep doing it then?" Muldoon said.

"Doing what?"

"Your trade. Why are you a soldier for hire?"

"There's no void here, no sir. Nice and bright. And besides, it's all I'm good at."

Then Fritz was screaming over the speakers.

"John Henry, blast those bastards! Terminate targets in forward sixty-degree arc!"

"JOHN HENRY HEARS AND OBEYS."

Muldoon straightened up and glanced right in time to see John Henry's torso, having pivoted, begin to shudder and make an awful racket.

"What the hell?" Muldoon threw the transmission into neutral and pulled hard on the brake lever, which resisted with a whine in the engine until he applied enough force to pull it down.

The Mule obeyed, treading to a halt, giving Muldoon a glimpse of a pair of giant sand crabs facing a rain of destruction that had the official seal of the holy wrath of God on it. Chips of shell as hard as rock flew away under clattering HMG fire, then fluttered lazily through the thin atmosphere to the ground. The cannon began to roar, then a series of rockets sprayed like fireworks in a concentrated fusillade. The crabs' shells splintered, shattered. The bottoms of the crabs exploded onto the sand, and their legs shuddered, broke apart and blew out to the sides. John Henry stopped firing, tendrils of smoke drifting off its blocky frame. The crabs collapsed to the sand in pieces as if they were a house of cards hit by a slight breeze, leaving only the smoking pieces of shell in twin pools of charred bluish goo that froze immediately.

"Wow," Fritz said. "That was Biblical."

The robot crouched, then advanced rapidly on the crabs and sprayed the remains with multiple quick bursts of napalm. After inspecting its work, the robot stood up to full height. Muldoon remembered Fritz saying something about John Henry being the only creature that could kill a man twice over, make him twice as dead.

"TARGETS TERMINATED. AREA PACIFIED."

"As you can see, Master Muldoon, John Henry is a mean motherfucker," Fritz told him.

"Yes, he is," Muldoon said, not sure of what he had seen.

"JOHN HENRY IS MEAN. ERROR. JOHN HENRY CANNOT SPEAK BAD WORDS."

Muldoon began to feel sorry for the Neverlandians.

ೲ

Four hundred Earth Standard years ago, when Muldoon and the ball turret gunner were considerably younger and enlisted men in War VI, the Xerxesian War Cabinet cautiously celebrated. After a life-and-death struggle in their own solar system, the Terran battlewagons were retreating back to their eyesore of a civilization. Only three ships remained, drifting—the Xerxesians concluded these were too damaged to move and were being scuttled. They were right. Soon, those ships disappeared from the screens.

What they didn't know was that the *Achilles* had fired a Doomsday Orb. The Xerxesians knew that the Federation had discovered how to manufacture antimatter, but were still eighty years away from the accomplishment themselves. Antimatter had never been used in known space warfare before. It was considered an unthinkable crime on both sides.

The Federation, however, was fed up after eighty-six long years of war, and could no longer tolerate a competitor so close to Capital Province. The decision to use antimatter was now suddenly considered a matter of long-term survival, not mass murder. Generations of historians and politicians on Earth would argue over that decision for hundreds of years, the privilege of being the winners.

A courier entered the Xerxesian Cabinet chamber and broke the news that the Doomsday Orb had been detected. Unfortunately, it was too late to stop it as it sailed at half the speed of light toward the planet. If they fired on it, they knew its smart antimatter charge would sense the attack, arm itself and explode prematurely, effectively destroying the planet anyway since it was so close. Instead, the Cabinet told the populace so that they could take their last moments to say their prayers.

Then they planned revenge, moving quickly. There wasn't much time to implement the Great Contingency they had never thought they'd need. Xerxesians didn't have a sense of humor humans could understand, but they certainly knew how to get the last laugh.

The Orb slowed as it passed the orbital kinetic energy weapons, dipped into the atmosphere, passed the ionosphere defenses, then the guardians of the stratosphere. It dipped into the clouds, tracked by anti-spaceship missile batteries. There was no panic on the ground. Three billion creatures lifted their nozzles to the blue sky and waited, consigning their life force to the Eight Gods that had forsaken them. Nobody cried, because they physically couldn't do so. Instead, they stomped their large feet gently, a final gesture of worship and farewell to *Idid-ethyua*, "Mother."

Three billion voices cried out as the planet exploded.

Far away in space, a cargo vehicle shed its boosters and the primary rockets fired, pushing it to safety while three billion kilometers away the Commodore of the Federation fleet committed suicide aboard the *Achilles*. Capping the vehicle was a machine.

The machine was intelligent. It held the consciousness of the aged Emperor of Xerxes in a small, heavily insulated cylinder surrounded by thirty-five tons of gadgets.

As the planet exploded behind it, the cargo vehicle continuously fired its rockets until it was safe to brake, then it landed on the nearest choice asteroid. It traveled with the asteroid belt on its wide elliptic course around the sun, using its chosen rock for building materials.

The machine needed building materials because it was a von Neumann robot. Small machines emerged from the cargo vehicle and mined ore, then built factories on the asteroid with the ore. The factories built more robots, which mined more ore and built more factories. These machines began transforming the asteroid into a sleek long spaceship with a rest mass of twenty thousand tons. All of this took about two hundred Earth Standard years. The Emperor bided his time in deep meditation, then acquired all knowledge, then grew bored, then went mad. During the long wait, stray hydrogen atoms were collected in a great latticework funnel, filling the new fuel tanks. The ship fired its rockets again, pushing off the remains of the asteroid with the aid of a laser to gain extra propulsion, and went into a trajectory that, at a velocity of eighty percent of light speed, would intersect Earth in another two hundred Earth Standard years. The

Emperor, an unparalleled scientist and happy to have something to do besides counting stars, had all of that time to catch up to the Federation by discovering antimatter combustion. With just five parsecs to go, the ship manufactured an antimatter charge and suddenly became a doomsday missile.

The Emperor, the last of his species, was determined to get the last laugh.

The ship could have arrived at Capital Province in short order if the Xerxesians had discovered and mastered the art of traveling through wormholes, the portals in space. Being pure energy rather than an organic life form, the Emperor would have survived the trip. But luck was with the Emperor anyway. He was immortal, and had plenty of time. Earth was going nowhere except round and round its sun.

The missile approached the borders of the Federation. Nobody cared much because the object would miss Capital Province by a long shot, and the space traffic controllers could easily keep the swarm of ships cruising around the Federation away from it. Only the star-gazers in the outer provinces scratched their heads at an object moving at such a high velocity, and sent out first one probe, then another that disappeared before sending back any useful data. The scientists ran out of money and stuck to their telescopes. Then an astronomer made a startling discovery with her radio telescope. The object was braking. Within a year, it rolled and changed course.

The object was heading straight for Earth's orbital path around Sol.

But first it would have to pass through the tip of Caulfield's Nebula.

Chapter 10
Liftoff

In all of his years as a professional soldier, the idea of mutiny had never entered Muldoon's mind. A man might well have asked him to go back to Grommet, slap a woman, fire on civilians and hang himself.

Yet here he was in his red, orange and black combat atmosphere suit with the helmet off, loading charge into his pistol, while Dobbs checked his own and said, "Let's go see the bugger, then."

"All right," Muldoon grumbled. "Let's get on with it, Sergeant Major. I'm not happy doing this!"

Dobbs smiled. "He'll thank us later. You'll see."

They marched down the west spoke corridor, checking their weapons one last time, their boots clocking against the floor. Once in the main building, they punched buttons and watched metal doors slide open with a hiss, then moved on to the next one. After a right turn and three more doors, they saw the sign that read, COMMANDER.

Muldoon took a deep breath and holstered his weapon, and Dobbs did the same, taking another moment to perfect the angle of his cap. After clearing his throat one last time, Dobbs pushed the button and the men walked into the Captain's office.

Williamson was in a familiar position to the men, slumped in his swivel chair facing the window.

"Who's there? You could knock next time."

"Sorry, sir," said Muldoon, at attention. "But it's important."

"It looks like the storm's letting up," Williamson said. "About time, I'd say." He turned his chair to face the men. "Well, if it isn't Sir Lawrence Dobbs and Lord Timothy Muldoon. You're both pretty duded up. At ease, men." He frowned. "I haven't seen you guys around for more than three weeks. Must have been out hunting crabs, because the miners tell me they didn't see even one during the feeding time last week."

"We have dispatched all crabs within forty square kilometers per the Captain's instructions, Sah!" said Dobbs.

"I said at ease. I knew you could do it if you applied yourselves. You know, now that that's done, you might want to get off this rock. The clock's ticking on you."

"Yeah, we have to go, but it looks like we'll all have to go," Muldoon told him.

The Captain leaned over his desk, his eyes narrowing. "Excuse me?"

"Trouble with the reactor," said Muldoon, staring straight ahead. "The Engineer has ordered us to evacuate the base."

"What the hell?" The Captain punched a number into a keypad. "Mr. Travis. Mr. Travis, report in." He waited. "He's not in the reactor."

"Well, that's like we said, sir," said Dobbs. "He's not working on the reactor at all. He's got a few robots in there to repair the leak. But he said we must evacuate at once."

The Captain eyed the men carefully for a moment. He leaned back in his chair.

"Okay, fine then," he said. "Let me get my files." He swiveled his chair away from them and opened a drawer. "And before we go, I want an explanation as to—"

"Please don't do that, sir," said Dobbs.

The Captain turned his head enough to see Dobbs out of the corner of his eye, then turned more to face him full, wide-eyed. The man held a pistol on him. The Captain saw the red sparkle above the barrel, could almost feel the red laser dot setting a nice target on his forehead. He was one quick squeeze away from oblivion. The classic zap between the eyes. He released the grip of the pistol in the drawer and raised his hand empty for Dobbs to see.

"I should have expected something like this." He said it calmly, like a man who had already gone through the anger phase and now accepted his fate. "If you came here to plug me, we can talk about it. Or you might just get it over with."

Dobbs and Muldoon glanced at each other.

"You're a brave man," Muldoon told the Captain.

"We haven't come to kill you," Dobbs said, "so long as you don't make

a fuss. As a matter of fate, you are now part of the endeavor to which
Sergeant Major Muldoon and I currently find ourselves dedicated."

"Oh, shit," the Captain said. "I was really hoping you'd be off this rock
by now."

"Now come along with us," Dobbs told him. "There's a good fellow."

The men marched back along the same route and came to the air lock.
Dobbs and Muldoon took turns pulling on their helmets and guarding the
Captain, who was then asked to put a suit on. They opened the lock, rocking slightly as the air was sucked out around them. Behind them, alarms
began going off, signaling a problem in the core of the base's nuclear
reactor, which within twelve hours would melt down and explode.

"Pay no mind to that, sir," said Muldoon, who was feeling sorry for the
Captain. "We're perfectly safe, and everybody else is on board." He
grinned. "Except Cook. We sent him packing to Camp Four with the rest
of the base camp staff—and a rover full of bean curd. The miners and the
rest of the Regiment have to eat!"

ॐ

The men walked to the freighter, passing several Crickets loading a car-
avan of robot trucks into the starboard bulkheads. Muldoon smiled at the
red dust swirling by at between forty and sixty kilometers per hour. The
desolation of the base at Siren was reminiscent of the mining world ghost
towns that came about whenever a precious mineral fell out of favor
because a newly discovered or synthesized material did a better job. Just
one month ago, this scene had inspired misery in Muldoon as a man who
relished the company of living things. Now that they were leaving, he
only smiled at it.

They entered the ship and waited for the bad air to be sucked out,
replaced by fresh air from the cylinders. When the gauge blinked green,
they took their suits off and entered the engine room, where they found
Travis, who waved an electrowrench in his excitement.

"I figured out how to soften our landing—oh, hi, Captain. We retrofire
with the laser used for hard take-offs. It'll penetrate the planet's crust for
about a kilometer, which will make a crater and trigger some seismic
activity, but we'll land like a feather." He tapped the nearest wall. "Good
hydraulics. They don't make 'em any better."

"Mr. Travis here has been integral to the success of our enterprise,"

Dobbs explained to the Captain.

"I'll bet the earthquake will shake up the natives," said Muldoon. "Make a nice show. And that crater will make a good natural defensive perimeter for our ship."

"Hey, what did you expect?" Travis answered, beaming.

"Where are we going?" Williamson asked Travis.

"We're going to a promising virgin world to make a new start for ourselves, sir," explained Dobbs.

"In the Beyond?"

"Aye, it is. Just a quick hop inside Caulfield's Nebula."

"Christ, I need a drink."

"Now, you don't have to be like that about it. Chin up."

The Captain looked around the engine room and frowned at the piping. "You went through all the trouble to outfit a stolen freighter for human flight to take you all the way to the Beyond, and you couldn't get a decent antimatter drive?"

Travis looked at his boots. "We're on fusion."

"You upgraded to deuterium and Helium-3, I hope."

The Engineer brightened again. "Why, sure. What'd you expect?"

ॐ

Dobbs and Muldoon led the Captain into one of the cargo holds, where a tall, lanky bearded man with long blond hair sticking out from under his gunner's cap was buckling robots to the bulkhead walls. He appeared to be arguing with the Mining Engineer.

"Captain," McDonough grumbled blackly, touching the rim of his cap. "Nice day."

"You too," Williamson answered, shaking his head. "I must have been asleep the whole time. This is treason, McDonough."

McDonough stared back at him with a bored expression and shrugged.

"We're trying to sort out where to put down some of the last equipment," said Fritz, after being introduced to Williamson. "We've got the scram and Mules bolted under those flexies. The rovers and repair robots are over there. I'm putting down the John Henry right here."

"JOHN HENRY RIGHT HERE," the machine blared.

Startled, Williamson glared up at the tiny red eyes of the robot, which bent its head a little to scrutinize him back, growling.

"I cleaned up some of the glitches," Fritz told Muldoon. "He's solid state now. If we had another few weeks, we could have cleaned out every crab on this whole crap planet."

"There's no need to overdo it," Muldoon scolded him.

"You do have the ammunition and weapons stored securely as well?" Dobbs asked.

"Yeah, it's all put down. Hey, Muldoni, watch this." Fritz kicked John Henry's shin, which resonated with a metallic bong.

"MOTHER-FUCKER."

The man winked. "I changed my mind about the bad words."

Muldoon explained to the Captain, "Fritz is—what did you call it? The Leonardo da Vinci of destruction."

"At your service, Captain."

Williamson shook his head.

"Don't worry," Fritz added. "Once we get to Neverland, the smart savages will stay in their beds. There won't be much of a fight, I can tell you that."

℘

Dobbs and Muldoon led the Captain up the elevator to the top decks.

"The Crickets who aren't loading the last of the robots are bedding down in one of the cargo holds," said Dobbs. "They wanted us to say hello."

"Everybody's pretty busy, sir," Muldoon said as if it were an apology.

"What the hell is this Neverland planet we're going to, anyway? That crazy gunner back there said something about savages."

"That's what they are, savages," said Dobbs. "They might try to interfere with our mission, which is to find the Holy Grail."

That term rang a bell with Williamson from somewhere in his past. "So you're not going there to settle, are you?"

"Well, not exactly, sir," Muldoon said sheepishly. "Sorry if we misled you."

"Muldoon, stop calling me 'sir' if you're going to hold me against my will. It's humiliating!"

The elevator stopped and the men marched down a long corridor which terminated at the flight cabin, where Kilroy and the Navigator tested their instruments. The walls were plastered with pin-up centerfolds of platinum blondes, except for the front wall, which was a solid mass of instrument gauges, lights, monitors and switches.

"Fuzzy logic my ass," Kilroy was telling the Navigator. "There used to be such a thing as absolutes in human thinking. The building blocks of morality, remember morality?"

Muldoon introduced Williamson and Kilroy shook his hand eagerly, while the Navigator merely sneered, a nearby monitor used to read invisible out-board radiation casting a sinister bluish glow on his bearded face.

"Commander, I have fly eyes," Kilroy told him with bravado, pulling a wilted cigarette from a pack in the breast pocket of his leather jacket. He torched its tip with a steel lighter.

Williamson shrugged.

Kilroy exhaled a cloud of smoke in front of his face. "I have fly eyes because I can look at this complete instrument panel, every little gauge and blinking light and monitor, and absorb it as a whole with kaleidoscope vision. I can stare at it for hours, the constant change. If one little thing goes wrong, I'll see it in a split second. You can bank on that. You're in for a safe ride with me."

"Emergency exits are on the sides of the ship," said the Navigator, and snickered.

Kilroy grew red in the face. "Tommy, go back to being absorbed."

"We'll be taking off in six hours on the dot," Dobbs reminded the men. "We will fire from the Coil Gun in another five, during which time we'll all go through the embalming. The reactor will blow its top about an hour later. Be sure you're right and ready, gentlemen."

"This is the sixth time we're checking this stuff over," Kilroy answered. "We're just killing time before launch." He turned to the Navigator. "Launch time confirmed. Synchronize watches, Tommy."

The Navigator, without looking up from an astronomical photograph he was studying with a loop, reached to the panel and punched a button, which responded with a click and rotated a series of numbers mechanically until they read 000.360.000.

"Commencing countdown at six hours," Kilroy said. "The gold rush is on. Make sure you're all buckled in a good thirty minutes before launch. You too, Commander. Nice meeting you."

"We'll be getting on, then," said Dobbs.

"I'm not one to judge anybody," said Muldoon, pointing to the centerfolds. "But I do want to remind you that we have ladies aboard."

Williamson blinked as Kilroy not only did not get offended, but appeared a little embarrassed.

$\wp$

After Dobbs and Muldoon nodded a farewell, the men found the women in the cargo hold that had been converted into the living quarters, busily retesting the cryogenic equipment to be used for the embalming that would turn the crews' bodies into inert objects for the duration of the flight. The women had learned a number of basic skills in the past three months, and had earned a place in the mission as full crew members to the extent that nobody had yet even thought to make a pass at them, which was a good omen to Dobbs.

Dariana ran to Muldoon and kissed him.

"Darry, you look happy today," he beamed at her. "Join me and the Sergeant Major in the farm before take-off, and we'll have some tea."

"I'd love to." She suddenly imitated Dobbs' accent. "That'd be smashing."

Dobbs winced and muttered, "Just keep feeding him, missus. That keeps him happy."

"Gold," Williamson said, as if remembering something he had long forgotten. "You've found a planet in the Beyond that has gold on it, and you're going there to steal it!"

Dobbs turned to the Captain. "Stealing, now really, sir."

"Five months ago, we ran into a certain astronaut who sold us the map to a planet that's stocked with gold," explained Muldoon. "We're going to take this ship to the planet, load it up with gold, and come back filthy rich. There's so much, we couldn't take it all, and if they're leaving it lying around, then they won't mind sharing it."

Williamson shook his head. "Amazing. So what will I do?" He added defiantly, "That's why I'm still alive, you need me for something. You can't make me do anything, you know."

Dobbs smiled. "We wouldn't dream of it, my good man. You may do as you like so long as you do not interfere with the mission. But we had rather hoped you might take a fancy to our enterprise and sign on for a percentage."

This seemed to confuse Williamson. There was nothing to be heroic against, nothing to fight, and nothing to stay for—the base would be a slag-heap within hours.

"I'll give it some careful thought and get back to you."

"Now there's a good fellow," said Dobbs, giving him a playful sock on the shoulder.

"Now that my long military career's finished, I suppose I'll need something to do."

"You wanted to get out," Muldoon said. "We're your free ticket. The planet's got a breathable atmosphere. It's nice and warm. You'll like it."

"So what do they do?" Williamson pointed at Rachel and Drew, who were smiling at him and whispering among themselves.

Muldoon led the Captain to the women and introduced him. "Commander, this is Rachel and this is Drew. Friends of Dariana's. Fine ladies and very good embalmers." He turned to address the women. "Rachel, Drew, do me a big favor. Talk to the Captain while we go up top and get us some tea." He turned to Dobbs. "And one last cigar!"

"Aye aye, sir," said Rachel with a mock salute, and took the Captain's hand.

Muldoon went back to Dobbs and Dariana, linking their arms with his and leading them along as if on a stroll. "That Captain really is a good man," he said.

"An all-around good fellow," agreed Dobbs. "A real corker."

"The hard work is over."

"Nice and easy, this is."

"And we can relax for a minute. I'm grateful."

"Some hot tea would go down well right now, thank you." Dobbs took off his cap gallantly. "Sergeant Major, we have assembled a crew, covered our tracks and taken care of the Captain. Now we finish the Retirement Fund and come back rich as Prefects."

Muldoon couldn't stop grinning. He was a fatalist and he accepted fate simply, yet he had chosen his destiny and was going to face it with the woman he loved at his side. This was the best of all worlds. One last adventure!

Dobbs couldn't stop smiling. The Holy Grail!

ൠ

Aboard *Macintosh*, men in short-sleeved blue shirts rushed in and out of the control room, chewing gum vigorously and some with cigarettes drooping from their mouths. Messages were handed back and forth, shoes squeaked on the floor, the Commander was shouting while filling a pipe, and a row of office machines went *clack clack clack* behind him.

Siren One had exploded. The reactor had gone up—the base was now just a boiling slag heap. Slowly, the men confirmed the safety of the mining camps. All but one had reported in. Anxious questions flashed from man to man. The room stank of sweat. Finally, the last camp reported in safe—the radio operator had been asleep, it being three o'clock in the morning local. This caused some relief, but it was still an unprecedented disaster.

The Commander tried to remember the Captain's name. Williamson, that's it. George. Good Navy man. He called the room to quiet, led a prayer, and tried to figure out what he'd tell the Commissioners who'd come all the way from New France, and whose ship was now docking.

He could at least tell them that the freighter had made it out okay and was preparing to launch toward the local wormhole.

৵

Buck Robinson ordered an excellent meal and a bottle of choice twenty-year-old New French scotch from room service, then went back to his radio to listen in on the traffic. Being an employee of Macintosh, he knew all the emergency frequencies by heart. It was a slow night.

His meal arrived and after eating he helped himself to two fingers of the scotch, leaning back in his chair and methodically stroking the back of Maxis, his cat. The calico purred gratefully and settled onto his lap.

"Let's see if those bastards have the stuff, Maxis. Don't you want to see if they have the stuff?"

His cat looked up at him with half-closed eyes, purring.

"Yes, of course you do, Maxis, you old cat."

The voices on the radio suddenly became more urgent. More voices plunged into the fray. Robinson downed the rest of his drink and listened. Soon, the emergency channel was jammed with frenzied voices.

Robinson threw back his head and roared with laughter at the ceiling. Startled, Maxis lowered his head and darted under the cot.

"You incredible bastards!" He clenched his fists. "You actually went and did it!"

৵

Four hours later, on the dark side of Danby, the Coil Gun was preparing to fire its thirty-thousand-ton steel bullet into space. The Coil Gun was an electromagnetic accelerator, a colossal four-thousand-kilometer-long tubular structure consisting of a series of coils held together by rods and an attached assembly of capacitors. The capacitors, each the size of a small space station, were the machine's batteries, now filled to the brim with energy that had been collected from Gamma Hades for the previous ten months.

With the freighter in place, the switch closed, completing a circuit that allowed electrical current to flow through the coils and create massive electromagnetic fields that began to act on the iron armature that girdled the freighter. The Coil Gun was ancient, built centuries ago when the name "Province of Good Hope" meant something, but its operation was still perfectly effective and reliable.

The freighter began to be pulled along the tube. It gained speed rapidly, soaring soundlessly through the circular coils, beginning its departure from normal definitions of space and time as it approached its final escape velocity of twenty percent of light speed, an acceleration of about 3,000g's.

The freighter escaped the fly-tube and plummeted into empty space, its rockets firing to begin the long push toward the speed of light.

ॐ

Aboard *Ultimatum*, a space station orbiting New France, the fifth planet from Gamma Hades and seat of government of the Province of Good Hope, Amazing Phil paced his room, still wearing his jacket. He had flung his boots in the corner to land on top of a pile of unwashed clothes. Finally, he flopped onto his cot and scowled up at the ceiling. A bare-chested platinum blonde smiled back at him from a poster he'd taped up there.

Sure, those bastards had paid him the balance, after he had completed his work to the letter. And a damn good job he did, too. But they'd paid him practically zilch for it.

Worse, that buffoon had insulted him. Muldoon. An even bigger buffoon than the other guy who had the goofy Marine accent. Dobbs. Phil decided he hated Marines.

The last guy who had the nerve to insult him like that, he'd . . . oo hoo hoo, oh yeah, that's what those guys need, he thought. The Fate Virus. Wait until they got back! I'll be long dead and buried, but I'll come down on them like a ton of Mars.

"You who think me dog can now call me god," he said aloud, and laughed.

Even better, what if they ran into a hard time while they were there? That'd be fun too. He was smart enough to figure out basically where they were going. A large ship like that wouldn't brake, roll and change course. It'd take forever to get to the Beyond, and they didn't have forever.

Phil launched out of bed and tackled his computer, furiously moving his gloved hands in VR gear until he'd hacked into *Macintosh*. They would have to stop there before going anywhere. It was routine, and getting the flight records would be as easy as telling a Gimp to jump off a cliff and watching the little monster do it.

Under the black-lensed goggles, he grinned. "Oo, they blew up the base. Neat."

He moved his hands furiously now like a mad young conductor, his mouth grimacing. "Ah, there you are. That's why it was hard. You fired out of the Coil Gun. Neat!" Must have a good engineer, he thought, to pull off a stunt like that. He downloaded the trajectory and heading of the ship directly into his memory chip, and plotted its course, his head hanging back and his mouth open. Then he grinned.

"I think I know where you're going. Pretty sneaky. This has to be worth at least the pay difference to somebody." He suddenly bolted upright. "They're going to get minerals there. I registered it for the Transplanetary Mining & Distribution Company. I am a genius!"

He threw off his VR gear and ran to the radio to contact the local branch office of Galactic Resources, Inc., the number two market share competitor to the TM&D.

৯

Siren One's cook and the rest of the base camp staff arrived at Camp Three and reported to Lance Corporal Harris, who was assigned at the post there with three other Marines. Cook told the story of how the reactor alarm had gone off, and how Sergeant Major Muldoon had told him to pack up all the food and get to safety. The other men were staying, Muldoon had told him, to make sure the freighter got out with its cargo as well.

"Blimey, seems the poor buggers couldn't get out themselves when it went all to cock," exclaimed Harris. "Poor bloody bastards."

Lance Corporal Harris and the other Marines took off their caps to fallen comrades.

∞

For kicks, the Emperor of Xerxes had just spent seventy-eight years curing *Mahhe-ee-jig*, a disease that had been a scourge on the Xerxesians since they had crawled out of the bellies of the tree slugs and evolved into intelligent life. Before that, he had designed a computer program that could play *Yees-pow* in nine dimensions, then played a single game for five months straight. Pure energy inside a cylinder, if he could have sighed out of an insane sense of boredom, he would have. The homeworld that had spawned the human species was still at least twenty-seven years (Xerxesian years; eighteen Earth Standard years) away at his velocity, with no braking time factored in since he was going to run smack into that world, blow it to smithereens and let the Eight Gods sort it out. He had calculated the trajectory so precisely that he had his target down to the centimeter, the width of the tip of his cone. For fun, he calculated the length of the rest of his trip to four hundred decimal places, then factored in a thousand variables.

Oh, but what is this?

He received input from his sensors. A probe. A military one this time, and as before, Federation-made. A box sprouting dishes, antennae, cameras, sensors and a rotating laser turret floating along in black space. The probe was old, chipped and scarred and battered by space dust and random debris, but it was still perfectly operational.

The Emperor learned its location, velocity and trajectory.

For my fathers, he thought, and pictured the probe destroyed.

Instantly, a gamma ray laser cannon sent out an invisible beam.

The probe's left leg was sliced off, then the machine took a hit in its chest smack on the Federation emblem, leaving behind a blackened scar which sprouted a trail of sparks. The probe went hurtling away in a tumble, its laser turret rotating crazily as it tried to fix a target.

No, the Emperor thought. *More!*

The ship's complete starboard armaments broadsided the probe as it soared by, the three cannons angling to focus the beams. In microseconds, the Emperor took parallax measurements, plotted points and then could then hit the probe easily.

The probe disintegrated with little fanfare in distant space, thousands of pieces of burnt foil, springs, wire and transistors floating away into the cosmos.

The Emperor was pleased. He had plenty of power for the lasers. He thought perhaps he should keep destroying things to keep himself occupied, and hoped more Federation space vehicles would come visit him. He was now only six Earth years from the *Iss-Ur* Nebula, where he could spread his scoops and gather more fuel. The *Iss-Ur* was full of unknowns. Perhaps the Federation had settled on a system inside it, or maybe its admirals had gotten wise to him and had their entire battle fleet arrayed for an ambush.

Now that'd be fun. For the first time in a hundred years, the Emperor was happy.

BOOK III

TO NEVERLAND

Chapter 11
Planet Ho!

Max Von Kleig was a veteran spacer and professional soldier. He wore his scars as badges of honor instead of having them repaired, but enormous sections of him had been replaced by biomechanical parts, including his right eye, now a red glowing disk. He carried a microchip in his head to help him with battlefield command decisions, another to stimulate the aggressive areas of his brain with microvoltage pulses, another to squelch pain, and a linguistic resonator chip to help him spot lies and even bullshit.

Smoking a cigar he'd recently pulled out of his black leather jumpsuit, he marched onto the metal grille bridge separating him and one of the tiered loading platforms surrounding the stacked sections of the cylindrical *Adversary*. A group of men stood on the platform, standing at ease without talking. His red eye scanned them quickly. Ten hard men in gray jumpsuits—three he spotted and knew well as veteran spacers, good men, the others he quickly sized up as common space trash. Another man, standing with his head at an odd angle and wearing a patient smile, was a combat-assassin android and probably one seriously ruthless bastard.

And the soft fat one in the business uniform who obviously didn't like being there could only be Felix Whitehead, the agent for Von Kleig's employer, Galactic Resources, Inc.

Whitehead introduced Von Kleig to his comrades and the men shook hands all around.

"It's good to have you working for us again, Max," Whitehead told him. "Sorry we couldn't give you time to pick your own team, but you'll find them of exceptional quality."

"Particularly the android," Von Kleig said. "Mr. Bova. He's your man, I take it." Corporations always sent an android on a mission like this as Troubleshooters. He had learned to sniff them out at the start of a mission, since they could be a wild card under stress.

Whitehead grinned sheepishly and shrugged as if to say so what. "Obviously, I can neither confirm nor deny that. But you know the drill. S-O-P." He chuckled.

Von Kleig nodded back, puffing on the cigar. He did know the drill. Almost all of his employers were transplanetary megacorporations involved in mining, agriculture, communications and transportation. They were a paranoid breed. But they paid well.

"The ship's crew—hand-picked men," Whitehead was saying. "The equipment, even the food and water—the best available. This is a very important mission to GR. The Board of Directors itself wants that planet. More importantly, they don't want the TM&D to have that planet. Do you have any questions as to what that means, or do I have to draw a chart?"

Von Kleig dropped his cigar and stepped on it. He shook his head.

"Then good luck, godspeed and make your claim for Galactic Resources," Whitehead recited with genuine pride, and they shook hands. The corporate agent then hurried off the platform, calling behind him, "Lift off whenever you're ready. Time is everything."

Von Kleig heard the corporate anthem play over unseen loudspeakers to wish them well in their mission, the sound tinny and distant as it was swallowed by the vast metal room. He entered the spaceship and headed straight for the cryogenics chamber while a crewmember secured the locks behind him. No need to delay in lifting off, if the ship's crew was as good as Whitehead had told him. And Whitehead was right. Time, and timing, was everything.

This was going to a very interesting mission. Very interesting. When Von Kleig had received the mission data and saw a man's name in the TM&D crew list, he'd known right away that Galactic Resources had been fooled by its informant, some hacker. The TM&D was not bankrolling this venture at all, even though the mission was in the Register under the flag of a newly incorporated TM&D contractor. Rather it was an old friend of Von Kleig's, pulling an independent score.

Von Kleig hadn't seen Lawrence Dobbs in more than two hundred Standard years, and was anxious to see him one more time. They had unfinished business to settle from a long time ago.

છ

The Captain of the Federation Ship of the Line *Undaunted* saluted the Admiral and marched away proudly, carrying the gold microchip that contained his orders in the side of his head.

Captain Antonio Malvez, tall, young and handsome in his dress reds, had gained his commission only two years ago, and now he had a real Type One mission straight from Admiral Armistead himself! He grinned, showing two rows of perfect white teeth against clean bronze skin. The Navy hadn't gotten a Type One mission in at least five hundred Standard years.

Captain Malvez was anxious to serve. After War VI against Xerxes, the Navy hadn't seen a lot of action, just an occasional planetary bombardment here and there that took months, sometimes even years, to complete. Hardly real action. Malvez had missed the last big naval war. These days, Space Cavalry had all the fun. He knew the jokes the other services told about the Navy. The one about search-and-search missions. The Federation taxi service. He thought them hardly fair. But this mission? This was high-speed.

Undaunted was to finish up her maintenance at the Yokohama Shipyard and fly into the Beyond, where an object continued on its path at 0.8*c*, or eighty percent of light speed, toward the borders of the Federation. The object had already destroyed two scientific probes without blinking, went into a clean roll maneuver and changed its course to intersect Capital Province. Not acceptable at all to the voters. Since then, a military probe had been destroyed, a quick kill that had deprived Local Command of useful information and increased the sense of alarm. Now the Admiralty wanted quick and decisive action.

Undaunted was the first line of defense for the Province—and for the Federation itself in this wide stretch of border with primitive unclaimed space. Captain Malvez would show Space Cav what a Ship of the Line could do. It was obvious just to look at one!

A Navy Ship of the Line, shaped like a long cylinder, had more than a hundred thousand tons of rest mass and held some four hundred officers and rankers, including five platoons of Marines. *Undaunted* boasted five separate batteries of laser turrets and six torpedo bays for attack; countermeasures for defense; hunter-killer satellites for planetary, moon and asteroid reconnaissance as well as attack; smart neutron bombs for planetary bombardments; and twelve boats for ship-to-ship, ship-to-station and ship-to-ground assault. Connected by five-kilometer steel rods on all four sides of the cylinder, kinetic energy cannons, similar to coil guns, were loaded with metal slugs that could be hurled at any target within a one-hundred-and-eighty-degree arc at a lethal velocity. *Undaunted* was propelled by a Wyoming antimatter drive, consisting of a reactor engine and superconducting coils attached to a magnetic nozzle used to direct the byproduct of antimatter combustion—pions dissolving into gamma rays—toward the rear of the ship. There was simply no finer ship in the galaxy for maneuvering, trading punches and coming out the winner.

After hitting the Beyond, he was to take *Undaunted* into Caulfield's Nebula, an excellent spot for an ambush, especially if he could meet the intruder around one of those young stars.

He marched between two Marine guards at the great marble doors of Browning Local Command and returned their salute crisply. Within a few hours, he would dine with his officers and together, full of excellent wine and good stories, they would make an earnest oath to destroy the intruder or die. Then Captain Malvez would stand and lead their traditional military toast to "Federation, honor and humanity."

Out there in the cold space of the Beyond, he knew, lay his destiny.

ॐ

In the Golden Age of the Federation, people enjoyed relative peace within the borders and few real threats from the Beyond. In Walker's view, the greatest threats to the future of the union were the megacorporations and the black market.

Christopher Walker was a Troubleshooter for the Federation Commission of Space Trade and Supply. The Commission, part of the Ministry of Commerce, enjoyed an enormous budget and broad executive powers. His immediate bosses worked in large offices on New France spending their time dreaming up new regulations all day that thwarted corporate rogues, smugglers, carpetbaggers, space-age snake oil salesmen, would-be robber barons, organized crime syndicates and other scalawags, continuously revising and adding to the Book of Trade Regulations that was already, in Walker's view, a Tower of Babel.

Walker's job was to go out and investigate serious violations of any of these regulations. It was a big job, with broad powers. Troubleshooters carried sidearms and psionic powers that came with a license to kill. They were level-headed, highly trained, the Federation's best. And with their reputation and track record, they were the most feared cops in the galaxy.

The megacorporations were often too smart to be caught outright. They fought their wars over resources at the discrete peripheries of the Federation, and the Commission often looked the other way and let them fight it out so long as the resources being fought over were not damaged. So most of Walker's cases involved the black market.

Walker saw reg busters as either harmless—even useful—or dangerous. Most cheaters were spacers who wanted to retire a little richer than the pensions allowed, and he saw no harm in that. Walker sometimes even appreciated minor cheats, because often no real damage was done and the offending loophole could be tagged and sealed up tight. It was a big game. But others were dangerous space trash. Before his time, the Federation had even had its share of pirates. People like them could not be tolerated for the simple reason that their activities would someday make the Federation collapse like a dome infested with Gimp fleas.

Walker didn't know exactly where to fit these two characters, Lawrence Dobbs and Timothy Muldoon. Excellent service record—God knew the Federation needed good Marines as much as it needed good Troubleshooters. Minor cheating of trade regs that made them a little money—so what.

For that reason, Walker had thought spending good taxpayer money on flight pay (which was time and a half) and fuel required for a trip from New France to Siren was a real big waste just to peg two nobodies who'd scammed the local liquor retailers. From the word go, he had categorized them as harmless spacer types out to make a small buck.

But a job was a job, and an order was an order. He had to go. He'd docked with *Macintosh* and heard the news: Siren One had blown up. The only good news, apparently, was that the freighter had fired from the Coil Gun just hours before the accident.

Walker pieced together the evidence and determined that Dobbs and Muldoon had blown up the base themselves and made off with the freighter.

Walker knew this because the freighter fired from the Coil Gun with a miniscule error in the trajectory required to meet the local wormhole. One degree at that distance meant about a billion kilometers in the final result. He alone had noticed it. He didn't buy the cook's story, and he figured the other men at Siren Base One had probably gone with Dobbs and Muldoon, since they'd need a crew.

Figuring out where they went would be a problem. After some research, he found the freighter now registered under a newly incorporated contractor for the Transplanetary Mining & Distribution Company. But the mission description was vague.

The local TM&D government relations man, a real glad-hander, offered no useful information. Walker doubted the TM&D had anything to do with it, and the corporations never told their government liaisons anything anyway to serve the age-old PR strategy of plausible deniability. Dead end. He was just following standard operating procedure.

Walker eventually gave up his detective work, which had consumed four months, and decided to start on the chase and hope he could correct himself later if he had to. The old atomic clock was ticking, and he had to get on their trail right away. Walker called the Commission astronomers and asked, if based on the logical assumption they kept going in the same direction after firing from the Coil Gun, where would they end up?

First was a narrow stretch of the Yokohama Province. Walker made a call to Border Patrol, and was referred to Space Traffic Control. A polite mission personnel supervisor told Walker that the freighter had just left the Province and headed into the Beyond, it was all in the records.

Then the astronomers arrived in a bustling train, spread out a series of astronautical charts and, using a stencil, showed him the most likely plotted course based on the starting trajectory.

The red line ended at the tip of Caulfield's Nebula.

Walker sighed. What a long shot to start with, and besides that he'd probably get there long after they did. But he had to try. To Walker and the Commission as a whole, the destruction of property—seeing how valuable anything man-made was in the colonies—was a mortal sin. To make things worse, the Siren mining operation was operated by the Commission itself, the previous owner having gone out of business. That made this a direct attack on the Government. Dobbs and Muldoon were no longer cheaters in his book. They were as bad as pirates. They would have to be hunted down, no matter what the cost.

Within two months, he and two hand-picked agents boarded the *Adam Smith* and embarked on a mission that would take them straight into the Nebula.

❧

Muldoon and Dariana watched the view-screen in the pilot and navigator chairs.

"It's just beautiful, Tim. Just beautiful."

Muldoon grinned happily and held her hand.

They beheld a starscape possible only at relativistic speeds—a small circle of stars, startling bright, many red, some blue. The rest of the screen was deep black around the circle. It was as if God had reached into their universe, grabbed onto all of the stars they could see, and compressed them into a small circular view for them, leaving the rest of the universe dark and empty.

"Perfectly romantic," Dariana added. "What a scheme you've cooked up!"

Two months earlier, when it was safe to do so, their bodies had been awakened prematurely while the rest of the crew continued to sleep. Blood had flowed back into their lifeless bodies, replacing the cryogenic embalming fluid and adding nutrients and anti-leukemia boosters. Their hearts began pumping again, and consciousness was stimulated with a timed series of microvoltages. Within two days, they were able to leave their armored pods and walk naked and dripping into the cold ship.

It had been Muldoon's idea of a surprise "weekend get-away," except they had two months before the ship would begin to brake hard and they would have to return to their pods. Muldoon would have preferred an entire year, but didn't dare use up that much food, water and power. Together, they performed inspections and maintenance on the ship in zero gravity, enjoyed a spectacular view of the starscape, and whiled away the hours talking and making love.

"So why are those stars red?" she asked, pointing at the starscape on the view-screen. "There are lots of those."

"That's the Doppler shift," Muldoon told her. "There are a few blue stars, too, but what we see are mostly red ones. They're red giants. We're also seeing cosmic background radiation, normally invisible, being shifted into visible light there in the center."

"They're so bright, they look like Polyphemus seen from *Macintosh*. Look, the biggest, brightest ones are in the middle."

"We're actually looking at a sort of cone head on, I'm told. So the middle of our view is more dense with stars."

Dariana smiled at him. "This is a fine adventure. Thanks again for bringing me. I know it wasn't easy to convince Dobbs the Scrooge."

Muldoon grinned and felt as if his heart would burst. He wondered what it must have been like for her, being raised and moved from one space station to the next by a single mother, deprived of a real education or even the chance to experience real freedom of choice over her destiny. Muldoon knew well that people without technical skills in the colonies usually fell to the bottom of society. He was proud to be able to show her the life he lived, and let her share in it. He had made the right choice in bringing her.

Dariana pointed. "Look! A star just popped out of nowhere, and those two are dimming! What's going on, Tim?"

Muldoon shrugged. "The eggheads say that's because of stellar aberration and geometric parallax." He grinned sheepishly. "Don't ask me anything more than that, Darry. My male answer syndrome only goes so far. But it makes the whole starscape animated."

"So you said this happens because we're moving close to light speed."

"Yes, that's true. If we continued to accelerate, the starscape would gradually compress down into a blob of light. We'd further leave spacetime as the rest of the universe knows it. It's amazing. In a sense, you're actually looking at time dilation in action."

"Oh, I wish you hadn't said that. Now the view makes my stomach feel sick!"

"Sorry, my love. Just think about what it'd be like if we could see it during the braking. As we slowed down, the starscape would unfold right in front of our eyes back to a normal view, showing us returning to normal spacetime. Picture it getting bigger."

"That's better," she said, resettling into her chair. "So because of time dilation, when we get back, Siren will really be about five hundred years older?"

"Yeah, almost four hundred and fifty Standard years," Muldoon agreed. "It's a little less than six light-years from Siren to Neverland. It'll take us more time to cross that distance for the return trip because we won't have the Coil Gun—we'll slingshot from a gas giant."

"Siren will be four hundred and fifty years older," she repeated. "But I'll only be less than a year older?"

"Yeah, that's right."

Dariana snorted. "I still don't believe it."

"You know I'm eight hundred and change Earth Standard years old, Darry."

"You say a lot of things to impress a girl, Mr. Muldoon."

Muldoon grinned and shook his head helplessly. "You knew what time dilation was, and what it would do to us. That's why you wanted to come with me, I thought."

"Okay, suppose you're right," she said. "What do you think the Federation will be like? Everybody'll probably be bald and tattooed or something. Who knows what fashion will be like?"

"It changes less than you think," Muldoon answered. "First, as you know, many of the people in the colonies can't afford and don't value luxuries. Plus things take their time happening in the Federation, it being so big and all. But on a flight like this, it could change a lot, especially the technology. It happened to me and Lawrence at least once. We could barely work a food processor! At the docks, it's traditional to say to spacers recently come back from a trip, 'Welcome back to the future.' But no matter what happens, the Federation is always there, it always has a Prime Minister watching over us, and it always has good cigars and beautiful women." He realized his mistake and hastily added, "That's how I met you, Darry, and now we're together." He squeezed her hand as insurance.

"I'm sure they'll still have sextechs," she said dryly. "In case you're interested. I'd bet my left boob on that."

"Well, I've played the game, I admit," Muldoon admitted, growing red. "But I don't make the rules. I'm a soldier and a simple man."

"Hm."

"And I'm not leaving you."

She squeezed his hand in return. "I know. You're a good man, Tim Muldoon."

"I love you, and that's a fact."

"Tim?"

"Yes, my love."

"If you love me, why don't we just settle the planet when we get there?"

"We're going to be rich, that's why. The gold will make us millionaires."

Dariana frowned. "Sometimes I feel really dumb, but I'm not, I'm just ignorant. So excuse a dumb question, will you?"

"There's no such thing between you and me, I swear it."

"Why on Mars are we going to get gold? It's pretty, but nobody uses it, really."

"You know, it was once used for money in ancient times before the Capital Credit System," he told her. "As money, then as backing for paper money."

"I don't believe you."

"It's true. And women used to wear it for decoration, all over their bodies, the way men and women wear gold bands on their fingers today when they get married. But only in Capital Province, never in the colonies— who'd put up with such a thing? I hear the women in Capital Province still wear it for decoration to this very day. But now it's mostly used as an industrial material. And it's worth good money to the right people. We're going to get the gold, come back rich, and buy our own planet!"

Dariana giggled, then added slyly, "Would your planet have a warm climate?"

"Certainly," Muldoon boasted.

"And a breathable atmosphere?"

"The best terraforming money can buy," he said heartily.

Dariana raised her index finger and made a show of trying to figure out a complex problem. "So, we're going to Neverland so we can come all the way back, get rich enough to buy a planet, when we could simply live on the planet where we're going that's the same thing."

Muldoon turned purple, confounded. "It's not the same!"

Dariana raised her eyebrows. "Well, I must be dumb then. Oh, or is it a guy thing like all the other things you talk about?"

"I know what you mean by that and it's not true! Don't even say it."

"You know, as in, there's like this competition to buy the biggest planet?"

Muldoon groaned and rolled his eyes. "Woman! Buying your own planet is just a figure of speech anyway."

Dariana laughed and squeezed his hand again. "Hey, don't worry, you didn't make the rules. You just follow them."

"I'm not wor—hey! Mars, woman!"

"You don't have to swear. Just think about what I said, okay? You love adventure, not money, and that's why I like you so much. Pioneers! That'd be an adventure. Dobbsy is the one who loves money."

"Don't call him that. He hates when you do that."

"Oh, I'm so sorry, my good fellow," she said, imitating Dobbs.

"And don't make fun of his accent."

"You started it."

"Almost all Marines have that funny way of talking—it's like spacers and their lingo. It's a service tradition going back almost two thousand years in honor of the first Marines who traveled to another star system, then fought and won against an alien species. The accent honors man's first conquest in space."

Dariana thought for a moment. "But think about the adventure, Tim. Colonizing a world. We could build our own little civilization, rename the planet Tim And Dariana One, its moon Mul-Moon, and live like Adam and Eve. I thought you liked adventure."

"But we'd never see the Federation again," Muldoon said sullenly. "I don't know if I could take that."

"I know, you're a patriot, aren't you? Our children could continue to build our civilization and enter the Federation later on. As planetary Prefects!"

This thought appealed to Muldoon, whose personal pantheon included Family, but he shook his head. "Darry, we have to get along for another seven weeks. Let's be nice and not fight. Because it's perfect when we don't."

"Who's fighting? I'm just thinking out loud, that's all."

"I don't want to think or talk about settling on Neverland. It's already handsomely populated with violent savages. And the real universe is back there. You and me, we're going to be rich." He regarded her uncertainly, noticing with some agony that she was pouting. "Hey, Darry, I could take you to Earth."

She blinked. He had gotten through.

"You know," he continued, "When Lawrence and I were stationed in the Commonwealth, you could look up at night and see Sol, Earth's very own sun, as a bright point of light in the sky. We used to talk all the time about retiring and going there. Seeing the Great Halls, taking long hot showers with unlimited water, visiting the incredible megacities that glow at night, bathing in its sweet atmosphere. Now I can go with you."

She didn't answer, but he felt a squeeze on his hand.

For the next seven weeks, Muldoon and Dariana sometimes talked about going to Earth. But most of the time, they fought over whether to settle on Neverland.

ം

More than a year later, the freighter, all of its inhabitants now in cryogenic sleep, approached Caulfield's Nebula, its particle beam accelerators cutting a swath through a dust swarm met through blind chance. Freighters were rugged space vehicles, designed and manufactured to withstand months of a sand storm on planets like Siren (at least according to the advertising), but a collision with dust moving at high velocities in space meant serious erosion of the hull.

Light panels flickered to life and the heating and ventilation system kicked into occupied mode, warming up the now cold occupied areas. The artificial gravity generator purred to life, providing Earth Standard gravity to the bridge and other forward compartments.

Within two days, Kilroy and the Navigator were awake, fed and at the controls. Kilroy couldn't stop grinning. Before his eyes, the vast swirling red clouds of the nebula filled the screen. He had lived to see a nebula close up.

"Look at that thing, Tommy. It's beautiful. It's the face of God."

They plunged into the clouds of hydrogen gas, then they could see inside the nebula, although if they stopped and turned around (a complicated maneuver), their visibility of the rest of the universe would be limited. The farther the spaceship moved in, the less visibility they'd have until the nebula itself would appear to become the entire universe.

Within three months, they guided the ship into the Neverland system.

"Seems the old coot wasn't lying after all," Kilroy said. "Things are looking up!"

His mouth full of grape gum, the Navigator pointed to his instruments and threw his hands up in frustration.

"All right, Tommy. I'll let the ship brake a little more, but I still want to do most of the final braking on the atmosphere to save fuel."

The Navigator shrugged and went back to a reference book on his lap. He'd been right—Buck Robinson's radiometrics were crap, ancient, so the smart move was to take it slow. An asteroid belt moved in a high-speed orbit along with four planets around the local spectral class G2 star, gleaming white and yellow like Sol. The asteroid belt was actually the product of one of the planets, the gas giant, due to the gravitational stresses it produced on the solar system—and something to watch out for. As the freighter passed the outermost planet, a frozen hell, the Navigator told Kilroy that the gas giant was now roughly at a Trojan point with respect to them, billions of kilometers away, which made for a safer ride.

The next planet, second from its star, was what spacers would call a rare gem. As the freighter's flight path was on the stellar plane, intersecting the elliptical orbits of the planets, the planet was now scarcely visible against the small burst of the local sun. But as the freighter closed the distance in the next three months, the planet and its two moons began to stand out in sharp relief until they filled the view-screen on the bridge. Being on the night side of the planet, there wasn't much to see, but Kilroy and the Navigator had been told that on the sunside it looked like a blue-white marble, as if they were visiting Earth or a terraformed world. The ship aerobraked on the atmosphere and parked in a geostationary orbit above where Graham's ship had reportedly crashed. The men launched probes, then they waited. They would see the planet in sunlight for themselves soon enough simply by waiting for it to rotate for another four hours.

"There is a God," Kilroy said seriously.

They had reached Neverland.

๛

"We are the luckiest spaceheads this side of the Magellan Clouds," Kilroy told Dobbs and Muldoon, smoking a cigarette that immediately overwhelmed the ventilation system and made the room unbearable for Travis, who was already feeling claustrophobic and therefore having trouble breathing. He'd never admit to the others that he was claustrophobic, because they'd call him a rookie and a grounder and there was no worse insult to a man who felt alienated among spacer types to begin with.

"See this?" The Pilot tapped a spot on an astronomic photograph.

Dobbs leaned over the photo and studied it in the bad light. "I see, yes. It's a fingerprint on otherwise perfectly blank empty space."

Kilroy leaned back in the pilot's chair, satisfied, and next to him the Navigator snickered. The Pilot exhaled smoke. "Tell 'em, Tommy."

The Navigator noticed Kilroy's move and also decided to lean back.

"Wormhole," he said, his mouth full of gum.

"Your astronaut friend thought it was the gas giant stirring up the soup in this system," Kilroy told them. "And I'll admit we agreed. The truth is this system has a wormhole almost right smack dab in the middle of it. I could put a message in a bottle, throw it out the window and it could pop out instantly at Capital Province. We almost flew right into the mother. How close were we, Tommy?"

"Less than a million kilometers."

"In astronomical terms, you know what I'm talking about. That's real close. We came that close to going in and coming out the other side a Flying Dutchman—another sad case of organic atomization. This whole solar system is like a freak of nature. Spooky."

"Well, we know it's there now," Muldoon said helpfully, but he was feeling irritable. It wasn't a good idea to go through embalming twice in a row in such a short period of time as he had—hibernating and waking up was like being taken apart and being put back together. To make things worse, Rachel had screamed from her pod that her right arm was missing, which turned out to be a bad joke. Then the alarms over the Captain's pod began going off—the computer was worried that he had too many toxins in his system, which turned out after some analysis to be alcohol. They'd had to leave him in his pod to detox, the computer working his blood over with a treatment of heavy nutrients.

"I just wanted to tell you, that's all," Kilroy said. He passed around more photos. Behind him, several monitors began scrolling endless lines of data, the blue light flickering into the room. "Your astronaut friend was right on the money with his astronautical data, though. As you know, stars move and we had to project where it'd be by the time we got here so we could travel the whole way in a straight line. We sailed right into the system like a dart hitting the bullseye with only minor course corrections in the system."

"That's a good omen, for sure," Dobbs told him.

"By the way, if you feel it getting warmer in here than you're used to, don't blame the HVAC system," the Pilot continued. "We're in a nebula, and we're surrounded by hydrogen and some helium. A nebula is where stars are born, the tropical zone of the galaxy."

"I like it," Muldoon said. "I'm used to the cold, but it feels about right now."

The men were passing around the photos.

"These radar map photos are from the probes me and Tommy sent into orbit that didn't get damaged from all the dust and junk in this system," Kilroy told them. "You should also know that we sent in an atmospheric entry probe, and that's it, we're out of probes. What you see behind me on the monitors is about a mile of crap that has to be analyzed. As you can see, we're conducting synoptic imaging and mapping in infrared and UV wavelengths, and we're conducting magnetic field measurements. We're not explorers or surveyors by trade, and we're lacking probes that can do the job the way it should be done, so we're sort of winging this planetology thing. But for now, we do know four things.

"First, the planet is inhabited. The infrared maps show where you can get a sense of population centers if you know how to look at these things. We made a rough conclusion that the natives are civilized and living in cities and outlying farms.

"Second, we're not far from the largest population center on this continent, possibly even the entire planet. So I think we lucked out again and hit a bull's eye the first time in.

"Third, the atmospheric composition and air pressure show we can breathe it. It's as good as what we humans breathe. I can't vouch for the water or food. For all I know, if you try to pick a berry it'll bite your finger off. And you should know there's something weird going on down there. There's a lot of electrical activity in the atmosphere, making some very funny weather. Electrical storms are pretty commonplace, and this planet gets a couple F-6 tornadoes as often as I change my shorts—all right, save it, Tommy.

"And four, seismological conditions are stable in a wide area we're standing on, so we can land with the laser retrofiring into the crust for a nice soft landing without triggering something worse than we want to trigger. Is that about the size of it, Bill?"

Travis beamed at the acknowledgment, pulling at his beard. "I checked it all out and you're on the money as far as I'm concerned."

"Excellent," said Dobbs, studying a map that showed various sprawls of colors. He put it in front of Kilroy. "Let's put her down right here, so long as there are no natives living there. Don't want to start a shooting war unless we have to. How does that sound to you?"

Kilroy laughed and jerked his thumb at the Navigator. "Give that crap to him, will ya?"

The Navigator accepted the photo, studied it with his face inches away from the sheet, and sneered up at Dobbs. "You're in business," he said.

Dobbs smiled back cheerfully. No amount of typical spacer attitude could snap his good mood. The planet was there, and it was populated, so Buck Robinson had been telling the truth so far, an obvious good omen.

All was going according to plan, and he had men of talent to solve all problems. The Holy Grail was within arm's length now, and it felt grand.

"Park it there, Mr. Peters, Mr. Kilroy," he said.

"Aye aye," Kilroy said, swiveling in his chair to face the controls. "You heard the man, Tommy. The rest of you better buckle up for the landing." Then he called after Dobbs. "Hey, Commodore! I got good vibes about this." He gave him a thumbs-up.

"You're the best I've seen at your trade, Mr. Kilroy. How was your view of the nebula? Much better than the inside of a black hole, I presume."

"It was spectacular."

"Carry on, then." Dobbs gave the Pilot a rough salute in return and went down the ladder.

"I love that guy," Kilroy said, laughing and shaking his head. "Predeterminists! Now let's park it, Tommy."

Down below, Dobbs and Muldoon hung the safety nets and buckled into their harnesses with the rest of the human crew—Fritz, McDonough, Travis, Dariana, Drew and Rachel. Then the Captain joined them, his hair freshly combed and with a spring in his step.

"Wow, I feel great," he said, and nodded to the women. "Ladies."

"*Cap*-tain," they said together, and laughed flirtatiously.

In the front two seats, Dobbs rolled his eyes and sighed, while Muldoon looked down at his hands in embarrassment. Then Muldoon turned his head and enjoyed the moment with a private grin.

"So how should we deploy, Sergeant Major?" Dobbs asked Muldoon.

"Since the lasers are going to make a crater, we'll head up the incline in rovers," Muldoon said, chewing his mustache. "Easier going. Make more of a show, too, not to mention the protection we get. You, me, Brandon Fritz, Bill Travis, Carl McDonough and all but three of the Crickets will go. Since we don't have battle armor, you and me will go in dress uniforms, even the swords, with the Crickets in standard dress. The important thing with a primitive native population is to make a grand show of it to impress them. The robot-trucks will follow close behind, ready to receive the gold. The Captain, Jim Kilroy and the Navigator will stay here with two or three Crickets to watch over things."

"That sounds like it will be suitable," Dobbs told him.

Muldoon turned in his seat to face Fritz. "How does it sound to you, Brandon? You're the war expert."

Fritz looked startled. "Oh, uh, I wasn't listening."

"So how are you feeling today, soldier?"

"Like one mean Kiki, sir!" Fritz replied, an old soldier's joke, and smiled sadly.

"Passengers, this is the Pilot speaking," Kilroy said over the intercom. "We're following orbit around the equator. The sun is just starting to peek around the planet, meaning the sun is rising over the landing zone, and it's a beautiful sight. But I gotta tell you, it's nothing compared to what Neverland looks like from up here. This is one gem of a planet."

Everybody cheered. Muldoon turned and caught Dariana's eye. She blew him a kiss and he slapped his cheek in response, grinning.

"There's some amazing storm activity on the ground, but at least five hundred kilometers north of the landing site and traveling northeast," Kilroy said. "As for our landing site, the probe tells me we've got clear skies, highs in the nineties and a light breeze from the southwest. Over and out."

The crew cheered again. Normally, visiting such a place—usually a terraformed planet, back in the Federation—would have meant a short, very expensive vacation for the likes of them, and here it was for free!

"You guys sure know how to throw a party, Mr. Dobbs," Drew said.

Dobbs turned and studied the faces, each excited, expectant and full of confidence.

"Gentlemen—and ladies—and oh, you too, Captain—welcome to Neverland," he said grandly, winking at Williamson. "When we touch down, and I'm told we'll land like a feather, we'll unload the equipment straight away and some of us will head toward what I'm told is a metropolis by Neverlandian standards. With any luck, we won't have to nuke any of the natives. We're going to try to trade them some of our equipment for the gold. All in all, I expect no fuss. Sergeant Major Muldoon and I have arranged your complete comfort, so let's have some fun at this party. Enjoy the warm weather, the air and the view. Then we'll load up the gold and come back the richest people in the Federation."

The crew applauded, and Dobbs and Muldoon bowed by nodding in all directions.

"Here we go," Kilroy said over the intercom. "Five, four, three—cowabunga!"

The freighter dropped into the atmosphere and began to free fall. The chemical rockets fired, jerking the ship and easing the landing a little. Nevertheless, it felt like falling in Earth Standard gravity in an elevator car with its cable cut. Then the lasers on the bottom retrofired at intervals, cutting their velocity into a series of short falls and bumps.

Travis began mouthing come on girl repeatedly. His reputation—not to mention their lives—were at stake.

Within twenty minutes, they felt the ship find a resting point and begin to settle. A distant hissing noise signaled the hydraulics easing the ship down onto its landing gear.

"Thank you, Mr. Travis and Mr. Kilroy!" Dobbs said.

"Hey," Travis answered, beaming. "What'd you expect? I'm two for two now."

Outside the ship and the smoking crater it had hammered into the ground with its lasers, within an area of twenty kilometers in all directions, the Neverlandians were screaming.

Chapter 12
The Neverlandians

Real air, and warm! Tons of space! A man could run naked in it. Muldoon walked down the ramp and stretched while the crew unloaded the rovers and supplies onto the soft dirt of the crater pit. The dirt was charred black, and small fires were still burning, billowing black smoke. He adjusted his ceremonial sword at his side to rest against the yellow stripe on his trousers, then pulled a cigar out of the breast pocket of his tunic.

Dobbs appeared at his right and lit the cigar for him, then lit his own.

"Looks like the party's on, Sergeant Major."

"Yes it is," agreed Muldoon. "Smell that air!"

Dobbs sniffed. "I smell smoke. The whole pit's on fire."

Muldoon grinned. "Have you ever smelled smoke like that before in your life?" Suddenly he sobered and blinked away a tear. "The air pressure—easy on the lungs. God, when was the last time we walked on the soft earth of a planet without an air tank?"

Dobbs patted his comrade's large shoulder. "Too long, chap. Too long. This is going to be like a vacation. Then we get back, and we can live as long as we like on the choicest terraformed worlds. No more barren rocks for the likes of us."

"Now that you brought it up, I was wondering if I could talk to you."

Dobbs forced a smile, not liking Muldoon's tone one bit. "Do tell."

"I was wondering, if it goes quick and all, if we could stay a little while."

Dobbs continued to smile. "Uh-huh. And why is that?"

Muldoon fidgeted. "Well, Darry's taken a liking to the notion of staying here to settle. I don't want to, of course, but I'd like to make her happy if I can."

Dobbs was still smiling, but his eyes were glaring wide, trying to pop out of his head.

"Aw, don't be like that," Muldoon told him. "You don't know her. She's had it rough her whole life. This is her first time on a real planet that has free air you can breathe."

Dobbs gave up the smile, it wasn't working.

"You can't rescue everybody, Sergeant Major," he said, shaking his head. "But I'll do right by you. Now put your cap on."

Muldoon brightened. "So that's a yes."

"What I meant was let's discuss it after we get the gold. I have to admit we've had good luck so far with the women. They've learned the basics of one or two trades, and they're pulling their weight. They will not work for us in any other way, I swear it." He reconsidered. "Unless they take a fancy to the men. I take a little to Drew myself, the cheeky cracker."

"Tim!" a voice called.

Muldoon turned and saw Dariana clapping her hands and laughing. "Yes, love?"

"Come here!"

Go on then, Dobbs thought, and rolled his eyes when Muldoon did. Holding his sword in its scabbard so it wouldn't bang against his legs, Muldoon ran across the pit to sweep up the woman in his arms and twirl her about. Dobbs turned, shaking his head in wonder, and drank in the air.

"Sergeant Major!"

Dobbs snapped out of his reverie and turned back to see Muldoon and Dariana standing by one of the ship's landing pads. "What's that, eh?"

"Darry has something to say to you."

"Yes, missus?"

"Dobbsy, this is the most wonderful planet. Thanks for bringing me!" Next to her, Muldoon was grinning as if to say, See?, happy that Dariana had thanked his friend and that all was well.

Dobbs scowled. Dobbsy. He called to Travis, who was walking aimlessly in his jumpsuit and boots with his hands in his pockets.

"Mr. Travis! Are you ready to depart?"

Thinking this was a test, Travis nodded vigorously. "I'm all set. No problem. Right now."

"Then let's take a walk up that hill and reconnoiter a little, shall we?"

Travis agreed and they marched up the incline toward ground level. The Engineer was breathing deep. "Ah, this air. It reminds me of New Maxis. We did a pretty good job there. We used orbital magnifiers to focus more sun on the place, blew the acquifers to get the water out in the open, spread black dust on the polar ice caps to get them to melt. The biologists had all the fun, introducing plants and stuff, but we had our share. When I get back rich, I'll never read another technical drawing again. I'm gonna write poetry. Fuck 'em!"

"Mr. Travis, I wanted to discuss something with you, and I'm afraid it is somewhat technical in nature."

"Sure thing. Shoot. I'm the answer man."

"Do you believe the inhabitants of this planet are far past the Stone Age?"

"There's a possibility they're in Bronze. That's about it. There's no way they could have advanced further in about a thousand years. But we can take them either way, right?"

Dobbs toked on his cigar. "I hope it won't come to that. No need to overdo it."

"Tim told me the idea is to march in there as emissaries of a foreign planet and offer trade."

"That's Plan A. Plan B is political. Plan C is military. If trade fails, then we get involved in local politics—you know, ally with the weak to topple the governing population, or reinforce the governing population who may feel their hold on power threatened. That usually cracks them. If that fails, then it's a shooting war. Straight from the *Protocols of Colonization of Worlds Inhabited by Intelligent Life*. We'll do this by the book."

"How are we going to make contact?"

"We're going to march right into that city on foot."

Travis fidgeted. "Is that safe? That doesn't sound safe to me."

"No," Dobbs told him, and winked. "It's isn't. But it'll make the right impression."

The Engineer seemed to consider this. "You're probably right, seeing how primitive they are. They've barely invented pottery. It'll be interesting to see their culture in—"

They topped the crest and Travis froze, his eyes widening. Next to him, Dobbs opened his mouth and the cigar fell onto the ground where it went out with a fiss.

Before them was a giant concrete pylon soaring fifty meters into the air, drawing their attention to the next one about a hundred meters away, then another, then another, receding into the far hills where a vast walled city sprawled like a distant myth.

But that wasn't the most amazing part.

Above the line of pylons, following them like a two-lane highway of air, steel hovercars shaped like zeppelins lumbered through the sky, blotting out the sun.

&

When they were finally able to look down, they saw the Neverlandians.

"I think this was a mistake," Travis said. "Oh God."

Dobbs shushed him. "Let's make a good impression."

In ranked formations less than a hundred meters away from them, a thousand squat bird-men holding painted spiked clubs and small round shields stood ready to give battle. They wore primitive battle armor made of plates of some type of brown hide sewn together, painted with elaborate designs. Some wore the furry pelts of ferocious local monsters, head and all, and carried standards. Their bodies were a mix of red-hued flesh and colorful plumes and feathers. These feathers splayed wide on their necks above the breastplate, implying aggression. Their black eyes shown with a dark intelligence, and their thick legs stomped the earth rhythmically in something like a war dance.

"We'll let them make the first move," Dobbs said.

"I think they're beautiful," Travis replied, forgetting his fear for a moment. "Like a cross between a velociraptor—an ancient Earth dinosaur—and Earth birds."

"Hm," Dobbs said, his hand near his holster.

The bird-men began screaming, filling the air with a thousand shrieks and caws.

"Get back to the ship, Mr. Travis," Dobbs shouted over the noise. "I'll hold them here. Tell Sergeant Major Muldoon we've got a shooting war!"

Abruptly, the screaming stopped. Dobbs and Travis held their breath and waited.

"Hello," a voice called. "Welcome to the ground! Are you Earthmen?"

&

The words hung in the air like an echo. Matter froze. Time stopped. Then, slowly, the motors of perception began turning again in Dobbs' head, and he laughed.

"It's happened! Too much time in space. I'm going balmy. Mr. Travis?"

"I heard it too, I heard it too. It said hello. Say hi back or something!"

"Wait. Something's afoot. Look there."

The warriors parted silently and a train of Neverlandians came through the middle, led by what Dobbs guessed was an older bird-man with the wildest mane of feathers he could imagine on any creature. The Neverlandian strolled slowly up to Dobbs and Travis, his head bobbing, his beak in a snarl and his black eyes glaring with menace.

"He's not angry," Travis stage-whispered. "I think he's actually smiling."

"If you say so, Mr. Travis. Let's play along." Dobbs bowed slightly to the Neverlandian. "Hello to you too, sir. I am Commander Lawrence Dobbs, sent to you by our Prime Minister to give you greetings. This is Mr. William Travis, an engineer who has come to bring you wondrous gifts of technology." He glanced up at the hovercars and hoped that last statement had some meaning.

Other old Neverlandians joined the first and together, they whistled, clicked and cawed. Then the first turned to Dobbs, spreading his arms and lowering his head.

"I said, 'Are you Earthmen?'"

Dobbs did a double-take, then said slowly, "Aye, we are Earthmen."

Travis gave him a nudge. "Say 'Yes' and give him welcome to us."

"Yes, we are Earthmen. Welcome. Welcome to us."

"Praise God," said the alien.

The old Neverlandians stomped their feet and screamed into the air.

ॐ

The group marched like a grand little army down the road, Dobbs and Muldoon leading the van on foot with the old Neverlandians and Travis, followed by Fritz in a Mule who in turn led John Henry. Smart in their crisp tan uniforms and caps, the Crickets marched behind in step, rifles on their shoulders. The robot-trucks followed this group, led by McDonough in the lead vehicle who operated the rest by remote, and an escort of one thousand Neverlandian warriors completed the procession, singing through their noses.

Dobbs and Muldoon once again found themselves marching on an exotic foreign world, but what they saw did not strike them as all that exotic.

The plants, for example, didn't look any odder than the myriad of species they'd seen on other planets. One species of Neverlandian bush was vase-shaped with thick barbed legs and large sagging flowers as big as Gimp heads. Dobbs did a double-take, however, when it appeared to him the bushes were backing away from the road as they passed, the tiny leaves trembling on brown twigs.

By the same token, the grass didn't look all that odd either, tall and shaped like stubby knives, a billion little aquamarine mountain ranges. The trees looked like giant blades of grass, barbed and green and fleshy like Earth cactus, the peak hidden by clumps of long leaves sprouting from thin, delicate branches. In a distant field, two potbellied furred creatures with two thick, stubby legs and a long snout sucked grass into layers of molars, then waddled toward the rest of the herd farther away.

Colonists fresh off the boat from Earth would have been amazed, but the sights were not strange at all for men who had seen many planets, many alien species and hence, many weird things in their time. Dobbs and Muldoon had learned to recognize the familiar before the differences. The sky color, plants, native life forms and the like may always have been different, but a mountain was a mountain anywhere, a hill was always a hill, a river was a river, an ocean was an ocean, a rock was a rock.

The most bizarre alien features of the planet were in fact things people of Earth took for granted but colonials like Dobbs and Muldoon rarely enjoyed all in one place like this—sweet clean fresh air, easy breathing thanks to an Earthlike atmospheric pressure, gravity where a man could walk on two legs properly, and lots of space to roam without wearing a suit, a bubble and an air tank. And the warmth! After studying the planet's axial tilt, Kilroy had told them it was the spring season in the southern hemisphere and the fall season in the northern (they were at the equator). Usually assigned to the rougher parts of the Federation, Dobbs and Muldoon had only a few times enjoyed such a climate since the Federation rarely terraformed and colonized a hot planet, usually a cold one. And the automatic climate control in the space stations and planetary bases could not compare.

"I wish Darry was here to see this," Muldoon said. "She'd be impressed. I'll have to get her a souvenir that doesn't bite."

Dobbs shrugged irritably. "I'd say she's already impressed by you or she wouldn't have picked you to get her out of that place. Take some videographs for her."

Muldoon frowned in thought. "I'm not sure whether to thank you or punch you."

"Be a sport, chap. She did come, didn't she? I suppose that's all that matters to you."

Muldoon eyed him uncertainly. "Yeah, that's true. But I don't like how you said that either. The truth is I hated leaving her behind. I'm worried sick now." He blinked. "God, I've never walked so far in a straight line in open air since my childhood!"

"She's with the Captain, and he knows to keep a special eye out for her safety," Dobbs assured him. "Plus a team of hand-picked riflemen. What could happen?"

Muldoon shrugged as if that didn't matter. "That weird bush just moved," he said.

"I'll tell you what," Dobbs said, rubbing his chin. "If we get to Capital City and the coast looks clear, we'll invite some of the crew to come visit and see things for themselves. You know, on a rotational basis. Right right?"

"That's an excellent idea."

Dobbs reconsidered, then added, "As long as she stays away from me."

"Great God," Muldoon said. "Look at that, Sergeant Major."

"I see it," Dobbs said, and laughed.

They had turned a corner in the road that cut two hills, and saw the soaring white walls of Capital City in the distance clearly now, far away enough to be a fantasy and close enough to be a dream come true.

Dobbs and Muldoon led their army through the city gates into narrow streets thronged with Neverlandians who eyed them with blank hostile stares while chattering and gesturing in their strange language. Many raised their arms and lowered their heads, screaming and stomping their feet. Others stood silently, babies peeking out of pouches in their stomachs. Muldoon stared forward with a fierce expression, playing the part of visiting general. Dobbs spared a few glances overhead at buildings that soared higher than any Federation building he'd ever seen, although he knew Capital Province had tens of thousands of such "skyscrapers" in the legendary megalopolises. The Neverlandians perched on thousands of balconies and made an awful racket that quickly gave him a headache.

"Mr. Travis, please stop grinning like that," Dobbs said irritably. "We're supposed to look imperious and make a good impression."

"They're beautiful," Travis said, wiping his right eye. "I've never seen anything like this in my whole life. Ralph told me—"

"Who's Ralph?" Muldoon demanded.

"Ralph is the old Neverlandian who talked to us in Standard Language," Travis told him, jerking his thumb toward the alien who walked next to him. "I'm serious, he calls himself Ralph, except he says it more like 'Ralp.' They can't say 'f' and I would suspect similar labial consonants as well."

"So he was introducing himself before," said Dobbs in wonder, glancing at the alien, then added to himself, "I thought he was chewing cud like a Kiki."

"Only a select few can speak Standard, like a private club, and they have human names," Travis continued. "How they learned it is a mystery, since there are no other humans—Earthmen—on the planet, I'm told. Anyway, listen to this. Ralph told me we came down from our perch in the sky at a good time. Do you hear that? They think we live in the clouds and came down to help them!"

"Ga-dam," the old Neverlandian blurted, then screamed the odor of some foul local dish into Dobbs' face.

"What the devil is he screaming about, Mr. Travis?"

"I think Ralph doesn't like your face. From what I can tell, expression is everything to these people, and you have to talk slowly and avoid sarcasm. They've got one mean aggression reflex if they feel at all threatened."

The streets and the perches above were packed with Neverlandians now, pushing and scratching for a look at them. Several began screaming "Ga-dam," then more took up the shout.

"What an awful noise," Dobbs said.

"Are they saying 'God damn'?" Muldoon grunted, disgusted. "We come six light-years to see them and here they are swearing at us!"

"No, they're not, really," Travis told him, almost doubling over with laughter and his eyes tearing up. "I get it now! They're not swearing, Tim. They're saying, 'Graham!'"

ࣰ

Ralph led them into an open courtyard that was the city square. In the middle were two buildings, one ten stories tall and another tiered structure that rose five hundred steps to a single room, like a pyramid. Groups of Neverlandians were sweeping around the base of the pyramid, and screamed "Gad-dam!" as the Earthmen marched past.

The men were given rooms on the tenth floor of the other building, a terrific climb through cramped rooms with low ceilings that reminded them of a spaceship interior. The Crickets, the Mule and the John Henry robot were left on the first floor to bed down in the straw with an odd assortment of domesticated local monsters.

"I go to talk to Council now," Ralph told them in his harsh accent, then let out a whistle. "You stay here. Wait a while."

Muldoon sat on the floor since there was little in the way of furniture. "I thought I was in good shape," he said. "After that walk and the climb up those stairs, though, I'm spent."

"It's damned hot," McDonough grunted. "I'm sweating like a pig over here."

Dobbs took a swallow from his canteen. "Actually, I think we're in a right spot of luck."

"You mean them speaking Standard Language, even if they do it like ten-year-olds," Muldoon filled in. "Is it all right to smoke, you think?"

"I mean everything," Dobbs said. "The language, them meeting us. It's perfect!"

Muldoon, deciding against consuming another of his limited stash of cigars, leaned back against the wall and studied Dobbs. He had never seen the man so animated, almost manic. His blue eyes were shining fiercely, making Muldoon think for a moment that he was back outside under the blazing sun.

Dobbs' eyes flashed at everybody in the room. "We come down and we don't even have to say take us to your leader. They just come and take us! It's like it's all been planned."

"Actually, you're not far off the mark," Travis said. "I could swear they were shouting Graham's name down there—listen, they're still shouting it in the streets."

"What a racket," McDonough observed, then laughed. "It sounds like they're saying 'God damn' to me."

Travis shook his head. "I have a theory. Picture this. Graham and his people land here and make contact. Robinson thinks they're dead and takes off, leaving them stranded. The ship fell from the sky, so the Neverlandians believe Earthmen live up in the atmosphere somewhere. The crew was probably all men, since it was common in those days to have the entire crew be of one sex or the other, never mixed, so they all die of old age. Graham teaches the Neverlandians Standard Language, and a religion forms around waiting for the return of the Earthmen—a rescue that never comes, of course—and a city forms around the religion, the exact spot where Graham's ship crashed. Hundreds of years ago!"

"We were prophesied!" Muldoon said in appreciation, making the others laugh. He turned to Dobbs. "But if he's right, then we're not going to make the impression we'd hoped. If the Neverlandians think we live in the sky, and they expected us to come, then it follows that us actually showing up isn't going to blow them over too much."

Dobbs rubbed his chin. "You're correct, Sergeant Major, but have no worries on that score. We're doing just fine. In fact, I think this puts us at an advantage."

"Is that how they got to build those hovercars?" Fritz asked Travis. "Because of Graham?"

Travis shrugged in embarrassment. "Who knows? Give me some time."

"It doesn't make sense," Dobbs said. He went to the large window and watched one of the giant bullets float serenely on thin air over a distant part of the city. "If they got the technology from Graham, or if Graham built it for them, why are they carrying around those spiky sticks and round things to fight with? It doesn't make bloody sense."

Fritz shrugged. "I've seen a lot of alien civilizations and they're all fucked up to me."

"Maybe they're ceremonial weapons," Muldoon added helpfully. "You know, just like we wear swords on parade."

"Aye, perhaps you're right, there." Dobbs turned from the window. "But if you are, then what are their real weapons?"

ॐ

Ralph led Dobbs, Muldoon and Travis onto the roof under the hot midday sun, where a group of Neverlandians sat on the floor in a circle. They promptly began screaming. One rolled onto his feet, strolled uncertainly up to Dobbs, then began snapping his beak, pulling himself back from lunging for his throat at the last moment.

"Er, welcome to us," Dobbs said, glimpsing little rows of razor-sharp teeth.

Ralph pushed his body against Dobbs and lowered his head in a beastly snarl. "He does not understand your language," the bird man said between a series of clicks and whistles. "Please. Sit. You are with 'riends. See? We are all 'ery happy you are here with us."

Dobbs, Muldoon and Travis sat on the ground on the striped hide of a monster, taking places in the circle with the Neverlandians. Each of these bird-men had different-colored feathers sprouting from tough reddish or orange-hued skin, which Travis guessed marked different races, and they wore a diverse collection of native costumes. Most wore gold on their wrists and ankles, and on each of their heads sat a gold crown of sorts. At the head of the circle was an empty object that looked like a chair, and on the chair was a strange metal object.

Dobbs' heart quickened. The metal object gleamed in the sun. It was made of gold too.

"This is their government," Travis explained, after listening to Ralph. "The Council of Leaders. Ralph says that as high priest he has been given the privilege of sitting here with them without being condemned to be eaten by some giant local snake. To speak for the Council."

He turned back to Ralph and talked further, while the council members stayed quiet, staring at Dobbs and Muldoon. One rolled his head from side to side as if trying to scratch his shoulders with his neck, while another picked up a bowl and slurped red meat.

"Sorry this is taking so long," Travis told Dobbs and Muldoon. "Ralph is very helpful, but he doesn't offer the whole picture, only little pieces that are sometimes misleading. You just have to keep asking questions and find the truth that way."

"You're doing splendidly, Mr. Travis," Dobbs assured him, his eyes set on the Neverlandian jewelry. "Do proceed."

As Travis went back to talk to Ralph, Muldoon occupied the time by trying different facial expressions on the Neverlandians. He made a funny face and one of the Neverlandian princes' head turned sideways, while another opened his beak and hissed until Muldoon saw his tonsils.

"Maybe I shouldn't bring Darry here," he wondered.

Travis turned to Dobbs and Muldoon.

"I get it now. I understand! It's fascinating. Their whole planet!"

"Come now, spit it out, Mr. Travis," Dobbs said. "Whole sentences, please."

"Their Emperor is dead. All of these leaders you see here are sworn enemies. The entire planet is in a state of civil war."

ℒ

Travis explained that the Neverlandians were ruled by a group of "factions" or ruling houses, and the men sitting with them were the faction leaders. They shared somewhat of a common culture, language and so on, unified by the hovercar system that allowed communication, cultural exchange, movement and trade. They met in Capital City to jointly rule the planet, since there was no Emperor. On the top floor of this building, where the Earthmen were allowed to stay, the largest and most powerful faction leaders lived, and so on to the bottom in a sort of pecking order (no pun intended). The whole society was set up that way, Travis told them, with about eighty social levels. The big cheeses got to live on the top floors of the skyscrapers and be, as Ralph had put it, "halfway between sky and ground."

"That's not the best part," Travis added, his face flushed and sweating in the hot sunlight. "They consider us to be loosely related to them, the people who live in the sky."

"Well now, that's good to hear," Muldoon said, then looked at Dobbs and shrugged.

"What I mean is that we're invited to join the Council as one of the factions," Travis explained. "To have a say in how the planet is run."

ℒ

Dobbs grinned. The sun kept shining, and good luck kept raining down on them.

"That doesn't explain this civil war," Muldoon asked Travis. "What civil war?"

"Apparently, they lead their armies against each other on the various continents to fight it out to determine the pecking order among nations. Nobody is strong enough to become Emperor, so it just goes on and on.

The wars are very ritualistic. Ceremony and ritual are part of everything with the Neverlandians. They continuously train themselves in the art of self-control."

Dobbs snorted. "You're forgetting about the one that almost ate me."

"You have to understand they have some real hopping genes prompting them to kill as a response to anything threatening, including facial expressions, tone of voice and subtleties of body language. They show affection and friendship in strange ways, which we don't know and would only get ourselves killed experimenting with. They're fiercely protective and kind to their blood relations. It's true they're nasty, but all of these rivals have enough self-control to come here to make decisions that must be made to keep the planet running. Alone, without protection. All bodyguards are left outside the city."

Muldoon nodded sagely. "Civil wars. That explains the big walls around the city."

"Actually, no," Travis told him. "Their Capital City is sacred turf, a neutral zone. Like I told you, the wars are conducted in a very ritual way, with set times, places and rules. The walls are actually to help protect them against the weather."

"What's this about the weather?" Muldoon said. "It's hot."

"They have electrical storms and big tornadoes all the time. The higher atmosphere is so full of electric charge there are no flying animals on this planet." Travis pulled at his beard. "Which makes me worried about the ship. You know that defensive perimeter we've got? The crater?"

"Yeah, what about it?" Muldoon demanded.

"If one of their storms—pretty common—blows through this region, our crater pit will fill with water. A lot of water. The crew'll be trapped inside, and we'll be trapped out here. Just as bad, we're going to have a lot of trouble making radio contact."

"Not a good tactical position." Muldoon turned and tried to shrug off a Neverlandian who was rubbing its beak against his arm. "I think this one likes me."

"That gives us a definite timeline, then," Dobbs agreed. "If it rains a lot, that explains why the city's built in the hills and all the streets run uphill to here."

"Not bad, Mr. Dobbs," Travis said, rubbing his chin.

"If you walk it, you can't help but notice," Dobbs added. "But Mr. Travis, we're lacking some vital information that affects our offer of trade. Have you been able to figure out the mystery behind those blasted hovercars?"

"I still haven't been able to find out anything," Travis admitted. "I ask Ralph and he says, 'We come from the sky, we come from the ground,' which I think is his way of saying that's the way it's always been. I could be wrong about some or all of this."

"No, you're doing splendidly, Mr. Travis. But ask them if there is plentiful gold around here. I notice they're wearing it. Tell him we've come to trade."

"Sergeant Major!" Muldoon admonished him. "We haven't even said hello properly yet. We don't know about the hovercars. We don't know what kind of advanced weapons they have!"

Dobbs watched Travis talk to Ralph, then said, "Sergeant Major, look at how God's taking care of us with his old Plan. I want to push our luck just a little. We don't have much time."

Muldoon shrugged. Travis began talking again.

"Once I got him to understand, he said sure, there's gold all around. It comes from that weird pyramid across the square. It's something like a church, or a temple."

"Ask him if we can see it."

"Sergeant Major!" Muldoon exploded, sending the Neverlandians into a fit.

Travis turned back, grinning. "He said sure. Just walk right over there."

Dobbs looked uncertainly at the edge of the roof, but he couldn't stop now. "Watch my back. I don't know if they can fly, but I sure can't. Not in this gravity, anyway."

He stood and walked to the edge. God, that heat was getting oppressive! The light dazzled his eyes. He paused, taking in a breathtaking view of the city from its highest point. In the distance was a great bridge leading to the city, which must have been an aqueduct, a large cylindrical building which may have been a stadium, and canals that served as communal drinking ponds and others as pools for bathing. Besides spaceships and space stations, Dobbs had never seen anything so big or grand in all his days in the service. A slight breeze refreshed him. Then, blinking, he leaned over the edge.

The gold gleamed into his eyes until he saw big purple spots in his vision. But he kept on staring.

"Crikey," he said quietly.

At each of the four sides of the Temple, a large hole emptied into a moat spanned by large bridges. The moat in turn channeled out of the square, where, Dobbs couldn't guess. Clean gold dust was spilling out of the hole into the moat, where it piled high, then was swept along the channel out of the square by squads of Neverlandians.

His mouth moving, and making a reasonable assumption as to the depth of the moat, he did some adding and guessed there were eighty tons of gold in his view alone.

A million miles of specification-grade wiring and plating, he thought.

"I've found it," he said. He turned, his arms raised. "I've found it!"

"What the hell is going on?" Muldoon demanded.

"The Holy Grail!"

The Neverlandians stood and started screaming.

"It's the Fountain of Youth!"

"Put your arms down and sit, Sergeant Major! They're going to eat you!"

ꕉ

Dobbs suddenly noticed that the Neverlandians were scraping their feet—great sharp claws—against the stone roof while they screamed and gestured. This led him to observe the bird-men's powerful leg muscles. A single leap with those claws splayed could tear a man's guts out, even through battle armor. He shuddered, sat down and smiled innocently.

One by one, the Neverlandians paced, snapped their beaks, and retook their seats.

Dobbs finally judged it safe and crawled on hands and knees to where he'd started, taking his place between Muldoon and Travis.

"You're grinning like a freak," Muldoon said. "What's the matter? There's some gold there? How much, Lawrence?"

Dobbs turned to Muldoon, his eyes blazing crazily again as if they still held gold in them. "Oh, only about eighty tons, I figure. We're rich, Sergeant Major. Rich, by gum!"

"Jupiter! We've hit the jackpot."

Travis nudged Dobbs. "They're ready to start talking."

"We knew that you would come in our time o' need," Ralph told them. "It is a time of great sorrow, 'or the world is without an Emperor."

"What can we do to help?" Dobbs told him. "Just ask, chap, and we'll fix it in a jiffy."

"Slower," Ralph said, and snapped his beak three times.

Dobbs repeated the question.

Ralph snarled. "Restraint. Union. Counsel. A new spirit that guides. It turn the wheels 'or us again. We belie'e it. We ha'e 'aith." He scratched at the leathery skin on his beak.

Dobbs told him to tell the Council they were sent by their Prime Minister to do good works and offer trade.

There was much cawing, chirping, hissing and whistling through noses.

Ralph said the Council's answer was that the people needed their good works and counsel, not technology, and that their input into the Council's discussions on an ongoing basis would surely resolve the planet's various crises. For that, they'd trade whatever they were allowed to, and with few exceptions the entire planet was at the humans' disposal.

"I said we're glad to help in any way we can, old boy," Dobbs said. "So you have a deal. It is a fundamental human responsibility to take care of alien species. In return for our good human counsel, however, we would like to acquire some of that gold down there."

"Hu-oh-gah-ch-caw," Travis said phonetically for Dobbs. "That's what they call it."

"You say gold," Ralph said. "I know word now. I lo'e words new to speak."

Dobbs felt funny talking to the alien as if the creature was an idiot, and felt worse hearing the alien talk like an idiot. He knew the priest was actually very intelligent. But such was a language barrier; it'd have to do.

"Gold is 'ery sacred to the people," Ralph said. "You ha'e all you want, ancient times. Temple brings more. Now, people are in sorrow because they cannot touch it. That is ancient Law."

Dobbs stifled a gasp. "But you'll let us have some, yes? As a downer for our guiding spirit, as it were."

"This time, you are saying. No. Sorry, old boy. Anything else you want?"

Dobbs' face fell, and Muldoon wiped sweat from his forehead.

"Can't have it? Why the devil not?"

"Gold belongs to the Emperor. He is keeper o' the Temple. The Emperor always gi'es it away. That was tradition, ancient times. But there is no Emperor now, so gold cannot be had now. So it is with many other things that only the Emperor can gi'e. The people are in sorrow because they cannot touch sacred gold. Penalty is death. Try again later."

"Okay, so we wait," Dobbs said, admiring his own restraint. "No problem."

"That means we can stay for a while," Muldoon said with satisfaction.

"You don't understand," Travis said, his face fallen.

"What's wrong, Bill? You're worrying about the ship going underwater. Well, that's a risk we'll have to take."

"No, that's not it."

"What is it, then?" Muldoon pressed. "They can't go on for long without an Emperor. Internal alien disputes usually work themselves out fairly quickly. Some strongman gets on top."

"It's different here," Travis told him. "In fact, they haven't had an Emperor in about eight hundred of their years. One of their years is one-point-two Earth Standard years. I don't think they're going to get a new Emperor any time soon."

Dobbs blinked hard in amazement, then screamed an obscenity.

He had screamed very loudly and earnestly, because the Neverlandians lowered their heads without raising their arms, a sign of respect.

Chapter 13
The Temple of Gold

Dobbs stared out the window at the Temple across the city square. The sun had set. Lights were blazing in the small room that capped the pyramid. Some distant machine made a drowsy *chug chug chug* sound that carried dimly through the warm night air.

McDonough appeared at his side, dripping with sweat and chewing on a toothpick. "That's a mining machine," he said. "And it's digging up pure gold from the biggest vein in the universe." He took the toothpick out of his mouth and pointed with it. "Right over there."

Dobbs looked across the square at the pyramid with longing. A moving river of gold was only two hundred meters away. It was within easy enough reach. He wasn't going to leave without it. And he sure wasn't about to wait another eight hundred bloody years to get it either.

"I don't buy this primitive society," the Mining Engineer went on. "Sticks and stones and ritual wars and ten flights of stairs and no air conditioning."

"What are you saying, Mr. McDonough?"

McDonough hooked his thumbs into the pockets of his jumpsuit. "I'm telling you that this is a high-tech society." He suddenly exploded. "Look at the hovercars! Listen to that mining machine, extracting ore, then refining it to purity! That's no torch up there in that pyramid, that's electric light! And God knows what else they've got up their sleeves."

"I can't explain it, but they really are a primitive society," Travis said behind them.

McDonough turned and waved a hand at the Engineer. "Feh! They're faking."

A Neverlandian entered the dark room, bowing close to the floor and carrying a glass box. The bird-man stopped in front of Fritz, who sat on the only furniture—a pedestal in the middle of the room. The Neverlandian began to growl and scrape his feet, his head still bowed and bobbing.

Fritz took the hint and stood. The bird-man put the box on the pedestal. It instantly filled with light. Fritz smiled. The Neverlandian shambled out.

"How do they keep doing things like that?" Travis said in a panic, his face bathed in the glow of the lantern. He turned and noticed the men staring at him. "Okay, if you want an answer right now, I say it's magic. We have nothing like this in the Federation."

"Maybe they can do it because they're a primitive society," said McDonough. He sighed. "So what are we doing here? It's damned hot. It's stifling, even at night."

Dobbs, still looking out the window, noticed a ceremony starting to take place down on the ground. Ralph had promised them a true Neverlandian welcome given only to high-ranking visitors. He watched several bird-men drag a large furry mooing beast shaped like a human hand into the city square, light it on fire and kill it with bronze-tipped spears while an immense throng of Neverlandians shrieked and capered.

"Great God," he said. "Bloody savages, every last one of them."

"Sergeant Major," Muldoon called behind him. "We need a conference."

Dobbs turned and saw the men facing him, their faces beaming with sunburn. This morning, they had been confident. Now they simply looked exhausted. And puzzled.

"Plan A was to offer trade," Dobbs explained. "We failed in that. And all they wanted was some advice! I'd give them tons of that for free. All righty then. Let's take stock of ourselves. Mr. Fritz, how's John Henry feeling today?"

"Like a hundred mean Kikis."

"Good. Sergeant Major, I trust the Crickets are keeping by their rifles."

"Morale is high. Pete says they really like the climate. Crickets don't get sunburn."

"Good. Mr. Travis, any contact with the ship?"

"We're getting nothing but static. It's the crazy atmosphere."

"That's not good. Mr. McDonough, how difficult will it be to move that gold?"

"Piece of cake. It's all right there ready to be scooped and loaded, if we ever get around to it. Should take about ten minutes."

"So the only glitch is we can't hail the ship. Suggestions?"

"I want to hear Plan B," McDonough demanded. "Let's get our asses in gear."

"Plan B is political," said Muldoon. "We have several options. We could bribe some of the factions to cover us while we get the gold. Or we could sign up with one of the most powerful faction leaders and declare him the Emperor."

"So which is it, then."

"It will reveal itself to us in good time. We must be patient. It means the difference between walking out of here waving to a grateful alien species or shooting our way out. And we still don't know what kind of weapons they have. We still need some missing pieces to the puzzle before we make our move."

All of the men nodded except McDonough. "I thought this was going to be easy," he complained. "We walk in, look down the barrels of our rifles and say give us the gold now. A planet robbery."

Dobbs resisted the urge to roll his eyes. "Patience, chap. These things require some finesse. No need to overdo it."

The Mining Engineer grumbled to himself.

"We don't have a lot of time," Travis said. "There's no way we'll be able to raise the ship, and if there's another storm soon, the ship will end up underwater for sure."

"Yes, thank you, Mr. Travis," Dobbs said, deep in thought. "The main problem, like I said, is that we don't know what kind of weapons they have. So we'll have to study their technology and make an assessment by deduction."

"If I could study some of their machines that I can understand, I can make a reliable deduction," Travis told him.

The room was quiet. Dobbs listened to the chug chug chug of the mining machine.

"I know where we'll find the key to this puzzle. We must go to the Temple tomorrow and have a look at their mining machine. Would that do it, Mr. Travis?"

The Engineer nodded. "Sure thing."

"Good. For now, let's get some sleep."

The exhausted men stripped down to their shorts and crawled onto their sleeping bags, sweating. Outside, an electrical storm burst into life, giant blue lightning bolts writhing in the air and splitting into hundreds of pieces like nature in torment.

"There's gonna be a big storm soon," Travis murmured.

Between the lightning, the heat and the wondrous mysteries of the world, nobody slept a wink except for McDonough, whose loud snoring made it all the worse.

જ

The next morning, Dobbs, Muldoon and Travis stood with the Neverlandian priest at the base of the great pyramid under a bright hot sun, looking up more than five hundred steps to the top. All around them, the people of the city screamed as they went about the daily business of living, reminding Dobbs of what Hell must be like.

"Come the de'il up," Ralph told them. "I will show you the Temple as you like."

"Mars, that's a climb," Dobbs observed.

The Neverlandian's head tilted sideways, rushing blood to where more was suddenly needed in the left hemisphere of his brain. "What is Mars?"

"It's an expression, a figure of speech."

Ralph clicked and shook his mane of feathers in a shuddering gesture.

"Mars is a planet in our native solar system," Dobbs explained. "Before it was terraformed, it was a real hellhole—it isn't now, but the expression stayed in use in the provinces, and—ah, what's the use!"

The Neverlandian bowed his head and growled at Dobbs, his teeth bared and his black eyes gleaming.

Travis pitched in, "It's the same as, 'We come from the sky, we come from the ground.'"

Ralph clicked again, looking from Travis to Dobbs, then added, "Ah, what's the use!" He started up the steps.

"Sergeant Major, you're being awfully quiet," Dobbs said to Muldoon.

Muldoon frowned, grunting as they finished climbing the first hundred steps.

"I'm in trouble, Sergeant Major," Muldoon told him. "In my head."

"Well, tell me what it is, and we'll get her all worked out."

"You'll probably just yell at me and call me a damned fool."

"Nothing's too big for you and me, I swear it. And you're no fool."

Muldoon stopped for a rest and faced Dobbs. "I'm getting too old for this. Listen, I've been doing a lot of thinking ever since we got here. I can't make up my mind."

Dobbs groaned. "You want to stay here, don't you, you dumb foolish bastard!"

Muldoon shrugged. "I'm thinking about it. Darry made a good point. She said if I'm going here to get rich and buy my own planet—"

"That's just an expression. You do realize how much that would actually cost?"

"Of course I do! But that just proves her point all the more. She asked why not just take this one and live here? It's a beautiful place. We know most of the food is edible and there's lots of free air, fresh water and sunshine, plus gravity and air pressure fit for humans. Our very own Earth. See? I told you that you'd just yell at me."

Dobbs scowled, pulled his canteen from around his neck and took a long swallow. The water appeared to be converted instantly a fresh wave of sweat on his forehead and armpits. He used to think of Dariana as all fur coat and no knickers, but she had proved to be very clever indeed. He had to admit she was right to an extent. For a moment he tried to imagine settling here, maybe with Drew, and carving an idyllic little utopia out of the wild, with all this gold just sitting here.

It'd drive him mad.

"I thought we promised to talk about this after we got the gold," Dobbs said, handing the canteen to Muldoon, who drank thirstily. "All right, then. Let's finish the job. Then you can go your own way. I can't stop you."

Muldoon nodded, wiping his mouth with the back of his wrist. "We're friends, by God."

"So it's all settled. You're sweating like a pig. Take it easy, there."

"It's damned hot. I'm soaked, just like you."

"We're not used to tropical planets, but we'll adapt. We're humans. We can do anything."

Muldoon nodded again, but he was far from settled, his soul pulled back and forth by the gods of his pantheon.

"I'm getting too old for this adventure stuff," he said to himself.

They made it to the top, gasping and weak-legged, and stumbled into a large room where shade offered some relief from the glaring sun. Then the men halted as if they had bumped into an invisible force field.

Occupying most of the room was a rover, a real antique, reduced to shards of rust.

"Graham's rover!" Travis said. "Show us more, Ralph."

The next rooms were smaller, cramped for humans, and contained various artifacts of Graham's expedition, including a pair of boots, a rover spare tire, plastic boxes and a wide assortment of other useless junk and equipment.

"This is Ga-dam's room," Ralph told them. He added proudly, "I am keeper o' it."

"Graham," Dobbs said. "Graham."

The Neverlandian scratched his beak and barked. "Gray ham."

"Graham," Dobbs repeated, patiently.

"Graham," Ralph said, and whistled.

"There's a good fellow."

"People will continue to say Ga-dam," Ralph said. "'uck 'em!"

Dobbs turned to Travis, who shrugged innocently. "He didn't get that from me!"

"Let's see if we can find something useful," Dobbs told him.

"Graham has always been one my heroes," Travis said. "One of the great Federation explorers in the early centuries. But I never knew he survived and actually lived the rest of his life here after he disappeared. Imagine him stranded here, marooned on a planet full of hostile aliens, befriending them and being worshipped as a god. Amazing!"

Muldoon pried open the lid off a plastic box and held up several audiochips. "Look at this, Bill. Is this useful?"

"Keeerist!" Travis said in amazement. "I'll bet they are. Hey Ralph, can we take these chips?"

"Sure thing," Ralph told him. "Graham, Graham. Graham."

Travis took the chips from Muldoon. "I think we can read these if they haven't crapped out from age in that box. Everything we need to know would be on them if Graham kept a log. I can't wait."

Muldoon threw him a meaningful look. "Let's be sure, Bill."

Travis turned to Ralph. "Can we go down below to see the mining machine?"

Ralph shook his mane, the feathers rustling. "Why the de'il do you want to do that?"

"Well, it's like this. We haven't been here on the ground for a long time."

The Neverlandian nodded sagely, a gesture of agreement that he had learned the day before from Muldoon. "Sure thing. We will go now. The way is long and hard."

"I didn't understand your explanation," Dobbs whispered to Travis.

Travis shrugged, laughing. "I just made it up to see what would happen."

Dobbs shook his head in wonder. "We should have tried that when they said we couldn't have the gold."

The climb down into the bowels of the Temple took even longer than the climb to the top.

ဇ

Travis ran from machine to machine, feeling the hot dripping metal of the pipes, hunched over others with his head bobbing as he took in details and created schematics in his head, crawling under some for a look at their belly. To Dobbs and Muldoon, the machinery merely looked like a bizarre museum of grotesquely shaped boilers, furnaces, pulleys and belts. The air was unbelievably hot, and soon they were drenched in sweat and steam. They'd been down there for three hours, moving from room to endless room. But Travis still wore an expression of pure bliss.

"Can't be, it's just carbon!" the Engineer shouted at nobody in particular, his face flushed and wet.

Dobbs and Muldoon exchanged a glance. Muldoon shrugged.

"When the sun rises to its highest point in the sky tomorrow, the Council will meet," Ralph told them. "We will all come together and begin sol'ing problems. You came in my li'etime! I am 'ery honored and happy."

"Looking forward to it, really," Dobbs assured him. "No fuss."

Ralph snapped his beak near Dobbs' throat, then growled. "Good."

"The pump just keeps going," Travis was saying. "But how does this air filter stay clean?"

"That machine brings the gold up," Ralph called to Travis helpfully. "E'ery se'eral moons, it comes out and we get a lot o' it." Then he threw his head back and howled, making Dobbs flinch and cup his ear.

The next room was the largest yet. To Dobbs and Muldoon, it looked like a factory built by a mad artist, all pipes and steam valves and giant wheels, each gurgling or spitting or turning with mysterious purpose. The

Engineer clambered over the twisted metal spaghetti and machines like a curious monkey.

They heard liquid rush through the pipes, followed by a distant metallic boom.

"Water hammer," Travis said, his voice echoing to them among the hills of humming motors. "Interesting." Then he disappeared into the steam.

Dobbs turned to the Neverlandian. "Listen, Ralph. I'd like to ask you a delicate question. Who is the most powerful faction leader here on the ground?"

Ralph made two loud caws, a click and a bark. "A good man," he added.

"That was helpful," Muldoon said. "God, the heat's unbearable down here!"

"Do you think we could help him become Emperor?"

"Sure thing," Ralph said. "It simple. To make a claim, a man stand at Council, to be higher le'el than them sitting. He walk up to throne and put crown on own head. Then Leaders decide i' they support him or want him dead."

"Would you act as our intermediary if we were to make an offer to help him?"

Dobbs thought he'd crossed the line. Ralph screamed a foul odor into his face, and stomped his feet, clawing the stone floor.

"What is 'inter-me-di-ary'?" Ralph demanded.

"I mean to say, would you speak for us and make the offer?"

The alien nodded sagely. "Oh. Sure thing."

Dobbs winked at Muldoon. "We've got a Plan B."

"But he will not accept your otter," Ralph said, and made a sound like a laugh, *ak ak ak.*

"What? Oh, our offer. Why the devil not?"

"I' he thought he was strong enou' to be Emperor, he would ha'e done so already, you dumb bastard. Your strength will make no di'erence to him. It will make no di'erence to any o' them. Try again later."

"Listen here, Ralph," Dobbs said, flustered. "When will you chaps get your act together and elect a new Emperor?"

Ralph hissed at him. "Pro'lly ne'er."

Dobbs' shoulders sagged. Plan B was a wash. Then he remembered Muldoon's words.

We could settle here.

It gave him an idea, but he needed time and information.

As if on cue, Travis stepped through a cloud of steam, his face hot and red from excitement, his hair and jumpsuit dripping with sweat and water from the steam jets.

"Listen to this one, guys," he said. "I've figured out the underlying principle of their technology. It's amazing!"

"Good show, Mr. Travis! You're a genius. Did you learn enough to tell us about the you-know-what?"

"Sure did. But I've got something better than that to tell you."

Dobbs looked at Muldoon, who shrugged. He turned back to Travis. "Well, spit it out, then!"

"Where they get the gold. There's no mining machine." He thrust his hand forward. His cupped palm was filled with gold dust. "Look. It's pure. No impurities."

Dobbs and Muldoon stared at him in amazement.

"Then where the hell do they get it?"

"They have a machine that makes it," Travis told them, and laughed.

"What?" Muldoon demanded.

"The Neverlandians have discovered the secret of alchemy."

ༀ

Travis knew that a big storm was coming as they returned to their room and fell exhausted onto the floor. The air seemed to grow thicker as night fell, and St. Elmo's fire crackled up and down the nearby buildings, while a glance skyward offered a spectacular view of the aurora borealis. Then the first of Neverland's moons rose over the world.

Putting on his headphones, he listened to the audiochips. The journal of Graham, the great Federation explorer. He heard the legend's voice, gentle but full of authority:

. . . *and we were able to observe the Julians assemble their forces, a hundred thousand men, on the plains outside the city. They pitched their tents and waited for the Emilians, those natives of the blue-and-gold-feathered and orange-skinned races. The martial music of horns and drums filled the air, and sacrificial fires were built, the smoke rising to please the people of the sky who watched over them from their perches. All was conducted according to the articles of war. This was a critical battle in the ritual campaign. Since the Julians had won three engage-*

ments against the Emilians, if they repeated their success here they would enter the city and loot it for its young, who would be absorbed into the Julian population and swell its ranks of young warriors in the future. . . .

Far away, thunder began to rumble like a distant battle. The Engineer glanced out the window and saw little sparks flash on the dark horizon.

"There's a big one coming," he murmured, his eyes fixed in a hypnotic stare as he listened to the next several chips.

. . . so that the hovercraft can easily be loaded with messages, silks, spices, gold, cattle, crafts and other goods for trade and distribution to the neighboring cities. . . .

. . . and when the King of the Agathans died, the Queen threw herself onto the pyre. . . .

Thirty years of history of a planet previously unknown to Man, Travis thought. The customs, culture and evolution of another sentient species.

. . . the gift turned out to be a two-handed sword, its edges jagged with the teeth of a monster, and they honored Luke by allowing him to kill the sacrificial cow. Luke hesitated, and he glanced at me as if to check whether this were proper, then before he received my answer he felled the animal with one cut to the neck. The natives were very pleased. . . .

Travis leaned forward, frowning.

. . . Ken died today, and we buried him in the catacombs. There are only two of us left now, Luke and myself. We know there will never be a rescue. Life is ideal here, but I sense a certain madness is beginning to overtake us. We are given full honors by the natives, regarded as something akin to gods but not quite, more like visiting relatives. But we miss human companionship dearly. Luke is particularly affected. He talks non-stop about the natives, their society, how he misses being a part of the moving stream of life instead of merely an observer. Then, with Ken laid to rest, Luke made the suggestion that. . . .

The Engineer's eyes widened. The voice on the chip no longer sounded authoritative, but full of self-doubt, as if begging the listener to understand.

. . . my dear listener, forgive me, I finally agreed to his request. . . .

"Bill, come and get some supper," Fritz called.

Travis shook his head wildly, still staring at the moving pictures created by his imagination.

He pointed out that it is very possible. The natives had done it already. Genetic engineering was their origin, back from the days when the Old

Ones took dramatic steps to save their species from extinction at their own hands. Although the natives had lost the knowledge of the technology required, just as they no longer understand most of the fantastic technology of their ancestors, the tools are available and we can understand them.

"Kee-rist," Travis whispered.

. . . but after three injections Luke is beginning to change. We will wait. Luke paced, he stomped his feet, he screamed at nothing. He flew into a rage when I tried to give him water. I was beginning to believe he had gone mad, but then I realized the truth. The injections are working. . . .

"You fools," Travis murmured.

. . . Luke ran away today into the surrounding hills. I despair of ever seeing another human again. . . .

The voice now sounded agitated, its tone hushed and urgent.

. . . I said four days ago that I despaired of ever seeing another human again. Now I know that I never will.

Luke is back. The injections worked. He has changed. His skin has turned bright red, his bones have shrunk and—and the flesh and muscle have both flabbed and toughened so that he has wrinkles and cracks all over his body. His face—how can I describe it? Once again, I wish our cameras had not been damaged in the crash. His hair has fallen out, and his neck sprouts a necklace of small stubby feathers.

I called him by name, and his black shrunken eyes flickered with recognition. But when he spoke to me, he spoke like one of them.

Luke has gone native in the truest sense of the word.

He told me he was happy, and his voice sounded like. . . .

"Mr. Travis, any results?" Dobbs asked him.

Travis removed the headphones, glanced up and saw the man standing over him, his face expectant and hopeful. He felt swollen with knowledge. It was at times like this that he felt real power, the power of information. He was not afraid; he did not dance on the outskirts of conversation, jumping high to catch a glimpse inside. He was the center of attention now, indispensable.

"Hold your rockets," he said, and put the headphones back on. "I'm onto something here."

Soon, Graham was dying. The voice sounded strained, out of breath, the eloquent descriptions in the entries deteriorating into fragments.

. . . Our medical supplies are used up. The natives do not have any type

of advanced medical care. They do not even sympathize with the sick. My broken leg is swollen. I'm afraid gangrene will set in under the splint. The wounds around my knee bleed pus every day, and I am in agony. I'm in agony!

I hate these people. I hate this world. I learned to love them, and I have learned to hate them. Every day I hear them screaming. They're gathered outside right now, waiting for my death, screaming! Luke visited this morning, and he has changed even more, presenting his three wives and eight children to me. I begged him to look after my wound. Luke studied it, and—oh, God—he—he—began to peck at it—little jabs—I can feel the pain still! Then he stabbed the wound with his beak, as if out of control, and I saw my own flesh in his mouth.

Damn this world! Where is the Federation fleet? Where are the Navy battleships?

I am still human!

I have been here thirty years. I studied them from a distance, as if they were part of my world, making room in my world and fitting them into it piece by piece. But I was always a part of theirs. I am their god, but they are the masters here. I was a fool to ever believe otherwise—I existed for them, the man from the sky. And I was arrogant to believe that by studying them, I would understand them, possess them, control them. A warning to my listener; there is a moral to this story, and it is this: Do not be arrogant to these people. Do not assume anything about them. There are greater things in the universe than Man.

This is where it ends. They will bury me here among their dead, in the catacombs of the Old Ones, on their soil, and I will be a part of their world forever.

The Captain rose early, stretched and walked down the ramp into the crater pit after a short breakfast. He felt the morning sun warm his limbs. Another glorious day!

"George!"

He turned and saw Dariana waving to him. Another glorious woman!

Williamson had heard why the women had come along in whispers among the crew. The men also knew that Muldoon had strictly ordered no funny business unless the women made an explicit offer to conduct it. For the Captain, he still felt a prisoner and had decided to mind his own business and simply play the tourist on this fine world.

He noticed Dariana looking at him strangely the morning the other men had departed with the funny Neverlandians. Then Rachel had approached him, a stunning redhead in a blue jumpsuit with the front zipper pulled down to her cleavage.

They made love on the rough grass behind some strange vase-shaped bushes, and when they were finished they noticed the bushes had moved twenty meters, leaving them lying naked out in the open. Williamson grinned in embarrassment, but nobody could have seen them from down in the pit unless they wanted to stroll.

Later, Drew approached him in the engine room, a tall blonde with piercing blue eyes, and they made love without even saying hello right there, she sitting astride him with eyes closed, he looking up and smiling at a giant pipe stretched along the dark ceiling.

Now Dariana was running toward him, and took his hand.

"Let's have a look up top, George," she said, winking.

"Okay," he agreed. What a glorious trip! But he'd never make a pass at Dariana nor accept one. Williamson had no qualms about caving in to the other girls, but Dariana was taken in his book and he was a sensitive man with a strong power of empathy for the "other guy."

Nearby, a Cricket screeched and followed them, toting his rifle on his shoulder.

"*Hu-im-grom-ak-grom*," he told Williamson.

"I'll take care of her," Williamson assured him.

The Cricket's head bowed his head in deep concentration for a few seconds, torn between Muldoon's orders to protect Dariana and his belief in the Captain's ability to do it.

The Cricket finally nodded. "*Rom-huma-mok-mih Wimsam.*" He reached into his holster and handed Williamson a pistol grip-first. The Captain accepted the gun and put it into the pocket of his jumpsuit, then nodded to Dariana and together they climbed to the top of the crater pit to enjoy the view. The bitter smell of the spiky grass brought back pleasant memories.

"My knight in shining armor," she said. "I feel simply safe around you, George. So how do you like the trip so far?"

Williamson looked at her green eyes, not her mouth, as she spoke, although her mouth was also exquisite.

"Heaven," he said, looking into those eyes for another moment, and laughed. "I was on a black list back in the Federation, you know, so this is quite a change of pace. You see—"

"Oh! This is so exciting. But first you must tell me what a black list is."

They paused to watch a lumbering hovercar head toward Capital City, framed by the clear blue sky dotted with large cotton clouds.

"Let me see if I can explain it, Dariana. I made a certain scientist pissed as hell at me. Some of the virgin colonies are under military rule or the rule of scientists until they become more established and can apply to become a province. The head scientist on this colony where I was assigned was selling medical supplies on the side, right during a plague of scurvy. I reported him and he was arrested, but he had powerful friends in on the take."

"So they pulled some strings and had you sent to Siren for being a Space Scout."

"That's right." He gazed at the towers of Capital City and whistled. "I've never seen a city that big in my whole life," he said. "I wonder how they're doing in there. Jim still can't get them on the radio because of the electrical interference. Hope they're okay."

Dariana snorted. "They're probably counting all their money. Money! It's only a middleman, not an end, George. Tim wants to buy a planet, and he has one right here!"

"It's just an expression," he said helpfully.

She ignored him. "Lord knows this is so much more beautiful than Siren, don't you think? People could settle here."

Williamson considered it. "Yeah, I wouldn't mind it, myself."

"Hm," Dariana said.

"Siren was an awful place," he continued. "I hated it every minute I was there. It got so bad I would drink so I'd forget. Drink a lot, actually. It was just another place the powerful sent their enemies to serve the Federation and be buried in red dirt. And to think it was once a thriving ocean world, teeming with life!"

"I don't believe you."

"It's true. The oceans died and left a barren wasteland. Mars, it sounds melodramatic but that's what happened to me, too. My soul died on that rock in a way."

"Now you're here," she told him, smiling. "How's your soul doing?"

The Captain shook his head, smiling in embarrassment. "I still can't believe everything that's happened. It's too much to take in. I mean, look at this place!"

"Yes, look at it. Let's be quiet for a minute and drink it in. I really want to."

They continued their stroll in silence through a forest of bushes for about two kilometers, then paused.

"Jumpin' Jupiter!" Williamson said. The yellow light gleamed into his eyes. He ran to a pit and dug his hands into an astounding pile of gold dust rising out of a shallow pond. "Where'd this come from? That Buck Robinson wasn't kidding. There really are rivers of gold here!"

"Too bad we can't tell Tim by radio," Dariana said. "And we don't have the trucks. We'll just have to leave it here. Too bad, it being so close to the ship."

Williamson's eyes followed the pit's length. It led all the way into the distant hills, to the alien capital. "They just throw this stuff away. Enough to fill a freighter." He shook his head in wonder and laughed. "Do you know how much all this is worth to the right electrical parts manufacturer?"

"George?"

Williamson tossed the gold back into the pit and stood. "Yes?"

"Looking at all this gold makes me remember a question I ask all the men I like. What's more important to you? Money or love? You have to pick one."

"Love, of course. Money happens all the time, more or less. Love happens only a few times at most. I loved a girl once."

"What happened? If I'm not being too nosy."

"Not at all. She was also a Marine, and she died from plague carried by some Olivian vermin that got onto all the ships in the Wolfshead in those years. That was before we had better booster shots to kill the alien microbes that could actually hurt our species. I was on a ship nearby in the same convoy that got the distress signal—Jan and I were never far apart, you know, because of the time dilation. But we were still a good light-year away, and by the time we got there, their ship was a ghost ship. The crew's bodies were stacked like air tanks. Jan had died with them."

"I'm sorry," Dariana said, touched. "That sounds dreadful." She had never heard a story like this one. It was touching. Most stories her customers told her were about daring exploits in the cosmos—dodging asteroids, repairing air leaks in free fall, crawling through ducts to repair a humidifier, last-minute recoveries from tumbles and the like—always men using brain and brawn to conquer the universe's many challenges.

Williamson shrugged. "It was a long time ago."

"So what is a 'Wolfshead'?"

The Captain laughed. "You're a pretty smart lady, Dariana, but they don't tell you much, do they? The Wolfshead Province is called that because its borders are shaped like a wolf's head. You know, that animal from Earth they use in the colony farms to keep away alien rodents. Olivia was big on farming before the wormhole was discovered there."

"Oh! I've never seen a live wolf, being in the space stations all the time. You know everything, it seems. I envy your travels. Now I want to ask you another question, George."

"Shoot."

"What's more important to you, money or a good life? Freedom?"

Williamson scratched his head and laughed. "I always thought that one got you the other in this universe."

"But if it didn't? If you were handed a perfect life, would you need money?"

"No, I suppose I wouldn't."

Dariana had the answer she needed. She began to seduce the Captain.

Humans were a rugged, adaptable species. They had learned to live in different gravities, breathe terraformed atmospheres that sometimes had a slightly different composition and pressure than Earth's, could live in cramped labyrinths, got used to the cold, and stood up to thousands of other challenges offered by life on spaceships, stations, moons, asteroids and planets. Human nature allowed the human race to first dream, then reach out across light-years of black empty space in great spaceships to tame the wild planets around Alpha Centauri A and B, Tau Ceti, Epsilon Eridani, Gamma Hades, Eta Cassiopeie, Sigma Draconis, Delta Pavonis, 70 Ophiuchi A and other stars.

But in the end, humans were still weak and foolish among their own species.

In the end, George Williamson was "only human."

He gave in.

જી

Alchemy.

For thousands of years, humans had tried and failed to make pure gold from ordinary lead or iron. It had always been a mystical science, filled with strange symbols, rituals and the belief that the alchemical process was an allegory of the transmutation of the human soul by God from sinful to pure. History had always shown it to be pure hogwash as well, with many stories from ancient Earth history of hoaxes, fooled political leaders and the like.

But on this planet, the Neverlandians had cracked the age-old mystery.

"Actually, the Neverlandians didn't do it," Travis told the men, now sitting in a circle back in their room eating their breakfast out of tins. "Not as we know them, anyway."

"Graham did it," Muldoon suggested. He hated waiting for punch lines.

"No, Graham didn't do it either. The old Neverlandians did it, the original people who lived here. It's all in Graham's tapes. Having spent half his life here, he got a lot farther in understanding them than we could."

Muldoon sighed in frustration. "Well, who did it then?"

"First I have to tell you about their technology," Travis said. "It explains a lot. See, the Neverlandians were once an advanced species that perfected the use of electrostatics."

Fritz shook his head. "Man, you lost me already."

"Electrostatics is as old as Tesla, who thought it up. The Federation tried it several times in its day, but no dice. The Neverlandians cracked it. They never discovered nuclear fission and then fusion. They went right from fossil fuels into electrostatics. The idea is simple, but almost impossible to achieve on a planetary scale.

"I can't get into the technical details without giving a three-day lecture. But take my word for it. The Neverlandians turned their planet into a giant capacitor. The result is the entire planet is charged with electric power from generators in the Temple and a lot of other places all over the globe. The atmosphere's so charged right now with the residue of this process that they get a mother lode of funny weather, and we can't use the radio."

"Why don't we feel it?" Muldoon asked. "The electricity, I mean."

"The voltages are at such a high frequency it's as harmless as static electricity," Travis explained. "If we could get a decent shower, I'm sure our hair would stand up a little when it dried in the sun."

"It'd be worth it," Fritz said. "We stink."

"The point is they have mastered the wireless transmission of power," Travis continued. "So they can put a glass box filled with gas onto a conductive pedestal, and it lights right up. They could put a food processor there, anything, and it would work, although human stuff like that would need a transformer. The hovercars operate on the same principle. There are probably a billion other wonders we don't even know about yet. Graham himself said he only scratched the surface. It was amazing to hear his voice."

"He would be proud of you right now, Bill," Fritz told him.

Travis beamed and said shyly, "Yeah, well I was saying."

"So what happened to the original people here?" Muldoon demanded. He hated when people stopped in the middle of a good story.

"Oh, right. I was getting to that. The original people built their entire civilization on electrostatics. They built the hovercar system to move goods and people, and probably went through a golden age. Since they'd mastered localized antigravity, they would have had space travel pretty quick if they'd kept going. But the process of electrostatics hurt them in some way—perhaps leukemia. It had to be a big problem, seeing what they did to save themselves. I can imagine some sort of cover-up, then they were in a Catch-22. Give up their entire way of life and go back to the Stone Age or slowly die off from disease."

"They wound up merging biologically with a flying animal," Muldoon said.

Travis stared at Muldoon as if he'd spoiled a long shaggy dog story by spilling the punch line. Then he nodded slowly with approval. "You are absolutely right, Tim."

Muldoon grinned with relief. He had guessed right.

"The birds were dropping because of the electrical activity," Travis said. "But the birds must have had a combination of genes that made them immune to the leukemia that the Neverlandians were dying of. So they merged these genes into their own and took the consequences. This is a lot of guesswork, because we're going back about more than a hundred thousand years or whatever, but it's Graham's only explanation. Much of the technology still runs fine—they'd mastered anti-corrosive ceramics that would knock your boots off—but it's obvious the Neverlandians got too much of the bird gene in them and don't understand their own stuff anymore. Besides some of their looks, the birds added powerful instincts to the original people's intelligence—and now you see the Neverlandians today, only at the border of real civilization.

"The Old Ones got more than they bargained for, because the bird genes dominate, but at least the species survived its first mistake. They're now living through the second."

"I'm willing to wager they don't have advanced weapons they understand," Dobbs said. "Well done, Mr. Travis. We have the answer we needed."

Travis nodded in agreement to all three statements.

"What about us?" Muldoon said. "Are we susceptible to this disease?"

"Not that I can tell," Travis answered him. "The frequency of the voltage isn't strong enough to damage our cells, which would create a risk of cancer. The only thing that might threaten us here might be native bacteria, and we've all gotten our booster shots. It's a remote possibility anyhow, and none of Graham's expedition died of a native disease."

Fritz took off his cap and ran his hand through his hair. "I got an interesting question. We can just copy their technology and take it with us. Then we could leave now, yeah?"

"I'd like to agree with you," Travis said. "I mean, I think I could copy it with the equipment I brought. I'm certainly going to copy the electrostatic generators. With a few improvements, they'll revolutionize the Federation like no other invention in history. You don't understand how I feel right now. What spacers call The Holy Grail, we engineers call a Eureka Moment. I've found two in one day!"

Muldoon laughed in appreciation, while the rest of the men grinned.

"So you can copy it," Dobbs prompted. "But. . . ?"

"But setting up a factory to make gold would cost millions. There's no getting around it."

"So we're back where we started," McDonough said to Dobbs. "I say we go to your Plan C and just take the gold and go. We got guns. They got sticks. We have the power to do it. There's nothing that tells us the Old Ones left weapons their descendants can understand."

"He's right," Muldoon admitted.

Dobbs smiled, his eyes twinkling. "Plan B is a go. I see it now."

Muldoon gave him the once-over. "When did you come up with that?"

"I just thought of it. But it all makes sense now since Mr. Travis is right—we'd need a lot of money to start our own factory. The problem is we want to leave. We just have to want to stay."

Muldoon laughed. "Don't tell me you want to settle here! I'd have a heart attack."

"That's exactly what I'm saying."

"I need a stiff drink."

Fritz reached into his pocket, pulled out a flask, and handed it to Muldoon, who accepted it gratefully.

"I didn't sign on for that," McDonough growled, turning red. "What the hell?"

"Oh, you'll get your gold," Dobbs told him. "And Muldoon will get his home. The people of Neverland want our good human advice, and I say we give them what they want."

"Mr. Dobbs, I mean Commander, what are you talking about?" Fritz said.

"The plan is that our faction will nominate an Emperor. A human one."

The men stared at him in amazement.

Dobbs smiled, the manic light shining in his eyes again, and said, "We're going to take over the whole bloody planet."

 و

The men were shouting. Disgusted, McDonough threw his cap onto the floor, stood up and walked to the window to observe a fresh electrical storm that boiled in hundreds of blue flashes over the dark horizon, past the rooftops of hundreds of tall buildings. A wind sprung up and cooled him off.

"We oughta teach the dummies how to make lightning rods," he grunted to himself, watching the ball lightning outside flicker as it floated serenely in the air.

"There are compelling reasons to stay here," Dobbs said. "Gentlemen, hear me out. First off, we want the gold. But we can't have the gold unless there's an Emperor. Nobody has stepped up to the plate in eight hundred years, and I'm told it's damned likely nobody will ever again. Graham was worshipped like a god, and they want our advice. So one of us will become Emperor, give them advice in spades, and let the rest of us have the gold. But I say we can do even better than having the gold."

McDonough turned from the window, grinning now. "Power!"

Dobbs nodded slowly, his eyes twinkling. "You will recall there's a wormhole in the middle of this system. We could ship all the gold the Federation would want through it in exchange for anything we want.

We'd have our own planet here to live on, and it's a nice place."

"We could build a city just for humans," Muldoon said. "A nice modern city with air-conditioning. We'd run the place from there! As kings!"

"With this much gold and the money it'd bring, we'd have power beyond our imaginings," Dobbs said. "Plus a perfect place where we can live like real men. Imagine common men like us, going to Capital Province, meeting the Prime Minister as equals!"

"I'm not common," Muldoon muttered, then blinked. "You think he'd meet with us?"

"We'd negotiate to have our system join the Federation as a full-fledged province. On our terms, of course."

"Well," said Travis, "what you're saying is feasible, but not—"

"I'm in!" McDonough roared. The man was red and full of tension, about to explode. "Kings it is, then!" He burst into laughter. "Why the hell not?"

"I—I—" Travis said.

Dobbs turned to Fritz. "How about you, Mr. Fritz?"

Fritz was startled by the question. "Wow, I don't know. What's your vote, Tim?"

"I'm definitely in on this score," Muldoon said. "I have my reasons."

"Well, I guess I'll go along," the ball turret gunner said. "I like it here. It's actually very peaceful. Lots of light. What about Jim and Tommy?"

"Oh, I shouldn't worry about them," Dobbs said. "But we can't give up our current ship until we're established, or we'll lose all our bargaining chips. Jim and Tommy will take the ship into orbit once we take over, so we can beat that storm that's coming. Mr. Travis, could you build a powerful transmitter that could send data through the wormhole?"

"Yeah, I think so," the man stammered. "The whole planet is full of the materials left over from the Old Ones. But—"

"Brilliant," Dobbs said. "If Mr. Kilroy and Mr. Peters or anybody does not want in, they can leave later when we buy our own fleet. So, Mr. Travis. What about you? Are you in?"

Travis frowned. "I like this place. And its people. Maybe we could help them, but—"

"Lightning rods," McDonough grunted.

Travis cleared his throat politely. "Actually, the towers used for the hovercars function very much like lightning rods," he said.

"Feh!" the Mining Engineer told him.

The Engineer continued, "I don't think taking over the planet is a—"

"Good," said Dobbs. "Now I'd like to nominate our Emperor."

"I volunteer," McDonough said.

"No, no, it must be somebody the Neverlandians look up to and admire. No offense, Mr. McDonough. They don't seem to take to me, I know that as well." Dobbs pretended to think deeply, then set his eyes on the Engineer. "Mr. Travis, for example."

All eyes turned to Travis.

"No, please, not me! Jupiter, this is all a big mistake!"

"Nonsense," Dobbs said, then addressed the room. "Gentlemen, hats off! You are in the presence of the Emperor of Neverland!"

Fritz clapped Travis on the shoulder, shaking him. "Wow, Bill, you're going to be the Emperor."

Travis stared at them wildly as they cheered him, and he felt afraid again, even worse as he realized that information did not make him powerful. It only made him a more useful tool, loved for what he offered instead of who he was. He thought of Graham's warning against arrogance toward the Neverlandians, the arrogance that the men and women of the Federation had taken with them to dozens of planets.

Neverland held mystery, and power. The planet moved on its axis according to the laws of nature, and its ancient people was as dangerous to tamper with as nature itself, as unpredictable as the weather. Right then, Travis knew it would swallow them whole, just as it had done to Graham.

Its rockets firing, the *Adversary* landed with a series of *whumps* onto the grassy plain. Then the roar quit as the rockets cut out, leaving behind a loud whine that gradually faded. Within a half-hour, Von Kleig stepped out and stretched, followed by three men in battle armor carrying large cylindrical blasters they held on their forearms like grotesque metal casts. The men fanned out as Von Kleig lit a cigar and enjoyed the warm sunlight and the air. He scanned the plain with his red eye, saw it stretch into a series of purple hills. No sign of life except for a faraway herd of some herbivore species. But beyond that, he knew, the great city of the natives lay, and he also knew that was where he'd find Dobbs.

Von Kleig turned his red eye toward the ship and nodded. Instantly, the rest of the men began unloading boxes and once the ramp kicked out of the cargo bay, a rover spilled onto the grass and revved its engine.

Bova, still wearing his gray jumpsuit, appeared at Von Kleig's side.

"Mr. Bova, you're a Company Man," he told the android, holding his cigar near his chest.

"I work for the GR, that is right," Bova said.

Von Kleig continued reading the hills. "Good. Then you can take a paint-sprayer right now and wash over the logo on the ship."

Bova turned his entire body and saw *GALACTIC RESOURCES—We Mine The Future* painted neatly on the side of the ship, spotted with corrosion from stray space dust.

"I don't think we need to advertise who we are, do you?" Von Kleig asked him, then put the cigar back into his mouth.

Bova could not turn red, nor could he look embarrassed in any way. His head snapped to regard Von Kleig at an odd angle, his eyes penetrating. "I am sorry, Mr. Von Kleig. But I will not take your orders. No. You take my orders. I work for the GR. I am, as you quaintly put it, a Company Man. You are a simple independent contractor."

Von Kleig nodded. He had sized up this guy correctly from the beginning. It was best to make things clear upfront.

"Then I'll take my men and go home."

Bova considered this by looking down, then his head snapped back up. "I cannot let you. No. I will not let you."

Von Kleig pulled the cigar from his mouth. "I know you can't. That's why you're here. You can't be bought. You're programmed to accomplish your mission at any cost. If I try to leave you'll break my spine in half before I can say amen. But you also can't avoid telling the truth about it later. Then you'll have to explain to the Company that you killed me, and caused the mission to fail, because I wanted you to paint over an advertisement to the whole planet that we're here to make a mining claim against the TM&D."

Bova considered this as well. He turned again and looked back at the ship.

"Mr. Von Kleig, there is something wrong with that ship."

"You don't say," said Von Kleig.

"Yes. I know what it is. It has the GR logo on it. We cannot have that get in our way. I will paint over it. It is a good thing I came along."

Bova marched back to the ship, wearing a patient smile.

Von Kleig knew androids well. Bova would be no problem. He listened to the men work silently and efficiently behind him. Somewhere out there, he knew, Dobbs was probably making a mess. The man had a classic problem of overreaching, leaving himself vulnerable. That suited Von Kleig just fine. He would clean up and make his claim for his employer.

To make the mission successful, Von Kleig needed Dobbs alive. Galactic Resources had no idea why Dobbs was here, what he was after. So Von Kleig could waste months doing a geological survey with a staff who were trained killers (not planetologists), or he could simply find Dobbs and get the information from him. That made it simple. Whatever the mineral was, it had to be valuable and there had to be plenty of it here.

Thinking of Dobbs made him chuckle. Together as partners, they had worked many jobs for the megacorporations in their youth. Dobbs had an iron-clad method for playing on their paranoia, pitting them against each other, raising the price in a bidding war for even small jobs. That and his occasional ruthlessness had earned him a nickname, The Dealer.

But when the man began to overreach, Von Kleig saw an opportunity to get rich as well as get rid of Dobbs in one fell swoop. He did get rid of Dobbs, but the man had been one step ahead of him that time, and Von Kleig had wound up losing both the money and his freedom in a Federation penal colony on Cantor V, the asshole of the galaxy.

The situation had created an old score to settle.

Yes, it would be pleasant to see his old partner again.

Within two hours, the Galactic Resources team was on the move toward the capital of Neverland.

Chapter 14
The Emperor of Neverland

The sun rose to its highest point over the western hemisphere of Neverland and shone straight down upon Bill Travis, claimant to the throne of the planet. He was sweating in his jumpsuit, now soiled from spending most of the morning in the Temple's guts, capturing the alien technology with infrared cameras, X-ray cameras, videograph recorders and other instruments. He hardly looked—and definitely didn't feel that day—the Emperor type.

Dobbs and Muldoon didn't realize that they already had the power to play a vital role in the destiny of the human race, he knew. Electrostatic power, if the kinks could be worked out, would revolutionize the Federation. Alchemy was nothing in comparison.

But Dobbs wanted his gold—he was blinded by it. Muldoon backed Dobbs because all he could think about was Dariana, who wanted to stay on the planet. And the rest backed them because they had nothing better planned, or like McDonough they wanted to see what it'd be like to be kings, even if their subjects were, to them, inferior savages of an alien species.

He supposed he could have told them about electrostatics and its real value to the human race, but why bother, he thought sullenly. He was good for giving information, but apparently had no say in how it was used.

So Bill Travis was about to become Emperor of Neverland.

Why was he going along with this? Why didn't he just stand up and say to hell with it? He wondered at his own strength and will power when it came to solving problems, his own fear and weakness when it came to danger and worse, dealing with other humans. He supposed that he was used to silently watching those in charge overreach, then take the consequences—he'd complain to himself, but would still go along with the crazy plan to fool with an entire planet's history and people. He'd been through enough to develop the mind-set common among a lot of Federation engineers—know better, complain to yourself, clean up the mess sometimes, watch the damage happen helplessly other times, give them a satisfied grin later that says I told you so, just before the asteroid hits the hull and we all go down.

An old story told by some engineers concerns a ship's captain who asks his chief engineer how long it will take to get their failed engines back on-line, since they are drifting without propulsion into the dangerous rings orbiting a gas planet. The engineer provides an estimate, then the captain tells him he has half that. The engineer pulls it off and the ship's crew is saved. But who gets the credit for nerves of steel, good judgment and command skills? The captain! And all the captain had to do was stand there and say, "You have four hours instead of eight. Out."

To Travis, engineers were the unsung heroes of the Federation, every last one unappreciated by the so-called decision-makers. Engineers made the wheels, then made them turn. Engineers were the builders, making each planet a fortress of light and civilization in a savage and entropic universe.

He snapped out of his thoughts with a blink. Horns were blaring throughout Capital City, hailing the hour of noon and announcing the arrival of the lords of Neverland.

"Here they are," said Muldoon, who sat next to the Engineer. Travis turned and watched the Neverlandians climb onto the roof in a silent dignified train and take their places. He saw them as Graham did—not comical aliens to be exploited, but Agathans, Emilians, Julians and the rest. Kings of an ancient civilization. Once seated, the aliens began talking and gesturing in their harsh language.

"Go on, then," Dobbs whispered to Travis. "No need to wait. You're on."

Travis shook his head, but stood up with a gulp. "Mr. Dobbs, I got a bad feeling about this," he whispered. "Let me explain. See, Graham—"

"Nonsense," Dobbs said. "They like you, Mr. Travis. You'll be splendid."

"What is my 'riend the engineer doing?" Ralph asked Dobbs.

Dobbs shushed him. "You'll see."

Travis began walking slowly to the chair at the head of the circle, where a gold crown lay on the seat, unworn for more than eight hundred years.

Travis glanced left and right and saw beaks dropping open as he approached. The babble began to fade, then the Neverlandians watched him in silence as he reached the throne and took the crown in his hands.

I can do this, he told himself. I'm not afraid. Fuck 'em!

Behind, he heard the Neverlandians suck in their breath.

The Engineer sat on the chair and picked up the crown. It felt like a hundred pounds, weighted down by thousands of years of history and the responsibilities of governing an entire planet. He gritted his teeth.

Fuck 'em.

The crown suddenly felt like a feather in his hands.

Travis held the crown high, the sun gleaming along its surface. Then he put it on his head, sat on the throne and stared forward resolutely like Muldoon had taught him, repeating his mantra in over and over in his mind: Fuck 'em. The crown, designed for Neverlandian heads, slid over his forehead and came to a rest just over his eyes.

The Neverlandians were quiet, staring. It was impossible to read their reaction. Black eyes flickered, appearing to take in everything they saw repeatedly. The sun blazed in the sky, and Travis realized he was sweating in waves. Some trickled into his eye and he blinked.

After five breathless minutes, one of the Neverlandians stood, whistled and left the roof.

"That's a good sign," Dobbs whispered to Muldoon. "We've got one on our side."

Two more Neverlandians left. One turned briefly, gave Travis the once-over, and barked. Soon, all of them were gone, leaving Travis alone with Ralph, Dobbs and Muldoon.

Dobbs stood and clapped his hands. "Excellent! Well, that does it. We're on our way, Mr. Travis. You did splendidly."

"I'm going to be sick," the Engineer said. "I feel faint."

"Nonsense. Now come down off that chair and drink some water. You look silly."

Dobbs felt a shove in his side and looked down at Ralph, who was growling.

"You have no manners, Mr. Ralph," Dobbs said, growling back. "Bugger off a minute, will you?"

"That was brilliant," the alien replied. "You surprise me greatly. What boldness!"

"Er, thank you."

"So where will your 'action otter battle?"

"What the devil did you say?"

"I said the de'il, the de'il did I say." Ralph cawed, thoroughly confused, then shuddered, his feathers rustling. "You wanted Bill to be Emperor, yes-aye? He wears the crown now."

"Very good then," Dobbs told him patiently. "So that settles it."

Ralph's jaws snapped shut an inch from his throat.

"If you do that again, Mr. Ralph, I'll put a zap right between your bloody eyes, I swear it!" He sighed. "Listen, old boy. The other faction leaders left, looking quite tamed. Nobody spoke a word of protest. They accepted what we offered, and now your planet will enjoy peace and progress in full under the benevolent guiding spirit of humanity."

The Neverlandian hissed. "The other 'action leaders rejected Bill, you dumb bastard. That is why they le't. That is why there has not been an Emperor in eight hundred bloody years. E'erybody else attacks the 'action leader who makes the claim." Ralph whistled. "He did good, though. Real good. I expected them to lea'e right away and not e'en consider it."

Dobbs grew pale. "So I'm a bloody fool. What happens now?"

"Now they will bring their bodyguards 'rom outside the city," Ralph told him. "You are not happy? Well then, it looks like you really screwed the Gimp this time."

Muldoon put a steadying hand on Dobbs' shoulder. "Listen, Sergeant Major. As much as I hate to see us go to Plan C, we're going to have to make a go at it. A few bodyguards doesn't sound like much of a scrap. We'll win the battle, then the faction leaders will accept Bill as Emperor. Right, Ralph?"

"Sure thing," Ralph said, *ak ak ak*. "You are the best soldiers in the galaxy!"

"So it's all settled," Dobbs said weakly.

Ralph scratched his beak and barked. "Yes, old boy. It will be glorious. The de'il I say."

"When are they coming?"

"If you do not go out to meet them in one hour, they will come here. I cannot wait!"

৶

Muldoon stood silently for five minutes, rubbing his chin. Then Plan C was set in motion. Just in case there was trouble after the takeover, he and Muldoon ordered McDonough to take the gold and bring it back to the ship for loading. While the Mining Engineer shouted obscenities into the atmosphere, working a remote control panel, the robot-trucks whirred to their places around the Temple moat and parked. Their ramps clanged against stone. Light bulldozers rode down the ramps, hummed up to the moat's edge, scooped up gold and brought it back to dump into the backs of the trucks. Hundreds of Neverlandians stood and gawked at them, screaming at the sun. Travis, still wearing his crown and looking miserable with his hands in his pockets, walked into the Temple and disappeared. At the bottom of the steps, the Crickets hurried to form ranks in front of Muldoon, who ordered them up on the double-quick. The John Henry robot marched after them, followed by Fritz in the Mule.

A robot-trucks' engines turned over with a loud whine, and they sped away into the city streets, programmed to find the freighter.

Trailed by a group of Neverlandian children who mimicked their movements, Muldoon and Dobbs studied the city square, took measurements, and developed tactical orders based on interlocking fields of fire. The Crickets began deploying in a square, two ranks deep, around the room crowning the Temple, about a hundred steps from the summit. From this height, their force had an excellent view of all approaches, and they enjoyed a strong uphill position. John Henry and the Mule would be held in reserve to rush to the side facing the most trouble.

The fleet of robot-trucks now full, they began to move while the bulldozers spilled lemming-style into the moat, making a loud racket of crashing metal.

But Muldoon didn't expect trouble. Back in the Federation, he knew, their tiny command would have been laughed at as a carnival act. But here, fighting little men with clubs, they were irresistible. Together, this tiny army would conquer a planet of several hundred million people by force of arms!

ରୁ

From the distance, drums began beating and horns blared and groaned. The Neverlandian civilians in the square scattered, disappearing in moments.

"What an awful noise," Dobbs said. He turned to see Ralph growling up at him. "Thank you for joining us, Mr. Ralph. Wonderful show of faith."

The Neverlandian spit on the ground. "I will ha'e the best 'iew 'rom here."

"Here they come," Muldoon said. "Let's see what these musicians are made of."

From all sides, the Neverlandians of all nations began marching into the square in ranks, standards waving over columns of fierce bird-men carrying great two-handed swords, barbed spears, spiked clubs and small round or large square shields. It seemed that thousands of horns and drums were each playing different songs at the same time.

"That's a lot of natives," Dobbs said, rubbing his chin.

The Neverlandians began to form into companies, a dazzling sight in colorful painted armor, their plumes splayed above their necks. Some wore masks that looked like human faces. Others wore the shaggy brown and spotted orange pelts of local monsters. The warriors screamed and whistled war songs through their noses. In the far rear, a group of bird-men sat on tall stools in front of easels, and began drawing the scene.

"How many bodyguards are they bringing?" Muldoon asked Ralph.

"Each 'action leader has 'i'e thousand elite warriors," Ralph told him, *ak ak ak.*

"Did you just say 'five thousand?'"

"Yes."

"Five thousand each?"

Ralph whistled. "Yes-aye! Are you dea'?"

"Wait a minute." Muldoon did some quick math. "That's sixty thousand men!"

Ralph nodded sagely. "It will be glorious. You are 'ery bra'e. My people salute you."

"I think we really did screw the Gimp this time," Muldoon told Dobbs.

"There's always a way," Dobbs said stubbornly, but he looked disoriented. "That's our motto, you're bloody right it is. Christ, I need to sit down." He sat on the ground.

"Something's happening," McDonough said.

Down below, a line of Neverlandians formed, holding odd-looking metal clubs.

"Sticks and stones," McDonough said. He had refused to go back to the ship with the trucks. "What's with you two? This is going to be a slaughter. Wouldn't miss it for anything."

A line of smoke erupted over the front line of Neverlandians with a loud report, and metal balls ricocheted off the walls behind them. Dobbs and Muldoon threw themselves to the ground as more bullets clattered off the flagstones. The Mining Engineer dropped next to them, shot through the throat. He was still grinning.

"Christ almighty! McDonough's had it!"

"Hold your fire until the assault!" Muldoon told the Crickets over the com link. "Save your charges. And stay flat. They've got metal projectile throwers."

"We could have just driven straight the hell out of here with the gold," Dobbs said, amazed. "Look, there's our rover, right down there."

Muldoon lay face down next to him, his hands on his head as musket balls whizzed overhead. "I think we're big stupid foolish dumb idiots, Sergeant Major," he told Dobbs.

"We've got a real fight on our hands now. I don't see how we're going to win this one." He snorted. "Sixty thousand men with clubs."

"Well, I guess we'll have a go at it," Muldoon said stoically. "Remember, we're Marines. Can't let the enemy see us sweat. And we won't scare in front of the men."

"Aye," Dobbs agreed, nodding. "We'll give these savages a fight they'll never forget."

Immediately, the city was quiet. The musketeers began to retreat.

"What's this?" Dobbs said, lifting his head for a look.

From somewhere in the city, a horn blared, and the Neverlandians charged forward with a wild scream, crossed the bridges over the moat in a single compact mass, and reached the bottom of the steps, leaping upward comically fast on their powerful legs, keeping formation, large square shields interlocked.

Muldoon and Dobbs jumped to their feet and hustled down to the firing line, which faced a rolling mass of bird-men screaming and waving their weapons.

"Prepare!" Muldoon said into the com link.

"*Ki-ka-ata!*" Pete echoed him.

"Ha!" the Crickets replied, raising their rifles.

"Aim!"

The Neverlandians screamed, doubling their charge.

"Fire!"

The sound of the rifles pounded the air like thunder, and the Neverlandians began to drop by the scores, the front ranks shattered and with it, any semblance of formation. The charge continued. Bird-men tripped over their falling comrades and spilled into the moat. Dobbs drew his pistol and fired down into the ranks, impossible to miss.

"Fire at will," Muldoon told his men. "Shoot straight."

The mass of Neverlandians rolled backward, the momentum of the charge broken, the front ranks falling in heaps.

Muldoon walked behind the Crickets, pausing behind each one and inspecting his work. "Take your time. Choose your targets."

Horns blared, and the recoiling mass of Neverlandians began to surge forward again in perfect formation, shields interlocked.

"The natives are good," Muldoon told Dobbs. "Excellent discipline."

"Hm," Dobbs replied. "I know just the thing to break their back." He switched on his com link. "Mr. Fritz, bring down John Henry for a demonstration."

The John Henry Class VII mining machine stepped slowly from the shadows of the columns. Fritz and the robot marched down to join Dobbs and Muldoon.

"JOHN HENRY IS READY TO FIGHT."

"Gee, that's a lot of natives," Fritz said.

"Let's get on with the show, Mr. Fritz," Dobbs scolded him.

"John Henry, terminate all organic targets in forward sixty-degree arc."

"JOHN HENRY WILL BEGIN FIRING."

Dobbs blinked as the robot unleashed a withering blast of rockets and machine gun fire.

"JOHN HENRY IS FIRING."

"Great God," Muldoon said, his words drowned out by the noise.

The Neverlandians wavered, explosions tearing holes in the solid mass of moving bodies, then entire ranks collapsed under the machine gun fire. Hit by exploding bullets, bodies broke into pieces spraying in all directions, while other bird-men relearned the art of flight in eruptions of stone and shrapnel.

"JOHN HENRY IS FIRING."

John Henry's upper torso rotated, fanning the area with its barrage. Then the tubes on its shoulders clicked.

"OUT OF MISSILES."

Through the smoke, Muldoon saw the Neverlandians climbing over hills of their own dead. John Henry angled its body to fire its machine guns at a slightly higher angle.

Click. Click.

"OUT OF AMMO."

A burst of light machine gun fire. *Click.*

"OUT OF AMMO."

The surviving Neverlandians, bleeding and wailing in pain, made a last-ditch effort to climb the steps. Driven onward by sheer courage, they came within thirty yards of Muldoon's Crickets. John Henry responded with an arc of napalm, filling the already hot air with smoke, screams of agony and the smell of burning flesh. Then the tube spit and coughed.

"OUT OF FLAME."

The robot slumped, smoke pouring out of its barrels.

"JOHN HENRY HAS NO VISIBLE TARGETS."

Dobbs let go of his ears and tried to see through the wall of burning bodies and black smoke. Muldoon received a report from the other sides of the Temple, and grinned broadly.

"They're running like hell on the other sides. Pete says no casualties."

"Excellent!" A breeze parted the smoke for a moment, revealing thousands of dead Neverlandians packing the bottom of the steps. "I've never seen anything like this. Not even when the Kikis came howling up at us through the airlock."

Muldoon shook his head in wonder. "I kind of admire the poor bastards," he said. "They've got plenty of spunk."

A horn blared, and the charge resumed.

"Here they come. Tactical Ten. Fire at will!"

Fresh waves of Neverlandians leaped through the wall of flame and ran up the steps, waving their two-handed swords and clubs.

"John Henry, let 'em have it," Dobbs said.

"OUT OF MISSILES. OUT OF AMMO. OUT OF AMMO. OUT OF FLAME."

Fritz was loading charge into his rifle. "John Henry's spent. I guess I didn't expect to be fighting a million savages who wouldn't know what fear was if it killed them twice."

"Sixty thousand," Dobbs corrected him, firing his pistol.

"Lay it on," Muldoon told the Crickets. He blinked. The Neverlandians were steadily making ground toward the top in a suicidal charge. "Switch to auto, Tactical Six. Fall back!"

The front rank turned and hustled up their stairs as the second rank fired, which in turn fell back as the front rank fired, creating a leapfrogging retreat.

"Lay it on, I said!" said Muldoon, firing his rifle.

Rank after rank of the bird-men fell, constantly replaced by a new wave bristling with spears, swords and flags.

Dobbs fired frantically. "Sergeant Major, how are we holding up on the other sides?"

Muldoon hurled a grenade. "The attack's very light on the other sides. They're hitting us here the hardest, using the smoke as cover."

"Then I suggest we bring out the Mule to our side."

"We'll have no reserve," Muldoon scolded him.

"I'd rather bring on the reserve now than when we're overrun and dead. We've retreated as far as we can go. We've got our backs up against the wall here."

Muldoon considered this. "All right, I agree. Brandon, bring out the cavalry."

"Yes, sir!" Fritz shouted, then pulled a remote controller out of his pocket.

The Mule stomped to the edge of the steps and lowered its turret guns.

"You may fire," Dobbs said.

The heavy machine guns on the machine's flanks began blazing, raking the mass of screaming bird-men with exploding bullets. Rockets, spraying trails of sparks and a thin stream of smoke, bucked out of their tubes and rained among the Neverlandians, falling to explode on the steps. The Neverlandians began to waver.

"I'll have him charge them and see how they like it," Fritz said. "We'll chase them out of the city and make good our escape."

"Good show!"

The Mule, swaying, began to march down the steps, then immediately lost its footing. The machine reached out a large pad into empty space, wavering while Dobbs held his breath and reached out his hand in a futile gesture of help, then it toppled to the ground with a groan and a loud crash. It rolled down the steps with a series of metallic bangs, its machine guns still firing in all directions. Dobbs and Muldoon heard the sound of glass breaking, then threw themselves to the ground as a brief barrage of bullets sprayed their area and the last rocket fired straight up like a flare.

The Mule finally came to a rest about halfway down the steps, still firing its guns, its legs plodding against empty air.

"Holy Mars, sorry about that," Fritz said. "I forgot about the roll when they walk."

"At least it's still firing in the right direction," Muldoon said. "It'll buy us a minute."

The Neverlandians soon learned by trial and error to avoid the Mule, and resumed their charge. Muldoon guessed that the enemy had lost at least ten thousand men, but he knew his own force was already exhausted and low on ammunition.

The Mule's guns clicked empty.

"*Grom-malakit-mi-prop!*" one of the Crickets cried.

Muldoon put a steadying hand on the alien's shoulder and said, "Stand your ground, men. You're the best in the galaxy. Remember your training."

But his stomach sank as he watched the Neverlandian charge gain ground. The bird-men were close enough that he could see their gleaming black eyes.

"Keep up your fire, but prepare to melee. Tactical Thirty."

The Neverlandians surged up the steps.

"Pete, send two men over to our side on the double-quick, we've got—damn!"

Muldoon watched as the first of a wave of bird-men leaped feet first directly at him, claws splayed, then blinked in relief as they were mowed down and thrown back down the steps. Several more made it through, waving their clubs at his face. Muldoon rapid-fired his pistol into their chests. He squeezed the trigger again, and the pistol whined and popped before it died.

"I'm getting too old for this!" He stepped back, drew his ceremonial Marine sword and thrust it through the shield of a nearby warrior. He smelled the bird-man's death-scream hot and wet against his face. Bringing his foot up, he kicked the Neverlandian in the stomach, which released the sword from where it was wedged in bone, and swiped it in a figure-eight to take off another's head as well as his hand at the wrist.

"JOHN HENRY WILL MELEE."

The robot stepped forward heavily and swung its metal arm clumsily, swiping three Neverlandians into their fellows down the steps. A warrior charged the robot, swinging his two-handed sword against its head, where it glanced off with a clang.

"MOTHER-FUCKER."

The robot swung its arm again. The little bird-man ducked easily, cawed and swung the sword in a wide arc until it rang harmlessly off the machine's breastplate.

"MOTHER-FUCKER."

John Henry punched the native high into the air with an uppercut.

Next to the robot, a Cricket screamed as three spears entered his abdomen, shoulder and throat at once. As he collapsed, a Neverlandian hero carrying a faction flag made it to the top, turned and waved it at his comrades, who redoubled their charge at the sight, screaming encouragement. Then his head exploded.

"Fuck 'em!" Travis appeared nearby, firing a rifle.

"Careful with that thing, Bill," Muldoon told him, then ducked the swipe of a two-handed sword. "Hail Mary!" He thrust and kicked, the Neverlandian falling back down the steps.

Bill fired wildly into the Neverlandians at point-blank range. "I told you so! I told you so!"

"Ah, who gives a damn!" Muldoon exploded, and was overrun.

‌⌁

Out of the corner of his eye, Dobbs watched in horror as three Neverlandians swamped Muldoon, tearing the front of his uniform open and raising their weapons for the kill.

"Ha!" One of the Crickets leaped into the fray, using his rifle butt to knock away the bird-men, then squealing as his skull was crushed by a large hammer.

"Fall back!" Dobbs screamed, but it was no use. Two of the Crickets were dead now, and the group was overrun. He continued to fire blindly, his eyes clenched shut, waiting for the end.

Overhead, thunder rolled and a dark cloud blotted out the sky.

The Neverlandians froze in their tracks. Muldoon, panting, stared up at a warrior holding a spear over his exposed chest.

A distant flash blinked into their eyes, moments later followed by more thunder. In shades, the sky quickly darkened until it glowed a neon green.

The warriors retreated, running down the steps and disappearing into the wall of fire and smoke. Within minutes, the steps were empty but for the dead and dying.

"What the dickens?" said Dobbs.

"Here comes the storm," Travis said, pulling pieces of bird-feather out of his beard. "Not electrical, though. Probably a tornado. They know the difference."

"Good luck, that," Muldoon said. "It was damned close there for a minute. I thought we'd had it."

Fritz took off his cap and ran his hand through his hair. "They break for a tornado but they run suicidally into the worst rain of death they could ever experience. What gives?"

Travis smiled grimly. "Wait until you see the tornado. And it's in their genes, their culture, to be afraid of them. Remember how their ancestors were killed by the weather."

"We're holding up on the other sides," Muldoon told them, listening to the com link. "They're the best there is, those Crickets."

Next to him, a Cricket's antennae stood straight up while he loaded his rifle with more charge. Then he reached down and patted the shoulder of a fallen comrade.

"Well, this storm will give us some time to rest," Dobbs said. He took out his canteen and pulled a long swallow down his dry throat. "Maybe some rain will cool this place off as well, eh?"

"Actually, we're even more screwed," Travis said. "If it rains big, the ship will end up underwater, remember? We'll be even more cut off than we are now."

"Thank you, Mr. Travis," Dobbs said.

"Ah, who gives a damn!" Muldoon shouted against the odds.

Dobbs sat on the ground, exhausted. He stared at Muldoon. "And what do you think you were doing, waving that bloody piece of metal around? Pick up a rifle!"

Muldoon grinned and did as he was told.

Lightning flashed, followed by a deafening explosion of thunder that echoed for a full minute. The sky continued to darken until they were in a gloomy mock twilight, the clouds coiling thick and black in the sky. A heavy wind rose up and blew the thick black smoke over them.

Dobbs leaped to his feet, coughing on smoke. "Mr. Fritz—the scramjet! Raise the ship and tell them to get the scram unloaded before it starts raining on us. We'll drop a bomb on these buggers when it clears up."

"Don't bother," Travis shouted over the wind. "We still can't get through on the radio, and besides, here it comes." He looked up at the blackening sky.

The rain fell in hard sheets, drowning the fire of the napalm and washing the steps clean of blood and entrails. The men retreated under the roof of the room that topped the pyramid, leaning against the columns. Fritz held his stomach as a thick carpet of dead came into view.

"God, this is the sickest spectacle I've ever seen," he said. "And I've seen plenty."

The rain fell for five full minutes, then turned to hail for another minute, stones as big as golf balls. Then it stopped as abruptly as it had begun. The sky began to lighten.

Slowly, the sun came out.

"Fancy that," Dobbs said in wonder.

Immediately, the horn recalled the charge.

ജ

"What beautiful weather," the Captain said inside the cab of the rover, and smiled at Dariana in the passenger seat. She smiled back and continued to scratch his head. It felt glorious. Drew and Rachel sat in the back of the cab, looking out the windows.

"That kind of rain will give us excellent crops if we set up filters," Dariana said. In the cargo hold of the rover, the entire hydroponics farm, fish pond and chicken hatchery were stored neatly with dozens of boxes of other equipment.

The rain turned to hail, and they listened to the hailstones clatter off the roof.

"Strong filters," Dariana said.

"Look, it's letting up," Williamson said in wonder, then restarted the rover. Its wheels crunched over piles of gold dust as it crossed the gold pit and continued its trek into the wild. "The sun's out again already. Strange!"

"It's so beautiful," Rachel said, wiping a tear. "Real rain. And the sun." She began to cry. "This is all a dream. Pinch me! Is this really our world now?"

"It's Eden, and we're like Adam and Eve and Eve and Eve," Drew said with a soft laugh, putting a comforting arm around her friend.

"This is a great idea," Williamson agreed. "And so simple and easy, too! I'm just sorry about the pilot. Old Jimbo."

"It had to be done," Dariana said.

"You know, this whole thing just makes sense to me. Dariana, I have to tell you, I may know a lot, but you're definitely the smart one here. I'll work hard and cherish all three of you, I swear it."

Dariana's eyes flashed as she toyed with his hair. "We're going to build a utopia, George. Our own little paradise on a brave new world."

～

"Gaw, if it's not one thing it's the next!" Muldoon said hoarsely. He watched the Neverlandians spill out of the nearby streets and into the square, heading for the steps.

Dobbs put his hand on his comrade's shoulder. "Here they come again. We're out of cards, it seems. We won't stand another charge. If it comes to us getting captured. . . ."

"I'll do the honors at the appropriate time if you like," Muldoon assured him.

"Thank you, Sergeant Major."

"But I don't think they want to capture us, if that's a comfort."

"No. I suppose it isn't."

"Let's just hope the others get out safely with the gold. My only regret is Dariana will never know I tried to take over a planet for her! At least she'll get rich and live a good life like she deserves."

"She knows how you feel, old boy. Now let's make our stand."

Ralph nudged Dobbs and whistled, making Dobbs almost scream when he saw a Neverlandian staring him in the face.

"What the bloody hell do you want?"

"You are doing 'ery well," the Neverlandian told him. "Your 'oes are impressed, *ak ak ak*."

"Well, now, that's good to hear. Now bugger off and let us die in peace."

Ralph crowed, "They will write songs about this and we will sing them 'or a thousand years!"

Dobbs shouted in the bird-man's face, "How about they just let us leave with the bloody gold, eh?"

Ralph barked back at him. "You look silly standing there. That is impossible."

"Ralph, get out of here," Muldoon said. "Men, hold your positions. Fire on my command."

The Neverlandians stormed the Temple, throwing themselves into the crashing sound of the plasma fire without fear of death, collapsing to form fresh writhing heaps of dead and dying in the sun. Despite incredible losses, they closed for the kill.

Ka-boom!

The men jumped as an incredible explosion tore apart the base of the faction leaders' building, the structure collapsing neatly downward into a pile of rubble on top of a hundred screaming bird-men.

"Look, it's a rover with an atomic thrower!" Dobbs said, and left his mouth open. Next to him, Fritz continued to scream and fire. Dobbs cupped his hands shouted over the noise to Muldoon, "It must be Mr. Kilroy and Mr. Peters! We're saved!"

"No, that's not one of ours, Sergeant Major," Muldoon told him. "Take it easy there, Brandon. They're retreating."

The rover plowed through the Neverlandians, sending them scattering, throwing away their weapons and squawking.

Fritz lowered his hot smoking rifle, wide-eyed and panting.

"Well, whoever it is, I'm grateful," Dobbs said. He took off his cap and wiped his forehead with his sleeve, leaving a black streak there.

The rover pulled up to the base of the steps and a group of men in gray battle-armor spilled out, firing into the Neverlandians with heavy weapons.

"This is disgusting," Fritz said, throwing down his rifle to clatter onto the steps. "I see it now. I'm the friggin' devil himself. The darkness is inside me, Tim." He looked at his hands in horror. "I'm not fighting anymore. I've had it."

"Don't be like that, Brandon," Muldoon said. "We'll make it out okay. Look, the cavalry is here. It's like a miracle."

Travis was staring at the hot rifle in his hands. "I didn't know I could do this. I feel weird about it, me being the Emperor and everything. I mean, I really like them. How'd I do, Tim?"

"You did just fine," Muldoon said proudly. "You fought like a Marine."

Travis beamed shyly. Hey, what'd you expect? Instead, he said, "Thanks, Tim."

It was time to take stock of themselves. Muldoon checked in with the rest of the men over the com link. Out of the original twenty-four

Crickets, only nine were still alive, and one of these was mortally wounded. The Color Sergeant said he would take care of it.

Muldoon heard the gunshot, and took off his cap. "Poor bastard."

Dobbs turned to Muldoon. "Sergeant Major, lend me your field glasses, and tell the men to hold their positions and stop firing or we'll start another war with these newcomers. In the meantime, I'll get a proper look at them."

Muldoon tossed the glasses to Dobbs, who caught them and brought the vision into focus. The men were well-equipped, the rover heavily armored. This was a well-financed expedition, with serious backers. Were they here for the gold? He knew they were. An armed freelance expedition didn't just go roaming around inside a nebula expecting to find a planet. He studied the area more carefully, looking for clues.

Stenciled neatly on the upper right corner of the rover's flank were the small words *GALACTIC RESOURCES—We Mine The Future.*

"Blast. I don't know if this will go very well for us," he said.

"Why?" Muldoon demanded. "Who is it?"

Dobbs surveyed the rest of the area with the glasses and focused on a tall imposing figure in black battle-armor, who stood smoking a cigar while studying the area with great interest using his biomechanical eye.

The head turned and the man appeared to look Dobbs right in the eyes. The man grinned and waved, then put the end of his cigar back into his mouth.

Von Kleig.

"It's a ghost," Dobbs said, paling. "Come back to haunt me."

Just then, the horn called the attack, and the Galactic Resources team found themselves fighting for their lives.

Chapter 15
Escape from Neverland

he Galactic Resources team deployed into a semi-circle bristling with heavy blasters, meeting the charge with a pattern of laser beams that glowed bright red. The blasters were not like the antiquated plasma-slug rifles still issued to the colonial soldiery on the backwater planets. They fired a beam that burned a clean hole through a man and asked for seconds. The Neverlandians, dropping by the hundreds, nevertheless kept up the attack, pressing on all sides and forcing the humans into a steady retreat up the steps, stumbling over the dead.

Behind his own men, Von Kleig walked calmly up the steps until he paused twenty meters below where Dobbs and Muldoon stood.

"That's close enough, Max," Dobbs shouted over the roar of the battle while squinting down the barrel of a rifle. "I'm in no bloody mood for jokes."

Von Kleig grinned. "Lawrence Dobbs, I presume."

"You're still a lousy bastard, Max," Dobbs said.

"You know this guy?" Muldoon said in disbelief.

"Aye, he's my old bleeding partner, come back like the prodigal son."

"But he's a mercenary," Muldoon said, glaring at Von Kleig. Mercenaries were looked down upon by the soldiery, who considered them vultures and bullies.

"It's good to see you again, Dobbs," Von Kleig said calmly as his men kept up their fire behind him. "It's been what, more than two hundred Standard years." He blew smoke and looked around him. "You don't seem very happy to see me."

"Oh, I'm chuffed as nuts about it, old boy. Really."

"What a mess you've made. I almost admire your work. No finesse, though." He spit on the ground. "But that was always your style, wasn't it. To overreach."

An unarmed and odd-looking pale man in a gray jumpsuit left the firing line and joined Von Kleig. "Who are these people, Mr. Von Kleig?" The man cocked his head to study Dobbs. "Why is he pointing a rifle at you? Why are we not progressing?"

"This is an old friend of mine," Von Kleig told the man. "Dobbs, I want you to meet Mr. Bova. He's with Galactic Resources."

"Aye, I saw your logo on your rover. Nice advertisement."

Von Kleig glanced at Bova in disgust, who turned, noticed he'd missed it after painting over the logo on the ship, and turned back with a patient smile.

"It does not matter any longer, Mr. Von Kleig, since you just told them who we are," Bova said with smug satisfaction.

"He's an android," Muldoon hissed at Dobbs. "Watch that one."

Dobbs kept Von Kleig in his target scope. "Max, I'd like you to meet Sergeant Major Tim Muldoon, my partner. And this here's Bill Travis and Brandon Fritz."

"A ball turret gunner," Von Kleig said with respect, noticing Fritz's uniform.

"This fellow dead at our feet was our mining engineer," Dobbs continued. "And that big metal man behind me is our angry robot. I'd like you to meet him too."

"They work for our sworn enemy, the TM&D," Bova said, looking at his hands. "I will kill them. I could snap their necks before they could get a single round into me."

"No," Von Kleig said, and spat. "We're going to talk. We can do business."

Bova shook his head. "Talk, talk, talk. That is all you humans like to do. I will show you how to fight."

The android abruptly turned and ran through the firing line, where the men labored over their lasers, and charged straight into the mass of birdmen, which appeared to swallow him whole. The Galactic Resources team stopped firing to cheer him on. Dobbs and Muldoon saw him take both sides of a Neverlandian's head in his hands, give a single fatal twist, drop the corpse to the ground and move on to the next systematically.

After twenty of their best warriors died this way, real irrational fear struck the Neverlandians for the first time. They broke and fled, while Bova pursued at a steady march for more than a hundred meters, grabbing more bird-men from behind and breaking their necks. Then he stopped, turned and jogged back to rejoin Von Kleig.

"That is how you fight," he explained once he reached the summit.

"Mr. Bova, thank you for quieting things down," Von Kleig said with a sigh. Behind Von Kleig, the mercenaries began to gather, holding their weapons at the ready.

"I'd like to talk, Dobbs," he continued. "I really would. Otherwise, we'll have to do business my way, and it won't go well for you. These are hard men behind me and they're good with blasters."

The mercenaries behind Von Kleig grinned. One patted his blaster.

Dobbs lowered his rifle. "Nice eye you got there. How was your time in prison?"

"You spend ten years on Cantor V and then we can talk about it."

"I heard you got out in four." Dobbs snorted. "Good behavior."

Von Kleig grinned and glanced up at the sun, squinting at its bright light. "Yeah, well. One week on Cantor V is enough. . . ."

"Small price to pay seeing as you got all the money and I was left marooned on Yuri," Dobbs told him. "Try getting yourself buried alive, and then we can discuss that too."

Von Kleig laughed. "Same old Dobbs. Big talker. I bet you'd like one of these here cigars."

"We'll take two, and you'll light them in the bargain."

Von Kleig walked up the remaining steps and stood face to face with Dobbs, his men following, then reached into his breast pocket and pulled out two cigars. As promised, he gave them to Dobbs and Muldoon and lit them.

Dobbs studied his cigar. "From Olivia," he said with appreciation. "We make the best. So how did you find us?"

"Galactic Resources doesn't want to let the TM&D have this planet."

"Will not let them," Bova added, his jaw clenched.

"I saw the crew list," Von Kleig continued. "Then I saw the real crew list, and your name was there. Naturally, I was interested in seeing my old partner again."

"Our Hacker sold us out," Muldoon spat. "Kids! Don't understand the oath of confidentiality."

Von Kleig nodded. "He's right. It's going to ruin the business."

"They should learn the way how," Muldoon added.

Von Kleig sighed in agreement. "Okay. Here's what we want. We want to know what got you out of bed and running into a nebula. There's some valuable mineral here, and we want to know what it is. Then we want to make the claim. Then you'll leave."

Dobbs smiled. "Listen, Max, you know we're not with the TM&D."

Von Kleig nodded. "It was a cover."

"So take the Godforsaken planet. You can have it."

"Oh?" Von Kleig sharpened the tuning of his linguistic resonator chip, which enabled him to spot lies, although he didn't need it. He still knew Dobbs like the back of his own hand. The man was sincere. "So the mission was a bust. You found nothing here."

"No, we found the Holy Grail and we have it by the tail."

Von Kleig's men stirred, licking their lips.

"Talk, talk, talk," Bova said.

Von Kleig exhaled a cloud of smoke. "You better not be screwing around with me." But his chip told him that Dobbs wasn't kidding.

Dobbs turned to the Engineer. "Mr. Travis, please demonstrate."

Travis dug into his pocket and pulled out his handful of gold dust, giving it to Von Kleig, who scrutinized it with his biomechanical eye. The man whistled. "That's very good metal. My employer will be pleased." He turned and handed the gold to one of his men. "Here, have a souvenir."

"Hot dog," the man said. "Thanks!"

"The Neverlandians have a machine in this pyramid that brings up the gold and spits it into that moat down there every couple months," Dobbs said. "Enough gold to fill the moat three times over. And it never stops. The gold just keeps coming, year after year."

"Amazing," Von Kleig said seriously. Then his eye narrowed. "So what do you want in exchange? I suppose you want a percentage."

"Actually, no. All we want is to get the hell out of here."

Von Kleig grunted, waiting for more.

"We've got our freighter loaded with gold right now," Dobbs explained. "We've got enough to set us up for life. That's all we need, and all we want right now, given the circumstances. So we'll leave you the planet, and you'll give us strong cover fire on our way to our rover down there in case the natives get restless again while we exit."

"No," Bova said. "That is not acceptable."

Von Kleig turned to Bova. "Mr. Bova, shut the fuck up."

"Not acceptable. That product belongs to the GR."

"Max, who is in charge here?" Dobbs said. "You or the robot-boy?"

Von Kleig's red eye flickered, and he chewed on his cigar. His face said nothing for a moment, but the men looked into each other's eyes, communicating wordlessly as they did in the old days when they were partners.

"I am, of course. But Mr. Bova here's just being a good Company Man."

"That's right. I am a Company—"

Muldoon brought up his rifle, sighted the android and squeezed the trigger. Bova shuddered, startled as he looked down and noticed he wore a smoking hole in his chest. His patient smile changed to a concerned expression. Muldoon fired again, clean through the head this time, and the android spilled backward down the steps, where he skidded to a rest against a heap of Neverlandians and lay stiffly.

Meanwhile, Dobbs had brought up his own rifle, covering the mercenaries.

"Hold your fire!" Von Kleig roared at his men, holding out his arms. When the men lowered their weapons, he added, "Mr. Bova had an accident just now. Understand?"

The men nodded. Accidents happened all the time.

Von Kleig turned back to face Dobbs. "I was wondering if you could still read the old signals."

Dobbs lowered his own rifle. "I can, and as you can see, Sergeant Major Muldoon can read mine."

"Thanks for getting rid of Bova. Androids are a pain in the ass."

"Always the wild card," Dobbs said, nodding. "Now we can get on with business."

"Good. So all you want is to get your ass off this rock with your stash."

"Aye. Then if you and me ever meet again, we'll observe tradition and drink our favorite scotch, and we'll settle some of our old scores. Hm?"

Von Kleig shrugged. "I know it was bad form to leave you stranded on that rock, Dobbs." He grinned. "But you know. Business." He looked around at the piles of dead aliens. "So how long have you been holding out?"

"Just a day," Dobbs told him. "We had it made, Max. But we hit a Catch-22 with Plan A, then Plan B backfired and now we have a forced Plan C."

"The military option." Von Kleig kicked a dead alien who lay at his feet.

"Sloppy, Dobbs," he continued. "You're getting even sloppier as you get older. You used to be a seriously ruthless bastard." He chuckled at private memories.

Dobbs shrugged. "That was a long time ago, Max. The days of my wanton youth. I offered you a deal, and I'm anxiously awaiting your reply."

Von Kleig studied his old partner. Did the man have any tricks up his sleeve? Couldn't be. He had the look of a man who'd just had his ass kicked. Not the type who held any real cards, just wanted to leave the game peaceably while he was a little ahead.

"We accept your offer, Dobbs. I think these funny little aliens have been bled white." His men laughed behind him. "We can handle them ourselves without you." Then he laughed. "Mars, you really do look like crap."

"Thanks, Max." Dobbs turned to Muldoon. "Sergeant Major, form the Crickets. We're getting out of here. On the double."

"You can stay with us, you know," Von Kleig offered. "Like old times. You get the gold back to the real world, and you'll retire. I know you as well as you do, Dobbs. Lust and seduction are as important as sex for you. Don't throw away your talent. Sign up with us, and you'll get your share of work with the Robber Barons. They pay well."

"I've got my share," Dobbs told him. "Now you go and get yours. Say, we have no more use for our angry robot. Would you like him? He scares the locals."

Von Kleig gave John Henry the once-over, and nodded, chewing on his cigar. "Nice craftsmanship on the retrofit. Yeah, we could use him, I guess."

Dobbs turned to Fritz. "Wind up our robot, Mr. Fritz, so that he'll be ready for an attack. We're going to leave John Henry with Mr. Von Kleig to help blow up the locals."

Fritz nodded. He opened up the back of the robot and set several switches and a timer. Nearby, Travis had found Ralph. The Neverlandian was busy snarling at Von Kleig and stomping his feet.

"I'll come down with you," he told Travis. "It stinks up here. I am sad you are lea'ing, You Celestial Majesty."

"Me too, Ralph," Travis said.

"Goodbye, Mr. Ralph," Dobbs called to him.

"Bye bye, you lousy bastard."

"You know, Mr. Travis, he's a lot calmer when he cusses me out," said Dobbs. "Tell him that's our human advice. Develop their language a little more so they can express their anger with words instead of body language, and then get more words to express a broader range of feelings. Make much less of a fuss. Now goodbye and good riddance."

Ralph heard and nodded sagely, appearing to be enlightened, then he whistled. "That Earthman sure talks 'unny, Bill. You know, you would ha'e made a good Emperor. Too bad. Better luck next time. Next time, don't screw the Gimp, okay?"

Travis grinned. "Thanks, Ralph. I'll miss you. Here, take this." He handed the crown of Neverland to the alien.

"Christ, I don't want this thing," Ralph said, and barked. He strolled up to Von Kleig, who looked down at him wearing an amused expression. "Here, accept our gi't, you lousy bastard. It is the crown o' the Emperor o' Ne'erland." His jaws snapped.

"Thank you, little fellow," Von Kleig said, entertained at hearing a five-foot-tall feathered alien speaking Earth Standard, and pulled a string of colorful plastic beads out of his pocket. He tossed them to Ralph, then studied the gold crown, grinning. "Emperor, huh?" He put the crown on his head, then removed it and laughed derisively.

The Crickets formed a line and they began to march to the bottom of the steps.

Travis stroked the back of Ralph's neck, a gesture he had learned that kept Neverlandians calm. "Come on, Ralph, let's go."

"'uckin' beads," Ralph said, gesturing with his hands. "He ga'e me 'uckin' beads!"

Muldoon called to them. "On the double-quick, Mr. Travis, let's move!"

"Goodbye, Dobbs," Von Kleig called after them, waving, his men behind him. "Lucky I saved your ass this time. Next time, don't over-reach."

"See you in hell, Max!"

Just then, the horn called a fresh charge.

"Jupiter!" Muldoon said. "Run for it, men! Tactical—aw, hell, just run!"

They scrambled down the steps, stumbling among the dead Neverlandians and reaching the rover head-long at about the same time as the bird-men. Dobbs glanced behind him and saw that Von Kleig wasn't providing cover fire as he'd promised. Instead, he was waving bye-bye at him. Typical Von Kleig. After all these years, he was still a bastard!

Travis and Fritz made it into the cabin. Travis covered his head with his hands while Fritz fired out the door over his lap. A Cricket screeched as a spear went through him and snapped against the rover's side.

Muldoon fired his rifle, making the spearman double over, then swung his arm and fired again, blowing a hole through another warrior's shield and dropping the man behind onto his back. Below him, Dobbs crawled among the legs and falling bodies.

"Fall back, men!" Muldoon shouted. "Into the rover if you can!" He fell to one knee and ducked the wide arc of a warhammer, firing into the warrior's abdomen. The bird-man cawed and flopped backward.

More of the Crickets disappeared, struggling and dying among the mass of Neverlandians. Pete was the last to die, throwing himself in front of a spear intended for Dobbs's throat. Muldoon continued firing, covering Dobbs as he was dragged into the rover's cab.

"Get in the damn rover!" he roared.

Muldoon felt a spear slice through his jacket at the same time a club glanced off his head. He staggered, seeing stars, then Fritz found his wrist and pulled him headlong into the rover as a two-handed sword sliced off his empty canteen.

"Get out us out here, Bill!"

The rover kicked into life and began plowing into the Neverlandians, who parted before the metal monster, stabbing it with spears and swords in an awful racket.

Muldoon began to come to. "What the hell is happening? What's that noise?"

"We're in the rover," Dobbs said. "And we're alive." He added somberly, "But it seems the Crickets have all bought it, Sergeant Major."

"They were a good lot," Mudoon said, blinking away a tear. "The best Marines I ever served with. Poor old Pete."

The rover lurched and bucked as it climbed a pile of rubble and crashed down to the other side, its wheels spinning gravel.

Muldoon dug into his pocket and found the ruins of the cigar Von Kleig had given him. He lit up. "It looks like your old pal sold us out back there, Sergeant Major. I lost good men because of that scum."

"Don't worry about him," said Dobbs. "We'll have the last laugh yet."

§

Von Kleig walked down the firing line, giving instructions to his men. The natives had lost most of their spunk, and his men were armed to the teeth, high in spirits, and safe and snug in battle armor. Thousands of natives were dying under interlocking fields of laser fire.

He smiled, amused at himself. That was twice he'd left that idiot stranded. But old Dobbs always got out of his messes—it's what made the man so lovable. He hoped they'd meet again, under similar circumstances, and resume their game.

More importantly, he felt close to cracking the locals and being able to solidify the claim for Galactic Resources. In all of his career, Von Kleig had never let down an employer. This time, he would hand over what had to be the biggest gold vein in the universe.

Or perhaps he'd take it for himself this time and say to hell with the likes of Whitehead. He had the crown of the Emperor, and maybe that meant something once he mopped up here. Who could tell? Perhaps he'd just take the whole planet. Now that was an idea worth chewing!

Behind him, the John Henry robot made a clicking sound.

"ALERT. ALERT."

Von Kleig turned and looked up at the robot's head, which bent down and scrutinized him with its own red eyes.

"You can talk. Are you ready to fight for us now or are you going to wait until it's all over?"

"SELF-DESTRUCT ACTIVATED."

The light shining from Von Kleig's red eye narrowed to a point of light on the disc. "Damn you, Dobbs. You're the devil himself. Damn you!" He kicked the robot in the shin, which resounded with a metallic *bong*.

"MOTHER-FUCKER."

The top of the Temple exploded, throwing debris and a large mushroom cloud of thick black smoke high into the air.

ᕬ

Muldoon turned around. "What was that noise?"

Dobbs smiled and winked at Fritz. "Oh, it's probably just your stomach rumbling again."

Fritz shook his head. "I think I'm starting to like my work again. You just have to be objective and realize the universe is full of people who need to be blown up."

The rover made a grinding noise, then began to shudder.

"What the devil is happening up there, Mr. Travis?"

"We're losing power!"

"Well, sod this for a game of soldiers!" Dobbs exploded. "Get it sorted!"

"It's still losing power. It's dying. Must have been all that rubble."

Muldoon leaned in. "Can you fix her, Mr. Travis?"

Travis turned around in his seat to face him. "Yeah, but it'll take me about two hours."

Dobbs groaned.

Travis turned away to enjoy a private grin. Actually, it would probably take him twenty minutes.

The rover chugged to a halt and hissed. They were still at least a good kilometer short of the ship.

"Aw hell, let me have a look at the engine," Travis said. "But don't expect miracles."

The men climbed out of the cab. Muldoon stretched and realized he was going to see Dariana soon, which made his heart race on its final reserves of adrenaline, erasing the pains of his wounds. It would feel like going home after a hundred years. He was bruised and bloody, and she would scratch his head and comfort him.

Jupiter, but he was exhausted. He thought he wouldn't need the cryogenic process—he'd probably sleep the entire seven years back on his own accord, he was so tired.

"I love that woman," he said out loud to himself, and laughed while shaking his head. "What an adventure this turned out to be. The best yet."

What a story he'd have to tell Dariana. He knew she'd be upset that they couldn't stay a while, but she couldn't accuse of him not trying—he'd fought sixty thousand aliens to try to make a home for her!

Out here, this far from the city, he began to notice again how beautiful the planet was. Green grass, breathable atmosphere, a nice warm sun shining over distant fields. He drank in the air in big lungfuls as he noticed those lumbering herbivores again, now waddling away as fast as they could. Muldoon thought they looked cute. Too bad he'd have to leave it all behind.

Wait a minute. They're waddling away as fast as they can.

Dobbs, Travis and Fritz bolted past him.

"Come on!"

He turned and saw a thousand Neverlandians running across the distant fields towards him, and behind them a great cloud of smoke was rising over the distant alien capital like an exploding volcano.

◊

Dobbs and Muldoon reached the crest of the crater and leaped over the top, hitting the muddy incline in a long skid. Below, they saw Kilroy shaking his bandaged head at them.

"Jim!" Muldoon called, sliding down the mud. "Is the gold loaded?"

"Yeah, it's all in there. It was hard as hell without McDonough, though. We left the rovers outside the ship down there. What the hell happened to you guys? The radio doesn't work."

Muldoon splashed into two feet of muddy water that immediately drenched his feet in their boots. "We've got sixty thousand screaming natives running after us, and we've got to get out of here right now. McDonough and the Crickets have had it."

Travis and Fritz splashed past them and ran up the ramp into the ship. A moment later, the three remaining Crickets charged out with rifles and began firing up at the crest of the crater.

"Okay, okay," Kilroy was saying. "Jupiter, you guys look like you've been through hell! But listen. Tim. Dariana's gone."

Muldoon put his hand over his chest. "What did you say?"

"She split with the Captain and the other women yesterday. Said they were going to make a colony here. Took a lot of equipment too, but it's okay, we don't need it. I tried to talk them out of it, really, but she pulled a blaster-pistol on me and then her friends bop-bopped me the head. Sorry, brother."

"She's out there all alone, Lawrence," Muldoon groaned. "I've got to save her or she'll be killed! You go. I'm staying."

"You're not going anywhere, Sergeant Major," Dobbs yelled back. "We're on our last legs and we're getting out of here. Into that ship on the double-quick! That's a bloody order!"

"I can't leave her here!" Muldoon looked around him blindly, as if trying to decide where to start. The sun hit him squarely, and he began to feel faint in the heat as his worst nightmare became a reality. Blue sky and brown earth swam before his eyes.

A spear, traveling in a wide arc, came crashing into the muddy water near the ramp.

"Hey!" Kilroy promptly pulled his antique .45 out of its holster and fired up at the Neverlandians until it clicked empty. "I'm out of here," he announced. "Let's go!"

Dobbs grabbed Muldoon's jacket and shook the man roughly. "She wanted to leave, you stupid bastard!" he screamed. "Let her go. You can't save her, you hear me? If we don't go now, we're done for!"

Muldoon's eyes rolled and he fainted.

The Crickets saw Muldoon collapse, then turned and ran through the boot-high water to help him up the ramp, rifles slung over their shoulders.

"*Agrota-mari-hota-ga-ti-grom Muggoon*," one of the Crickets said.

"Get him into the ship!" Dobbs shouted from the bottom of the ramp, firing with his pistol at the heads along the crest of the crater.

An awful racket of drums and horns called a new charge, and a swarm of Neverlandians bounded down the hill, shrieking and waving clubs. Musket balls ricocheted off the ship's hull with a sharp clang and a puff of smoke.

Dobbs suddenly froze, unable to move. He was the thinker; Muldoon was the brave one who got them through the gunfire and slaughter. Without Muldoon, he panicked, spears raining around him until his instinct for self-preservation overcame his fear with a gasp.

He braced his legs, sized up the lead bird-man, and brought him down with a clean shot through the head. His arm darted left, his finger squeezed and another Neverlandian flopped backward, holding his throat. He glanced right and saw a third splashing into the water toward him, close enough for him to see the bloodlust in his black eyes and hear his personal war-song whistling through the nostrils of his beak.

"Mommy!" Dobbs shouted, and shot the Neverlandian point-blank through the chest.

The Crickets exchanged a few words in their harsh language and abruptly dumped Muldoon onto the ramp. One threw away his rifle— which had jammed—drew his knife, and led the three, their tan uniforms splattered with mud, down the ramp toward Dobbs.

Dobbs turned in time to see them close on him with deadly speed, and almost shot the lead Cricket between the eyes out of reflex when the man barreled past him, splashed through the muddy water, and charged up the hill to meet the enemy. The last Cricket paused long enough to turn and shove Dobbs roughly toward the ship, then followed his comrades.

"Come back here, that's a bloody order!" Dobbs screamed after them.

"Ha!" the Crickets shrieked, doubling their pace. Firing from the hip, they cleared the hill of Neverlandians, the bodies dropping in the mud, and disappeared over the top. Several painful seconds of quiet ticked by, then there was a storm of rifle reports and screams.

Dobbs lingered for another moment, torn, then ran up the ramp to help Travis drag Muldoon, still unconscious, into the ship.

"She was her own woman, Sergeant Major," Dobbs told him. "She made her own choices. I thought that's why you bloody brought her here. Now you be your own man!" He turned and shouted, "Are you all in one piece, Mr. Travis?"

Travis nodded weakly, got into his harness and laughed insanely. Then he felt inside his pocket. Graham's audiochips. And all of the data about the technology. He had been the Emperor of Neverland!

Dobbs noticed Fritz getting into his seat. "Mr. Fritz, I see you're still alive. Good show."

Fritz smiled feebly and gave a thumbs-up. "That was Biblical. But I'm ready to retire now, thanks very much."

Dobbs turned back to Muldoon and shook him roughly. "And how about you, you dumb ox? Are you still alive and ready to retire now that we're stinking rich?"

Muldoon opened his eyes, blinking rapidly. "I threw away my honor," he said, as if in the middle of a bad memory. "I failed to protect my fiancée and lost all of the men in my command in a single day. Finish it for me if I botch this."

Dobbs watched in horror as Muldoon reached into his holster, but it was empty. So were the scabbards that had held his sword and service knife.

"I can't win, godammit," Muldoon said, staring straight ahead.

"Don't even think it, you big stupid ox," Dobbs told him. He hated seeing Muldoon like this, and wanted to say something, but there was no time. Instead, he ran to the ladder and climbed up into the bridge.

The ship trembled as the rockets on its bottom fired.

"She's not made for hard takeoffs on planets with a real atmosphere," Kilroy said, his eyes darting from one gauge and monitor to the next. "Let's hope that engineer is as good as he made himself out to be. Fire the lasers on my mark, Tommy."

In the seat next to him, the Navigator stuffed wads of purple chewing gum into his mouth one after the other until his left cheek bulged, all the while calling out numbers.

Dobbs held onto the back of Kilroy's seat. "Will we be able to pull up?"

"You look like Gimpshit," the Navigator sneered, showing purple teeth.

Kilroy turned and frowned at him, noticing him for the first time. "Commander, I suggest you find a seat and get in your harness if you want to survive this takeoff."

Dobbs returned to the passenger compartment and strapped himself in with Muldoon, Travis and Fritz. The sound of the rockets firing up was suddenly drowned out by the ear-splitting sound of groaning metal.

"Think she'll pull up?" Dobbs shouted at Travis over the din, the room shaking in front of his eyes. "This ship looks like it's been in an asteroid fight and lost!"

Travis turned to him, pale and dripping with sweat, and smiled. "Of course!" Then he went back to staring straight ahead and mouthing come on girl over and over.

Dobbs nodded uncertainly and patted Muldoon's shoulder. "Hang on, there."

"I've gained and lost so much in one day," said Muldoon.

"We're doing fine, chap."

"Whoa, here we go!" Travis said.

Dobbs felt the ship begin to lift, shaking violently as its own mass, the atmosphere and the gravity of the planet bore it down like an anchor. He closed his eyes, but saw the Neverlandian warrior splash through the muddy water towards him again, his feathers splayed, painted club and shield in hand. His eyes popped back open.

"Ahhhh," he said.

Travis was screaming: "The lasers are firing! This is it!"

Dobbs felt as if he were in an elevator that suddenly shot upward into the atmosphere at a hundred kilometers an hour.

They had escaped Neverland.

Chapter 16
The Duel

Kilroy cheered as they left the atmosphere and entered orbit. He clapped his hands.

"Only a month to go, Tommy, and we can slingshot back home-free."

The Navigator merely shook his head and pointed at the view-screen, chewing rapidly. The Pilot followed his finger and his smile evaporated. He slumped in his harness.

"That's a big problem, Tommy."

The Navigator nodded, then activated a small hologram that showed a cloud of blue dots in three-dimensional space. Two red dots—spaceships—were near a blob the size of a ping pong ball—Neverland. Then a third dot entered the hologram.

"Ever have one of those years, Tommy?" He sighed. "It's not going to hit us, is it?"

The Navigator gave him an incredulous stare: As if.

"I feel like I could reach out and scratch its head, it's so close."

The Navigator gave Kilroy a scolding look for doubting his word.

"So what's that third ship coming onto the screen?"

The Navigator shrugged.

Kilroy sighed. "Might as well tell the boys. We really screwed the Gimp this time." He flicked a switch for the intercom. "Dobbs, Muldoon, report to the bridge. On the double."

৭

Down below, the men were cheering. Dobbs studied his comrades.

Their faces were covered with soot, their hair clotted with dirt and blood from cuts. Muldoon's jacket was ripped in a dozen places, the buttons torn open to expose the graying hair on his barrel chest. Fritz looked as if he'd been beaten with a club and hung out bruised and wrinkled to dry. Travis' hair, thick with dried sweat, was standing at odd angles, and he still had pieces of broken feathers in his beard.

Dobbs smiled, guessing that he too must look quite a sight. But they had pulled it off. This ship was carrying the Holy Grail in its belly like a baby safe in its mother's womb. After a brief sleep in the cryogenic chamber, he'd wake up a millionaire.

At that very moment of reflection, he heard Kilroy on the intercom. He didn't like the tone of the man's voice. In fact, it made his hair stand on end.

"Mars, what is it now? Come on, Sergeant Major, chin up. We're rich!"

Muldoon obediently rose and followed Dobbs up the ladder into the cramped bridge. The room stunk of stale cigarette smoke, sweat and grape gum. Travis and Fritz followed.

"What's the ruckus, Mr. Kilroy? Care to celebrate?"

The Pilot pointed at the view-screen. "That. That's the problem. They've got us dead to rights."

"Look at that," Muldoon whispered.

They were looking at a Federation battlewagon, as big as a silver crayon on the screen, the sunlight gleaming along its long frame and cutting shadows among its architectural details. The men held their breath.

"Don't worry, we won't collide," the Navigator said defiantly.

Muldoon watched the warship fire its rockets, leaving a short fuzzy trail of light behind it on the screen. "Look at her move," he said with admiration.

"We can't win, can we, just for one bloody minute," Dobbs said in amazement, rubbing the bump on his head. Then he sighed. "Mr. Kilroy, what are our options?"

Kilroy lit a cigarette and blew a stream of smoke into the stale air. "Hm, that's a tough one. We resist and be destroyed, or we give ourselves up."

"We can't give ourselves up."

Kilroy turned full in his seat to face Dobbs through a cloud of smoke. "I don't think you heard me. The Feds have us dead to rights. We resist and be destroyed, or we give ourselves up."

Dobbs' face contorted in agony. But there was always a way—wasn't there? He started to hyperventilate.

"Mr. Kilroy—signal the ship—we—we—"

Kilroy waited.

"Surrender," Dobbs finished.

"Aye aye. You heard the man, Tommy. Use radio and Morse code, and flash our lights."

The Navigator nudged Kilroy with his elbow and pointed at the screen.

A pair of torpedoes were launching from the ship's rear ports, signaled by a twinkle of light. Moments later, they exploded in a flash. The men blinked.

"Who's she firing at?" Muldoon demanded.

"Somebody who's good with a laser," said the ball turret gunner. "The torpedoes barely made it fifty thousand kilometers before getting zapped. Can anybody see what's chasing her?"

"The ship's retreating?" Muldoon said. "Nonsense."

Kilroy nodded. "Yeah, now I see it. Her engines are on fire. She's limping. Look."

"Everybody can put a lid on it," the Navigator said, silencing the room. He threw down his head set and turned the radio dial to channel its signal to the intercom circuit.

"Mayday, mayday, this is the Federation Ship of the Line *Undaunted* in sector four-alpha-two-seven-eight-niner, Caulfield's Nebula." The radio operator gave out the ship's spatial coordinates. "In action against intercepted hostile alien vehicle. Request assistance from any Federation military vehicles in this sector. Engines on fire. Laser banks damaged. Taking evasive maneuvers. Mayday, mayday, this is—"

Muldoon picked up the radio. Dobbs grabbed his wrist.

"Don't you answer that, Muldoon!"

Muldoon flicked his hand away. "Get your paws off me. That's a Federation ship and we're going to help them. If there's no other ship in this sector, it'll take years for anybody to hear the message, and more years before anybody else can get here."

"How are we supposed to fight the enemy? Smile at them? If whatever it is happens to be beating the tar out of a Navy battlewagon, what on Mars are we supposed to do with a freighter?"

Muldoon's jaw was set. "That's a Federation ship and we're going to help them in any way we can. Maybe we can help evacuate their wounded to safety."

Dobbs stepped back and pulled out his pistol, pointing it unsteadily at Muldoon. The red target laser dot swept around Muldoon's forehead. "I'm tired of your bloody emotions and your bloody heroics! Don't touch that button! There's nothing we can do. We've got a belly full of gold. We're getting out of here, right now!"

The other men watched them in stunned amazement. Muldoon glared back into Dobbs' eyes. "You want to give me a zap between the eyes, do you? Go right ahead. This is about honor." He hit the button on the mike and hailed, "*Undaunted*, this is Federation freighter 77X19 in your sector. We're in orbit along the equator of P2. We're ready to provide assistance. Over."

Dobbs groaned, his face contorted, then holstered the pistol. A part of him felt ashamed. Most of him still simply wanted to away with the gold. Muldoon was starting to become a variable problem-generator, but he couldn't be stopped.

The radio crackled with static. More flashes popped on the screen.

"BIG BERTHA, get off this channel. We are a military vehicle requesting assistance from other military vehicles. Over."

"Is there anything we can do to help? Over."

"Get out of this system. Be advised we are taking evasive maneuvers— Mars, what the hell was that?" There was a breathless pause. "BIG BERTHA, evacuate this system immediately and take precautions to avoid convergent course. Over."

"I'm on it," the Navigator muttered to himself. "As if I'd let him hit us."

"For Federation, honor and humanity," Muldoon said.

The radio operator replied dutifully, "For Federation, honor and humanity. Over and out."

Muldoon holstered the mike back onto its place on the console, then leaned against Kilroy's chair. "They'll pull through. That's the best ship in the known universe."

"You're a big dumb ox," Dobbs told him, but his words lacked force. "Mr. Kilroy, get us out of here." He turned to the Navigator. "Mr. Peters, where is that gas giant we need?"

The Navigator pointed to a bright dot of light beyond *Undaunted*.

Dobbs took off his cap and threw it to the floor. He pointed at the battleship. "You mean the only way to pull the slingshot will be to go around the Feds?"

"Yes, that's exactly what he's saying," Kilroy said. "Either that, or we enjoy crossfire if we sail between them. We don't have the fuel to get home without the slingshot, or it'll take us thirty years of space flight with the extra acceleration. Look!"

A series of massive soundless explosions tore apart the rear of *Undaunted* like firecrackers popping through a paper bag, scattering a swarm of giant pieces of debris that glittered in the sunlight until dissipating into black space. The ship pitched, its nose pointed downward at an angle, then the pitch jets fired, trying to correct its orientation.

"One of her reactors blew up," Fritz said. "Classic. Whoever the bad guy is, he's real good with a laser. He's working *Undaunted* over like a surgeon."

"That debris might hit us," Kilroy told the Navigator. "I don't care about a coffee mug or even a chair. Anything bigger, and this girl has had it. Do what you can with the particle accelerators."

The battle reached a climax as a long series of flashes popped soundlessly on the screen.

Fritz shook his head in wonder. "I've never seen anything like this. *Undaunted's* throwing everything she's got at him. Go, girl!"

The radio crackled with static for another moment, then erupted into sound—fire extinguishers, men shouting, boots tramping against the floor.

"BIG BERTHA, why aren't you moving? Evacuate this system immediately! Evacuate immediately! We're done!"

"Damn it!" Muldoon said in agony, his hands clenched into fists.

Undaunted was taking hits in her side, signaled by incredible flashes of light, leaving giant blackened holes sprouting bodies and space junk and sparks as the vacuum sucked the insides of the ship into open space. The ship was out of control now, drifting and shoved a little harder each time a powerful gamma ray laser beam found its target and streaked along her flank.

The radio went silent.

Undaunted continued to drift into space, growing smaller on the screen, finally visible only as a flickering orangish dot. Then it was gone.

The men slowly took off their caps.

"What a waste," Fritz said, wiping his eyes. "Not even enough time to launch the lifeboats."

"Well, whoever nailed *Undaunted's* now in our flight path," Kilroy reminded them. "And we're in his!"

❧

Muldoon wanted to pace, but the small room was filled with men, and they were staring at him and Dobbs, waiting for a bright idea.

"Brandon, you have Navy and Space Cav experience," he said. "What are our options?"

"This ship has a few particle beam accelerators to destroy space junk, which won't do much in a real fight. We essentially have no weapons. So basically we don't have any options."

"Jim, is there any way to avoid the enemy? Let's get around to the other side of Neverland. Maybe he won't waste his fuel on a chase."

The Pilot shook his head, dropped his cigarette onto the floor and stepped on it. "You know spaceships aren't hovercars. We're at low velocity right now, so don't worry about brake time. But by the time we roll and change course, he'll be right on top of us. We're in orbit around a planet. This is not an easy place to pull maneuvers, especially with a freighter full of metal. In fact, it really sucks." Then he pointed at the hologram to the right of the Navigator, where a red dot was slowly creeping toward a second red dot—their ship.

Dobbs picked up his cap, dusted it off against his leg, and put it on, trying to feel dignified instead of scream.

"Do it anyway, Mr. Kilroy."

"Aye aye," the Pilot said. "You may feel a little pull. Reverse, then centrifugal. Brace yourselves."

"I've got an idea," said Fritz.

All heads turned to him.

"Well, we never used the nukes. We could load up the scrambler with them and send it right at him like a jury-rigged space mine, yeah? We program the computer so it drifts, then fires its rockets when it's close enough to the bastard. Even if he scored a hit in a quick amount of time, the explosion could still do enough damage to put him out of action."

"And how do you propose in millions of kilometers of empty space to have it drift and then 'run right into him'?" Kilroy demanded, while focusing on the roll maneuver.

"Well, we'd have to make a run for it, which we're doing. If he chases us, he'll follow in the wake of our flight path. That narrows it down. Hey, I know it's a long shot."

"Excellent idea, Mr. Fritz." Dobbs turned to Travis. "There's always a way. Mr. Travis, you may proceed."

"I can't," Travis told him, and laughed insanely.

"Why the devil not?"

"It'd take me only like eight hours—at least—to try to do what you're describing. It doesn't sound like we've got eight hours. I can do it, but it'd take time. I'm serious."

"He's right," said Kilroy. "He'll be right on top of us in about thirty minutes."

Travis threw his hands in the air. "It'll take me half that long just to get to the cargo holds. I'm not a miracle worker." He gritted his teeth and added, "I can't do it."

"We shouldn't assume he wants to destroy us," Muldoon said. "We're a commercial freighter, and no threat. Maybe he'll ignore us."

"If it's an alien ship, how the devil will he know what we are?" Dobbs asked him.

Muldoon shrugged and pointed. "There's the radio. We call him up and tell him."

Dobbs rubbed his chin. "Give it a go, then. Not that'd we could expect them to understand or speak Standard Language. But it could at least buy us some time to think."

Muldoon took the mike and with the Navigator, hailed the alien space-ship on a broad range of frequencies. After a moment, the radio crackled and a choppy computer-generated voice answered in Standard Language:

Be quiet, Earthlings. I am thinking.

Kilroy patted Muldoon on the back and the men wrung their hands, hoping for the best.

I have finished recording data about your vessel. You are a cargo vessel and have no significant armaments.

"Thank God, we're saved," Dobbs said, grinning with relief. "You're a genius, Sergeant Major. I'm sorry I ever doubted you."

You will therefore be much easier to destroy and scatter to the Eight Gods.

Dobbs' face sagged. "Ask him. . . ." He couldn't finish the sentence, overcome by nausea.

Since I have already had to brake to destroy your battle vessel, I am at leisure. Are there any settlements on this planet?

"An independent civilization," Muldoon told him. "They're not part of the Federation."

Well, we'll see.

"Who are you?" Muldoon said.

I am Ooe-egh Loess Nepthyua, of the House of al-Nepthyua, He Who Sits on the Thrones of Prosperity, Justice and Accord, and Protector of Our Mother—Grand Emperor of the Nations of Idid-ethyua.

The ball turret gunner shuddered, as if confronted by his past sins made flesh.

"Xerxes," he murmured.

"But Xerxes was destroyed hundreds of years ago," Muldoon said.

I alone, now immortal, escaped the great fire and built this ship, and I too have discovered the art of collision of opposite forces, Earthman.

Fritz put a hand against his heart. "Antimatter. He's discovered anti-matter."

For hundreds of your years I have journeyed in solitude among the stars. Now I enter your possessions and will turn Earth into dust, so that your Mother may become a tiny dust nebula like our Mother. Oh, I see you are turning. Are you trying to escape me?

"Yeah, I suppose we'll try," Muldoon told the Emperor. "That's called human nature." He struggled for a moment to remember something he'd learned long ago about Xerxesian culture. "Can you give us some time to pay homage to our planet before we meet our maker—I mean, join our fathers? Then we'll try to escape and you can destroy us."

I suppose that would only be just. But I like talking to you.

Muldoon switched off the radio.

"That alien fellow's a crackpot," Dobbs said. "Mr. Kilroy, how are we doing?"

"This is going to take time."

"Ram," said Muldoon.

He watched the men turn and stare at him. "I said we ram him. We've got enough mass to carry through. Piss on his lasers."

His comrades didn't share his enthusiasm. They looked at their boots.

"Come on, men. Earth is at stake here! And we're goners either way."

Dobbs considered this. He wanted to cynically believe that Muldoon was overdoing his self-redemption routine, but the man was right in all he'd said. "Actually, all of Capital Province would be damaged. The Federation itself would fall apart, each province its own kingdom. Civil war, and without the guiding light of Capital Province, a thousand years of barbarism. It'd be the end of the Federation. I need to sit down." He sat on the floor.

"I'll join you," Travis said.

"What you're saying is possible," Fritz told Muldoon. "But that guy can strip down a ship like ours in no time. If we headed straight into him, with the power of his guns I think he could slow us, strip us and evade, then destroy us at his leisure."

"But it's possible, Brandon."

Fritz took off his cap and ran his hand through his long hair. "Yeah, I guess it is."

"We're all agreed then," Muldoon said resolutely.

"Not so fast," the Pilot said. "I've got an idea. You're not going to like it either."

"Do tell," Dobbs said wearily.

"Muldoon, you get on the radio and keep him busy. If he's been flying for a long time, he's bored and lonely as all hell. Just six months in open space is enough to send me and Tommy howling like Sky Whales. We'll get him to chase us for a while, make a game of it. Because although he's discovered antimatter, he doesn't know about something else."

"What's that?"

"He doesn't know what a wormhole is. That wormhole I told you about before is a quick hop away from here, er, astronomically speaking."

"And you say we're going to trick him into going in?" Travis said. "That's impossible."

"No, I'm not saying that. I'm saying we go in."

"You're mad!" Dobbs told him. "Only unmanned ships go through wormholes. Organic life forms are atomized. The ship pops out of another wormhole like a Flying Dutchman. Everybody knows that."

"Oh, you'd rather try to ram him and have him play with us, maybe push us into the atmosphere so we burn up?"

The Navigator turned, wide-eyed, and screamed, "What did you say?"

"We go into the wormhole with him right in our wake," Kilroy continued, putting a hand on the Navigator's shoulder. "He won't be able to brake in time, see. He goes in. Here's how I see the outcome. He could end up atomized. If he can somehow stay alive inside the wormhole, he still doesn't know how to navigate through one. He could end up in a star system far away—I mean, there are a hundred billion stars in the Milky Way to choose from. He might even end up in another galaxy—there are more than ninety billion of those."

"In any case, he's nicely screwed," Muldoon said, twirling the ends of his mustache in admiration.

"And besides, I'm almost done with the roll maneuver," Kilroy said. "If I try to turn her around again, he'll get suspicious and he'll probably attack." He forced a grin. "So. Anybody want to see what it's like inside a wormhole?"

Muldoon turned to Dobbs. "What do you think? I say we have a go at it. We've got nothing else planned."

Dobbs steeled his nerves with forcible effort. "Do it," he gasped. "If you're so determined to get yourself killed."

Muldoon grinned. "That's the spirit, Sergeant Major. Chin up. We're in God's hands now, all part of the plan. Nice knowing you."

Dobbs nodded weakly. "The Holy Grail. I had the mother right here in my two hands."

"We're getting a signal," the Navigator said. He switched on the radio.

I appreciate your prayers to your Mother, but I do not have much time.

Muldoon picked up the mike. "Mr. Emperor. What you are about to see is us firing our rockets. This is a Federation ship, the envy of the civilized universe. We're going to outrun you and escape. Goodbye."

I am thinking. Wait. Wait. You are using a concept called sarcasm. No, irony. Wait.

Kilroy swept his hand across the room. "Everybody grab onto some-thing along that back wall and say Hail Mary. We're going to get some serious *g*'s in here when we accelerate—enough to break ribs—so it's going to be rough."

Suppose you are not 'kidding' me. But I have to ask a question.

The men braced themselves against the back wall that would receive the *g* force.

"Fire when ready, Mr. Kilroy," Dobbs said.

"Aye aye."

Can you outrun a laser beam traveling at the speed of light?

The engines whined and the rockets began to roar. The ship trembled slightly and within moments, the men felt the gravitational force of accel-eration push against them. Kilroy was making the engines give every-thing they had, to hell with fuel. The gravitational force increased steadi-ly until it pushed the flesh taut on their faces and it became difficult to breathe. One by one, and then in one massive pile, the Navigator's reference books flew off the console at incredible speed and smashed into the wall over Dobbs' head, sticking there.

"Chuffin 'ell!" Dobbs screamed.

"How long do you think you can chase us before you give up and go home?" Muldoon said into the mike, his words garbled as his lips were pulled back from his teeth.

I do not have a home—nor do I have a lot of time. This is an enormous waste of fuel. I am not having a pleasurable experience. Are you sure you do not want to just talk instead?

"To a Xerxesian? Somebody from that planet of losers?"

I understand. You are taunting me.

"I meant to say, 'that planet of idiots?'"

I do not like talking to you any more. I will begin destroying your vessel.

"Keep him occupied!" Dobbs cried.

"Did you know that the word 'gullible' is not in the Standard Language dictionary?"

Wait. Wait. Wait. Oh, I see.

"Good one, chap!" Dobbs told Muldoon, laughing.

Here is the entry for 'justice.' Do you believe in 'justice,' Earthman?

"As a matter of fact I do," Muldoon answered the voice.

Then why stand in its way? Your species destroyed my planet. Three billion innocent people. I will make the Earthlings pay for this act. Do you not agree that genocide calls for genocide? Is this not justice? Please answer. I would like an answer.

"If ten men run an army and they order it to commit atrocities, do you destroy the entire army and their families and their descendants? Or do you punish the ten men? You can't hold five billion innocent people responsible for the actions of a few men hundreds of years ago. It doesn't wash!"

That is an interesting argument.

"And now look at you. Blaming us for what happened in the bargain!"

I am thinking. Wait. Wait. Wait.

"I think you got through to him," Dobbs said in wonder.

Perhaps you are right. But we have a saying similar to one of your proverbs.

Muldoon couldn't use the mike any longer due to the gravitational force. It was now plastered against his shoulder.

An eye for an eye, Earthman. I am firing.

The ship trembled under the impact of the Emperor's laser.

"Oh Mars," said Muldoon. "Me and my big mouth!"

I am firing.

Near Muldoon, Travis groaned, his eyes clenched shut and the flesh pulled taut on his cheeks.

Are you there, Earthman?

Kilroy, barely able to move his head now, continued to check the monitors. "Tommy! Align target for particle beam accelerators. It's worth a try!"

"Aye aye!" The Navigator, his face contorted, worked the controls. "Ready to shoot!"

I know you are still there. I am coming.

"Shoot on my command, four, three, two . . . Shoot!"

"Shooting!" the Navigator shouted.

Idid-a-laam! That was a nice shot. I took a hit.

The men cheered, a chorus of hoarse grunts.

I am firing.

The ship bucked, then continued its acceleration, climbing higher than five *g*'s.

"He nailed our accelerator guns," Kilroy announced.

"He's a surgeon!" Fritz reminded them.

Where are you? Are you in your hydroponics farm?

The ship bucked again.

I guess not. Oh. Maybe you are in the cryogenics chamber.

This time, they heard the explosion over the roar of the rockets.

"God, please don't let him hit the cargo holds," Dobbs was saying.

"Or the engines!" Muldoon said.

Let me see. There are so many choices.

"How is he hitting us on the roof?" Travis said. "He's behind us."

"No, he's a little above us too," the Pilot shouted back. "So he doesn't run into us after we're destroyed. He could hit us here in the bridge if he wants!" The acceleration suddenly became unbearable. "But the bastard's still—coming—in with us."

I am firing. I am firing.

The ship trembled under the impacts, jarring their bones.

I am firing.

"Kilroy—damn it—how long now—until the—wormhole?" Muldoon

said, barely able to breathe.

"Almost—there!"

I am so close I can sense you. Is that you, Earthman?

"Mars—we're done for!"

Yes, yes. There you are. You are in the bridge. Fresh meat.

"For Federation—honor and—humanity!"

"Cowa-bunga!"

I am—

The freighter disappeared into the wormhole, welcomed by a deafening roar.

Chapter 17

Inside The Wormhole

The spaceship disappeared from normal space into the wormhole dimension with a deafening crash. Instantly, the stifling gravitational force was released, but without throwing them forward to be turned into spaghetti against the far wall. The men had instinctively clasped their hands over their heads at the horrible noise, luckily for Dobbs, who was then showered with the Navigator's books that had previously been held against the wall above his head. The ship shook violently with subsequent booms that pounded them like cosmic thunder. A blinding light flashed into the room from the view-screen, as if it were a window, bathing them in an eerie blue glow.

The men prepared to be atomized.

"I changed my mind!" said Travis. "Don't do it, Jim!"

"Hail Mary!" Muldoon roared.

"This is the end," Dobbs cried. "It's God's own hammer. Don't do it, God!"

"Cowabunga!" Kilroy shouted back into the thunder.

Then the noise faded, replaced by a strange moaning sound as if they were being blasted by a forceless wind. Instead of being afraid, the men now felt horribly cold and alone. The atmosphere was eerie and oppressive, pulling at their emotions like a blind puppeteer. Slowly, they stood again and patted their bodies. The Navigator stayed huddled in his chair, shaking his head slowly and staring into the light.

"That was Biblical," Fritz said, shuddering. "We're still here. We're still alive, right?"

"Yeah," Muldoon agreed. "But where the hell are we?"

Kilroy was grinning insanely. He pounded the instrumentation panel nearest him, and a row of lights blinked out. "Don't worry, she knows where to go! I've never seen a ship go through so much. I'm going to have to buy her from you with my share if we get out of this." He turned to the Navigator. "Hey, chin up, Tommy."

"Suit yourself," Dobbs said weakly. "You can have her for free if you like. Mars, that light is too bright. And is that weird Emperor chap still behind us?"

"No way of knowing," Kilroy said, checking the monitors. "The instruments are going wild. We're breaking the gauge on velocity. The guidance system tells me we're a quadrillion kilometers long, in pure blank empty space, no stars, no dust, no junk, no nothing. Say goodbye to the laws of physics as we know them. Wild."

"So there's no way to navigate," Dobbs said. He touched the bandaged cut on his head gingerly.

"I do know where we are, though."

Dobbs and Muldoon looked at Kilroy expectantly.

The Pilot laughed. "We're inside a friggin' wormhole and talking about it. This is a miracle!"

"I'm truly tickled that you're happy," Dobbs told him. "But I'd truly like to get the hell out of here and go home." He turned to the Engineer. "Mr. Travis, what are our options? You know something about wormhole physics."

Travis was methodically rubbing his shoulder and neck, as if to keep checking that he was still in one piece. "Technically, we, being organic lifeforms, should have been atomized," he said. Whether it was so that he wouldn't be atomized, or because of the cold eerie light, he whispered. "I still think that's what will happen sooner or later. Plus every other ship that's gone through a wormhole had about a billion lines of sophisticated navigational computer code for getting out. We don't have that. So even if we can actually get out of here, like Jim said before, we could wind up anywhere in the universe there's a wormhole. The odds aren't good at us winding up in the Federation."

"It'd be like winning the Capital Province lottery about a billion times in a row," Kilroy agreed, nodding.

Travis sagged even further. "In other words I think we're as good as dead or at best, buried alive. Remember that the cryogenic chamber's probably fried."

"That's good," Dobbs said dryly. "That's quite good. If we had an easy way out of this jam, I would have had a heart attack. Well, at least we're alive for now. I think."

Muldoon clapped Dobbs on the back. "There's another bright side."

"Do tell," Dobbs said wearily.

"We saved Earth, didn't we? We saved the entire Federation." He looked at each man in turn. "We should be celebrating! We did it!"

Dobbs took off his cap and threw it to the floor. "You and your crummy heroics!"

Muldoon shrugged. "So I wanted to save Earth and we did. Sorry. Why don't you just shoot me in the head?"

Dobbs' shoulders sagged and his arms flopped to his sides. "We had it all and we lost it," he bawled. "So that's the end of His plan for us, to be buried alive. Oh, I don't care anymore!"

"I got what I wanted," Kilroy said. "That was better than flying down the throat of a black hole."

"Maybe you lost your chance to retire rich," Muldoon told Dobbs. "But I lost Dariana, and she was everything to me. The point is I'm feeling bad too. So quit your blubbering."

Dobbs wiped his nose with his sleeve. "All right, old man. I apologize. I apologize for everything. I was unraveled. If it hadn't been for my bloody greed, we'd be living in a paradise."

Muldoon shook his head. "No, it was all my fault. I should have said goodbye to Dariana back on *Macintosh*. It made me want the whole stupid planet to give her. I was the one who overreached. If I hadn't, we'd be on our way home with the gold safe and sound."

"Well, I apologize just the same."

"In any case, it all worked out. We lost everything, but we saved the Federation."

"Hm," said Dobbs.

Muldoon thought for a moment, chewing on his mustache. "I want to know something, Sergeant Major."

"I swear to tell the whole truth."

"You weren't really going to give me the zap back there, were you?"

"Of course not, my good fellow," Dobbs replied, his eyes twinkling.

Muldoon regarded him uncertainly. "Sometimes I think deep down you really are a ruthless bastard. Well, no hard feelings, I guess."

"And none here," Dobbs said, feeling his breast pocket for a cigar. "I guess there's nothing left to do but wait for the end."

Muldoon set his jaw and exhaled through his nose. "We're still friends." He thought about it and laughed. "You're all I've got!"

Dobbs nodded. "Same here. I think that's how it's always been."

Kilroy said, "I wish the girls were still here."

Fritz pointed. "Wow, look at that. It's beautiful."

The light had diminished in intensity, giving them a view of a giant tunnel whose walls seemed to coil and move like thick purplish smoke as the ship flew past at an incredible velocity. The tunnel made turns side to side and up and down occasionally, making them flinch, but the ship kept its course straight down the middle of the tunnel.

"Mr. Travis, what do you make of this?" Dobbs asked, holding onto the back of the pilot's chair.

The engineer frowned, struggling with his words. "We're in a cartoon, that's my explanation!"

A voice suddenly thundered:

WELCOME

"Who said that?" said Dobbs, looking around the room. He looked at Kilroy. "Was that the Navigator?"

WELCOME TO THE FUTURE

Muldoon jumped. "Look at those things in the tunnel."

In normal space, what they saw would have meant they were flying straight into a star cluster at close to light speed. Being spacers, they found this bad on the nerves. The brightest ball of light in the center began to pulse. It appeared to be spinning rapidly.

YOU ARE IN OUR UNIVERSE

"So this is it," Muldoon said in wonder. "Too many years in space."
"We all see it," Dobbs told him.

YOU ARE LOOKING AT US

Dobbs shielded his eyes with his hand, squinting into the light. "Can you hear us, too?"

YES

"Who are you?" Muldoon said.
"They're amazing," Kilroy was saying.

THIS IS OUR PLACE. THIS IS OUR TIME

"We're just passing through, really," Dobbs said.

OTHERS FROM YOUR DIMENSION HAVE COME HERE

"Now what have we gotten ourselves into?" Muldoon wondered.
A chorus of other orbs of light began pulsing:

WE WERE ONCE FEDERATION NAVIGATORS. WE DECIDED
TO STAY. WE ARE WITH THEM NOW

"What're that energy fellows talking about now?" Dobbs said.
"Something about everybody else deciding to stay."
"I'll stay!" the Pilot said. "Hey, you!"
The ship continued to zoom down the tunnel, although the cluster of
lights stayed at the same distance. The ball of light in the center of the
cluster began to pulse again.

IF YOU STAY, YOU WILL KNOW NO PAIN AS YOU ARE NOW
FAMILIAR WITH IT. NO WAR, NO POVERTY, NO GREED, NO
MONEY, NO EVIL OF ANY KIND. THE EXPLANATION IS SIMPLE.
THE CONCEPTS THAT ARE CONSIDERED NEGATIVE IN YOUR
UNIVERSE DO NOT EXIST IN OUR UNIVERSE.
WE ARE ALL EQUAL IN THE EYES OF WHO YOU CALL GOD
AND WE CALL. . . .

The men saw an exploding ball of fire like a supernova in their minds,
accompanied by a sound like an electrowrench fighting a drill-hammer.

STAY, AND YOU WILL LIVE IN OUR TIME, WHICH IN YOUR

TIME IS CALLED FOREVER. WE WELCOME OTHER LIFE FORMS
TO JOIN US IN OUR EXISTENCE. THE TRANSLATION FOR
HUMANS IS DESIRABLE. WHAT WE CONSIDER NORMAL EXIS-
TENCE, HUMANS CONSIDER PERFECTION.

The other orbs of light chorused:

HEAVEN AWAITS

"I don't know what to make of this," Muldoon said to Dobbs. "What do
you think? It sort of sounds like Gimpcookies to me, I don't know. Like
those Sirens the Captain told us about that time in his office."

"That's what I was thinking," Dobbs agreed. "Those very words. I don't
trust the buggers for some reason. And it doesn't sound like a fun place
at all, does it? Pure energy my ass. We've got The Holy Grail itself in our
cargo holds. And he wants me to turn my back on that?"

Muldoon squinted into the light. "Why are you doing this?"

WE HAVE NO REASON NOT TO

"What is life like here?"

HUMANS ARE WELCOME

"If we can't feel evil, or greedy, or the like, can we feel good or gener-
ous? Can we feel love?"

HUMANS ARE WELCOME

"How can you know what good is if you don't have evil? Love if you
don't have hate?"

HUMANS ARE WELCOME

"Ask him if humans are welcome," Dobbs said in disgust.

"I'm going in, guys," Kilroy told them, smiling. "Thanks for the ride."

"Are you sure about this, Jim?" said Muldoon.

The Pilot paused. "It's the perfect end—which is really the beginning.

It's been real. We really did find The Holy Grail. Not the gold." He winked. "The experience."

"You're a master of your trade," Dobbs said with admiration. "The best I've seen."

Kilroy winked again. "See you on the other side some day." He stepped forward, then turned. "Tommy. Tommy."

The Navigator shook his head and mouthed no, his eyes wide.

Kilroy walked slowly over to the Navigator, leaned and took his hand.

"I'm afraid, Jim," Tommy told him, blinking into the blue light.

"Don't be afraid." Kilroy tugged on the Navigator's hand, who obeyed, standing up out of his harness as if in slow motion.

Dobbs held out his hand. "Wait! Are you sure you want to do this?"

Kilroy ignored him. "Eternity," the Pilot said, and pointed. "Look, Tommy. The Fountain of Youth." Together, the men walked toward the window until a blinding flash of blue light consumed them. The men had disappeared.

"Jupiter, did you see that?" Muldoon demanded, pointing at the floor. "There goes our pilot and the Navigator."

"That's why the other explorers never got through the wormholes," Dobbs said, rubbing his chin. "They weren't atomized. They were seduced by these guys. Nuts!"

Fritz wiped his eyes with his palm, staring into the light. "No war?" he said.

Dobbs and Muldoon watched in amazement as he stepped toward the window.

Fritz took off his cap and jacket and flung them to the floor. Then he pulled out his pistol and tossed it onto the jacket.

"Now hang on there a minute, Mr. Fritz," Dobbs said.

The ball turret gunner raised his arms and said, "Take me into the light!"

Dobbs and Muldoon were blinded, then Fritz was gone.

"God, that was quick," said Muldoon, shuddering. "Didn't even say goodbye."

They slowly turned and regarded Travis, who was sitting on the floor hugging his knees.

"Well, I guess that leaves you," Dobbs said. "I give up. Go on and join the others if you like. We've all got our problems."

"He means we won't hold it against you," Muldoon assured him.

"I won't go either," Travis told them. "Speaking of energy, I have a gift for humanity I have to deliver." He giggled. "I am Prometheus. Not going in there is my eternal punishment. You guys go. It's the deal of a lifetime, trust me on this one."

"Not bloody likely," Dobbs told him. He turned to Muldoon. "What about you, though, Sergeant Major? I have the gold, that's what I've always wanted. Maybe they have something you want. Don't let me hold you back. I won't judge you."

Muldoon shook his head slowly. "I can't. There's nothing for me here. With Dariana gone . . . aw Mars, don't make me say it again. You're all I got right now. I'm not the kind of man who throws a good friend away."

Dobbs gave him a sock on the shoulder. "All right then. Say, if they let us go and we somehow make it back and get our cash, we'll visit Earth. What do you say to that?"

Muldoon's grinned. "That'd be excellent," he said. "If they let us go, I agree. I might even be able to get the Muldoon clan back on Earth, to settle. Now that'd be a sight!"

"Do you hear that?" Dobbs shouted at the balls of energy. "That's what we want!

YOU HAVE REFUSED US

"They sound like they're pissed," Muldoon said. "Buckle up!"

PREPARE TO BE BANISHED FROM OUR DIMENSION

The Marines sat in the pilot and navigator chairs and strapped into the harnesses.

"Hold on to something, Bill!" Muldoon told Travis. "They mean it!"

FROM OUR DIMENSION. GO!
FROM OUR TIME. GO!

The freighter trembled, then roared into a blinding chaos of bright lights and blue sparks and rainbows. Dobbs and Muldoon were in an alien universe that violated every law of physics, and its vast unfathomable space seethed in front of their eyes impossibly framed by the smoky tunnel.

"Hail Mary!" Muldoon roared, closing his eyes.

Dobbs stared straight ahead. He screamed.

The ship was flung into that sea of light, an ocean of colors grinding and crashing.

BOOK IV

HOME AGAIN

Chapter 18
Home Again

obbs stared wide-eyed out the window of the bridge, next to Muldoon, who had his eyes clenched shut. Both held their armrests for dear life. He saw a trillion pixels, each a separate color, which popped and stretched into lines as they soared forward. Their ears filled with an incredible roar. The ship bucked wildly as if it were about to break into pieces.

Then, all at once, a dull boom made their ears pop, and Dobbs saw plain black space again dotted by thousands of bright points of light.

Muldoon's eyes flipped open. "God in a Rocket," he swore.

Dobbs nodded dumbly and turned to see Travis sitting on the floor smoking one of Kilroy's cigarettes and hugging his knees.

"They told me I should never smoke," Travis said with a shaky voice. "Fuck 'em!"

Dobbs nodded again and slowly turned back to the instrumentation panel, staring at the controls, monitors and gauges without understanding.

Muldoon began to make a noise like a rumble. It turned into a chuckle.

Dobbs choked out a giggle, then another, then he and Muldoon looked at each other and roared with laughter.

"We're alive! We escaped."

"Yeah," agreed Muldoon. "But where are we?"

Dobbs shook his head and studied the panel, saw a giant wad of grape gum stuck to the outboard radiation gauge.

"That Navigator chap was a—ah, here we are. We're just outside the Yokohama wormhole! We're back in the Federation! Those fellows gave us a helping hand."

"But how long were we in there? Check the atomic clock."

"Twenty-five minutes. I think I've gone mad."

"No," Muldoon said, shaking his head slowly. "You're the first man to ever go through a wormhole and tell the tale."

"So what I think happened did happen." Dobbs turned to Muldoon and added uncertainly, "It did all happen, right?"

"I was there! Every bit of it happened. We discovered alchemy. We fought an entire planet. We saved Earth. Then we went through a wormhole!"

Together, they turned to the Engineer. Travis's cheeks were flushed.

"We sure did!" he told them. "Boy am I glad you guys didn't leave me out of this."

Muldoon dipped into the breast pocket of his tunic and produced a battered cigar. Dobbs did the same.

"My last one," Muldoon said.

Together, they lit up and enjoyed a moment of silence.

"There's always a way," said Dobbs, then laughed.

"Yeah. I wonder where that Emperor ended up. Far away, I hope."

They set course for the planet Moravia, the trading center of the province.

ᔐ

Three days later, with the men showered and rested, the freighter docked with the traders' space station *Major Tom* orbiting Moravia in the Yokohama Province. *Major Tom* rotated slowly, a giant cross inside a wheel. On the view-screen, they watched construction workers in spacesuits yoking on a new set of rooms to the modular structure. Dobbs and Muldoon shook hands with Travis and made arrangements to credit him with his share after the trade. Travis didn't want to go to make the sale. He headed straight for the Federation patent office.

The customs officer met them in the airlock, and the inspection and endless scanning began. Muldoon studied the man curiously. He was bald with a goatee, he had diamond-shaped black tears tattooed under his right eye, and his earlobes were elongated. His badge read MITERRAND. The customs officer studied them just as curiously.

"Who are you guys supposed to be, Rip Van Winkle?" Miterrand said. "Welcome back to the future. How long you been out in the cold?"

"About two hundred Earth Standard years," Dobbs told him. "In the Beyond."

"Don't know why you went in the direction you did," Miterrand said, shaking his head as he ran a laser pen over a page of bar codes in his clipboard. "There's nothing in that nebula but dust and hydrogen. The Federation's going the other way. We added two more provinces while you been gone, Doreen and Manchester. You want to know more than that about what the Federation's like these days, you go find out yourself. I'm not the answer man around here. Call the Reintegration Office." He pulled a card out of the breast pocket of his jumpsuit and gave it to them. "The latest vid address."

"You could tell me one thing," Muldoon said. "You're bald and your ears are long."

"Yeah," Miterrand said incredulously. "And yours aren't. At least put a cap on or something. Most folks are bald these days; the complete look is called Stone Age. No more questions, please. This ain't a tour."

Muldoon's face sagged. "It's happened, Lawrence, like I said it would. Everything's changed. We're helpless!"

Their boots clomped as they marched together to the cargo hold. Dobbs winked at Muldoon and opened the door, and they saw a wall of gold sparkling under the customs officer's flashlight. Several buckets full of gold dust spilled out and reached their feet.

Miterrand promptly doubled over and laughed, the sound ricocheting off walls dimly lighted by blinking panels.

"What the hell?" Muldoon demanded.

"What's the matter?" Dobbs asked the customs officer casually, leaning with his elbow against the wall. "Never seen the Holy Grail before?"

"Rip Van Winkles," Miterrand told himself, cooling off. He sobered, shaking his head. "Guys, I don't know to tell you this, but gold's been replaced. The material of choice these days is a new ceramic polymer called Ibramax!"

ॐ

Dobbs and Muldoon entered a strange new galaxy.

Gold prices had plummeted after new superceramics made their way out of Capital Province to the colonies and became economical. The freighter, battered as hell and fairly outdated itself (almost all ships now ran on an antimatter engine after prices fell about ninety years earlier), was still worth in scrap and spare parts about half the value of its cargo. Luckily, the Transplanetary Mining & Distribution Company had gone out of business a century earlier and had no creditors, so they didn't have to pay the company its twenty-five percent share. They sold both, paid off Travis, and after Dobbs reduced its real value for inflation, they ended up only a little ahead of where they had started two hundred Earth Standard years ago.

"Don't sweat it, Tim old boy," Dobbs told him at Maxwell's, a restaurant aboard Major Tom. "We're only a little older. And we're no worse off than when we started."

"But now even the alchemical machine is useless!" Muldoon replied.

"We had some high times though, didn't we? But we need to think of our future now."

"Rich we were to be," Muldoon groaned. "And I lost Dariana in the bargain."

"If I can stop sulking over the gold, you can start getting over her."

"I'm over it. I really am. I just hope she's okay. Left on that planet with hostile savages. That Williamson better take good care of her."

"She looked like she could take care of herself just fine. I'm sure they're okay."

"I suppose you're right," Muldoon agreed. "She always wanted an adventure. She's got one now. If she's happy, I guess I should be happy for her."

"There's a good chap. You know, once we learn how to navigate inside the wormholes, if you want we can go back and visit. It'd be an easy ride."

"Thanks, brother. But that part of my life is over. I'm staying away from women until we figure out a way to retire."

"You'll find somebody else easily enough. I know that once we retire, I'm going to marry into the wealthiest, most aristocratic family I can find in Capital Province."

Muldoon shook his head and grinned. "You might even marry somebody you love."

Dobbs frowned back. "Of course! What kind of fellow do you take me for?"

"Actually, what I was thinking is that we should have gotten into the food business. I hear Maxwell's now has restaurants on space stations

Federation-wide."

"Aye, and too bad we didn't have enough cash when we were younger to pull off a Prodigal Son Account." The expression translated as, "It doesn't matter." Dobbs was referring to the old way spacers used to set up their retirement—put some cash in very safe low-growth interest accounts and by the time they got back after a trip that represented hundreds of Earth Standard years, they could be millionaires. But a Federation law had put an end to that after spacers began retiring in droves after only one mission.

"So we sell our story about how to get through wormholes," Muldoon suggested. "Get a royalty if the Federation sets up toll booths. Is that what you're planning?"

Dobbs shook his head, then read his menu. His eyes flashed at Muldoon. "You're going to love the food. They really know how to cook here in the future."

Muldoon began reading his with satisfaction. "I'm so hungry I have to decide what I don't want from the menu. I remember Maxwell's fondly from our days on Mac." Then his face contorted. "Jupiter. Half the choices are bean curd! Is that what they eat these days!"

Dobbs snickered. "We can't sell our story about the wormholes. Who'd believe us?"

Muldoon sighed. "I suppose you're right. They'd lock us up in a nice pink rubber room with a guy who thinks he's Maxis the Great."

"For the same reason, we can't tell anybody we defeated the Emperor of Xerxes."

"Aw, who gives a damn!" Muldoon exploded. "Okay, so we saved Earth, discovered a planet of gold and two scientific breakthroughs to boot, we turned down immortality, and we get nothing for it except bean curd in our face. Fine! Do they at least have cigars in this century?"

"Don't worry," Dobbs assured him, his eyes narrowing. "We'll see who gets the last laugh."

ॐ

After getting a good financing package, Dobbs and Muldoon leased a small ship and went through the wormhole again. This time, no utopian energy beings accosted them and the trip inside was uneventful. After a few mistakes, one in which they almost ended up sucked into a black hole clear on the other side of the universe, they mastered rudimentary navigation.

"Think of the good we could do with this," Muldoon said in wonder. "Men traveling through wormholes! We could change the Federation. Think about it!"

Dobbs shushed him.

"Men could colonize the entire galaxy in no time," Muldoon added. "Scientists could study time at the brink of black holes, then hurry back and publish their findings in the same year! The human race could make easy contact with new alien species! Find the edge of the universe!"

Dobbs shushed him. "I've got a plan," he said. "How would you like to see Earth?"

Muldoon blinked. "You better not be kidding. Let's go!"

They parked the ship at the New York City Spaceport and together, they toured the Great Halls of Earth, the soaring skyscrapers that glowed at night, the air filled with beams of light and the hum of airships, the clean wide tree-lined streets bustling with exotic people and commerce. Earth was a paradise now, terraformed a thousand years ago to rid itself of the industrial pollution of earlier times and the radiation left over from Earth's War III in the largest, most ambitious and most expensive project ever undertaken by Man. Earth itself had become a space-age Wonder of the Galaxy. The people in Capital Province enjoyed a quality of life these men from the hard colonies had only dreamed about.

Hydrogen trains zipped them around North America, leaving them in towns and cities where they drank in the sights and sounds and air in full. There—miles of corn stretching into the horizon! There—authentic Earth animals out in the open, raising their heads as the train zipped past! There—a thousand varieties of trees in a massive forest, flanked by cities soaring into the clouds, the clouds themselves dominated by airships and rockets! Earth reminded them of Neverland, but a more temperate Neverland populated and cultivated by humans, with every building and bridge and airship and farm and rocket demonstrating *Pax Humanus* in this arm of the galaxy. On Earth, they saw their dreams for Neverland fulfilled, as if they had returned to that planet after fifty years of cryogenic sleep—in time, Neverland would surely have been as beautiful and industrious.

In Chicago, they caught a glimpse of the Minister of Trade at a public appearance. A real band played the Federation Anthem and Mudoon sang along loudly and patriotically with the crowd in his baritone, tears rolling down his face and his heart about to burst. In Kansas, they visited a zoo stocked with real exotic Earth animals and non-sentient aliens in special atmosphere chambers. In Denver, they hiked in the mountains with the grounders, and found the Terrans to be an open, honest and friendly people. In Arizona, with jet packs on their backs, they studied the Grand Canyon, and in San Francisco they sat on the beach staring speechless at the endless blue ocean until Sol set and Luna rose to light a path on the choppy surface.

At the end of the trip, Muldoon felt as if his life had been fulfilled. He had seen his species' native sun—and beautiful it was—his native moon, his native planet. Only a tiny fraction of the Federation's colonial population had ever been to Capital Province and could match his experiences.

Dobbs, meanwhile, had gained something he could take with him. All along the trip, he had learned about new technology, processes and culture. To him, his life wasn't fulfilled, it was just beginning the good part.

During the ride home to the Yokohama Province, the men dreamed silently about their memories and when they talked, they planned their future.

After their ship docked with *Major Tom*, Dobbs promptly bought certain commodities and technology stocks on the local exchange. He was at least two to four years ahead of fresh Earth information as it splashed, then rippled outward slowly through the provinces. These ripples made big changes in the local stock markets. As each splash that Dobbs knew about reached Yokohama, Dobbs was ready to sell and make a killing. He and Muldoon moved to the finest hotel aboard *Major Tom* and lived in relative luxury, while building a new Retirement Fund that slowly climbed toward an ambitious new target.

Their goal was to make enough cash to live on Earth itself. They had promised themselves, and they deserved it!

҉

Three years after their first trip to Earth, Muldoon was reading the twenty-thousandth anniversary issue of *Davy Jones* in their room. He had just finished watching a holovision movie about the legendary Captain Antonio Malvez of the Navy Ship of the Line *Undaunted*, who had sacrificed his own life to save the Federation from a hostile alien intruder in

Caulfield's Nebula. Then the door slid open and Dobbs entered, wearing a sour look.

"You'll never guess what holo I just watched," Muldoon said.

Dobbs walked to the middle of the room and threw his cap onto the floor.

"Won't need that anymore. Hair's back in style."

Muldoon set the magazine aside. "Oh? I heard earlobes were going to go a centimeter longer next year. Everybody's talking about it."

"That won't happen either. Normal ears are coming back too."

Muldoon frowned. "Really? So what's the news? You're back early from Capital Province. Next time, I'm coming."

"It's too expensive for both of us to go, I told you. We'll be living there soon enough. Anyhow, our Mr. Travis has set some new trends."

"You mean Bill—that engineer?"

"Oh, aye," Dobbs said dryly. "He's a fashion-setter now. For the whole Federation."

Muldoon waited for the punch line. He shrugged. "I don't get it."

Dobbs told him that Travis had recently unveiled his patented Travis High-Frequency Oscillating Generator. Thousands of them were now being manufactured by Macron Power Generators & Turbines, Ltd. The new invention was a dynamo that turned planets into giant capacitors to provide the wireless transmission of cheap and plentiful energy to their inhabitants. And as his signature, Travis had figured out how to operate the machines without causing electrical storms and other funny weather. As a result, the Minister of Trade had just announced, the Federation could potentially double its economic output within two centuries.

"Good for him," said Muldoon. "I liked that man. But how is he setting fashion trends? You never answered that. Not that I'm ungrateful he's doing it."

Dobbs shook his head and said patiently, "Within just a few years, every time a man activates an HVAC sensor or every time a family turns on the holovision panel for a good show, Mr. Travis will earn a royalty. Any time electricity is used for anything. He's already the richest man in the Federation, and he's actually going to buy his own bloody planet."

Muldoon threw back his head and laughed at the ceiling. "Which one?"

Dobbs tried to smile with him. "He found The Holy Grail, my friend. We ended up with a wash and Mr. Travis scored the Grail."

"Eureka Moment," Muldoon corrected him, chuckling.

Then Dobbs laughed with Muldoon, and together they chalked it up to fate.

"We'll get our fair share," said Muldoon.

"Aye, we'll get the last laugh yet," Dobbs agreed. "I just bought a hundred thousand shares of Macron Power Generators & Turbines Ltd. on the Yokohama exchange. Within a year or two, when the news about the invention gets here, we'll be very rich men ourselves."

Then, their life's work complete, they could retire and live on Earth.

They believed it was their destiny, pure and simple.

∾

Six months later, the Fate Virus announced itself in a videogram in their hotel room, the image of the Hacker's face grinning at them in a ridiculous close-up.

"YOU SHOULD HAVE GIVEN ME THE FOUR HUNDRED THOUSAND."

"Look, there's that Mr. Chip fellow, the Hacker," said Dobbs.

"Yeah, it is," agreed Muldoon. "Amazing Phil. The kid with the Jovian ego."

"EVEN THOUGH I'M DEAD, YOU CANNOT ESCAPE MY POWER."

"I wonder what he wants."

"It should be important, since he's been dead for at least two hundred years."

"He could have gone into hibernation too," Dobbs said doubtfully.

Muldoon snorted. "He just said he's dead, Sergeant Major. And that kid was afraid of his own shadow. He'd never go anywhere near the speed of light."

Muldoon was right. The Hacker was long dead.

Two hundred Earth Standard years ago, the Hacker had injected his Fate Virus—the mother of revenge—into the InfraNet. It spent the centuries hopping around the Yokohama Province and the Province of Good Hope, looking for Dobbs and Muldoon, patiently waiting for their return. Now, a little less than two years after the men had sold the gold and the ship, the Fate Virus was dumped into the Moravia LocalNet and found their names. It activated itself.

It went off like a bomb.

A pair of dice flashed on the screen, tumbling in a sea of stars.

"WE'RE GOING TO PLAY THE COSMIC FATE GAME, BOYS. ODDS, YOU GET GOOD ODDS. EVENS, I GET EVEN."

"What the hell is he talking about?" Muldoon wondered aloud.

"YOU WHO THOUGHT OF ME AS DOG, NOW CAN CALL ME GOD."

"Now there's a fellow who thinks he's Maxis the Great," Dobbs said.

"Dumb kids. I'll bet they're still dumb, even here in the future."

"STAND BY FOR A DEMONSTRATION OF THE FATE VIRUS."

The dice continued to tumble, settled and accelerated off screen. The videolink went blank.

"What was the number?" said Dobbs.

"A five. Three and two."

"Are you sure? I thought for a moment it was a four. Three and one."

"Who gives a damn!" Muldoon exploded. "It's a bunch of space junk."

The videolink burst into life less than an hour later. It was a videogram from Skytech Ltd., shouting at them with a blast of trumpets that they had won a new Arrowhead 5000 hovercar, worth eighty-three thousand.

"I didn't enter any sweepstakes," said Muldoon. "Wow, what luck!"

"Aye, it was a five," Dobbs said thoughtfully, rubbing his chin.

Slowly, he began to shudder in horror. He reached out and groped until he found an armrest of the nearest chair, and sat down. The chair, manufactured by General Ergonomics Inc., immediately molded to his size and contours to fit him perfectly and support excellent posture. Even so, he slumped.

Variable problems made his hair stand on end. He had just been introduced to the mother of all variable problems, Pandora's Box itself.

The Fate Virus haunted them for the next three months. It proved fickle and uncaring, and worked in more mysterious ways than the Lord. Dobbs and Muldoon lost clearance to their hotel room three times in a row. At Maxwell's, the owner came to their table, saying the meal was on the house and begging for an autograph and if they would please sing for the other customers—which, after a free bottle of excellent scotch, they did. Later, a hundred pizzas were delivered COD, and they began receiving a free subscription to *Davy Jones*.

Muldoon didn't tell Dobbs, but he thought it was all fun. Harmless pranks.

But slowly, the stakes began to go up as the Fate Virus learned more about them and their environment. The presents stayed the same, but the punishments got nastier. Dobbs could scarcely get out of bed in the morning, wasting away. They were less than a year away from becoming millionaires, and every minute was agony. All of their countermeasures—virus hunters, attempts to change their names—had failed. Then the Moravia barracks received a peculiar message in Morse code that had come all the way from Local Command.

A-W-O-L. STOP. SUBJECTS A-W-O-L. STOP. APPREHEND AND DELIVER—

❧

"I'm going mad," Dobbs said two days later in their hotel room. Half the commodity stocks they'd bought that day had skyrocketed, the other half had plummeted.

"Rich we were supposed to be," cried Muldoon. "I lost Dariana. We didn't collect on the gold. Now I don't even have my own free will. They don't even make cigars anymore!"

"No worries," Dobbs told him. "There's always a way. Isn't that our motto?" But he sounded tired now, his voice hollow.

"We're not insignificant men," Muldoon said, his jaw set. "We'll fight back. To Earth or bust!"

"Aye. We'll see who has the last—"

Just then, the doors burst open and the MPs hauled them off to the barracks, and they once again found themselves noncommissioned officers in the Colonial Marine Service.

❧

The Emperor of Xerxes re-entered black space and immediately saw an amazing view of billions of stars clustered together. If he could have blinked, he would have. This was no typical starscape squashed down by going close to light speed, because his velocity was far from that, and he didn't dare use up his remaining fuel for acceleration until he'd determined his location. He was actually looking from a distance at an incredible cluster of billions of stars.

The Emperor received input from his sensors. The stars were densely packed, a thousand stars per cubic light-year, a vast swirling stew of gases. A ring of gas, produced by ancient violent explosions, rotated around the whole like a whirlpool, and another of lower density surrounded that. At the center, he deduced an incredible black hole.

Fathers! he swore. *I'm at the heart of the galaxy, the core of the spiral, the Great Furnace itself from whence the Eight Gods came. But what arm of the spiral am I in?*

He was able to determine that he was in the right arm of the right galaxy in about three hours of intense calculations. From there, he plotted a course to Earth.

It was an impossibly long distance. Twenty-six thousand and change light-years.

Idid-a-laam! I am forsaken. Ah, well.

He spread his scoops and began collecting hydrogen atoms to fill his fuel tanks. He soaked them up fairly quickly—the space around him was rich with the foodstuff of starship propulsion. Nonetheless, it took him several years. He thought about those strange energy beings that had taken him into their dimension and tried to recruit him into their society.

They said I could have immortality. And here I am immortal, trying to die! Idiots!

The Emperor figured it would still take him more than twenty-eight thousand years at peak velocity just to get to the Federation border. And because he didn't know the exact location of Earth from where he was, he'd have to replot his course at some point in the future, brake, roll and then accelerate all over again. That would take time as well. A long, long time. By the time he reached Earth, more than two million years would have passed on the planet.

But the Emperor was patient. He had plenty of time. And Earth was going nowhere.

Wait for me, Earthlings. I am coming again.

The Emperor of Xerxes, the last of his species, was determined to get the last laugh.

৯

By the time Christopher Walker, Troubleshooter for the Commission of

Space Trade & Supply, reached Neverland, he had missed Dobbs and Muldoon by a full year in space and fifty-four Neverlandian years. He followed a radio signal beacon that could only have been sent by humans, and landed during the night to find a thriving colony of eighty-four people and a lone, ancient-looking Cricket. He was welcomed by a young man who called himself the Captain—which turned out to be the title of an elected office—but it didn't take him long to realize it was just a figurehead position in this matriarchal society.

Walker asked the people what had happened to Lawrence Dobbs and Timothy Muldoon. They laughed, delighted, and pointed at the sky. So they'd left, he said. Where did they go? he asked. Where are they now?

The Captain shook his head patiently and grinned. He pointed at the brightest star in the sky. "Dobbs," he said. Walker then followed his finger to the largest moon. "Muldoon."

Printed in the United States
108228LV00004B/130-186/A

9 781930 486799